TRIGGER
MORTIS

ANTHONY
HOROWITZ

An Orion paperback

First published in Great Britain in 2015
by Orion Books
This paperback edition published in 2016
by Orion Books,
an imprint of The Orion Publishing Group Ltd,
Carmelite House, 50 Victoria Embankment
London EC4Y 0DZ

An Hachette UK company

3 5 7 9 10 8 6 4

A CIP catalogue record for this book is available from the British Library.

ISBN 978 1 4091 5914 8

Typeset at The Spartan Press Ltd,
Lymington, Hants

Printed and bound in Great Britain by Clays Ltd,
St Ives plc

www.anthonyhorowitz.com
www.ianfleming.com
www.orionbooks.co.uk

Contents

PART TWO: ... MUST COME DOWN

Prologue

It was that moment in the day when the world has had enough. The sun was sitting on the horizon, a soft red glow creeping over the tidewater while, high above, a flock of birds drew random patterns against an empty sky. The wind had dropped and the afternoon heat had become oppressive, trapped in a haze of dust and petrol fumes. Cutting through the middle of it all, the dark blue Crosley station wagon was suddenly alone, spinning along Route 13, heading inland from the coast.

The Crosley was an ugly little car with its over-pronounced nose, slab-like cabin and rust already eating through the steel bodywork. The driver, hunched over the wheel with his eyes fixed on the road ahead, had bought it for three hundred dollars from a salesman who had sworn he would get forty miles to the gallon and speeds of up to fifty miles per hour too. Of course, he'd been lying... with the perfect teeth and the friendly smile of every small-town hustler. The Crosley could barely pick up momentum when the road dipped steeply downhill and here, close to Virginia's Eastern Shore, the landscape was flat for miles around.

The driver could have been a professor or a librarian. He had the look of someone who spent much of his life indoors with pallid skin, nicotine-stained fingers and glasses that, over the years, had slowly sunk into his nose until they had become a permanent part of his face. His hair had thinned out, showing liver spots high up on his forehead. His name was Thomas Keller. Although he now carried an American passport, he had been born in Germany and still spoke his own language more fluently than that of his adopted country. Without letting go of the wheel, Keller turned his hand and glanced at the Elgin 16-jewel military watch that he'd picked up in a pawnshop in Salisbury, almost certainly dumped there by some GI down on his luck. He was exactly on time. He saw the turning just ahead and signalled. In an hour from now, it occurred to him, he would have enough money to buy a decent car and a decent watch – Swiss-made, of course, maybe a Heuer or a Rolex – and finally, a decent life.

He pulled up in front of a diner, a sleek, silver box that looked as if it had been delivered off the back of a truck. The name – Lucie's – was spelled out in pink neon above the same four refreshments that defined the whole of American cuisine for most of its population, no matter which state you happened to be in: Hamburgers, Hot Dogs, Shakes, Fries. He got out of the car, his shirt briefly sticking to the vinyl upholstery, and dragged his jacket off the front seat. For a moment he stood there in the warm air, listening to a snatch of music from a jukebox, and considered the journey that had brought him here.

Thomas Keller had only just graduated with a degree in physics and engineering when he had stumbled onto what would become the great passion of his life. It had happened at the Harmonie Cinema in Sachsenhausen where he had gone with a pretty girl to see Fritz Lang's new film, *Frau im*

Mond, The Lady in the Moon. Five minutes into the film he had forgotten all about the girl and, for that matter, his hopes of groping her afterwards in the cinema car park. Instead, the sight on the screen of a multi-stage rocket leaving the earth's orbit had woken something within him and from that moment it consumed him. You could say that he was propelled, with the same irresistible force, first to the University of Berlin, then to Verein für Raumschiffahrt – the Society for Space Travel – and ultimately to the Baltic coast and the seaport of Peenemünde.

At the time, German rocket research was already well advanced, for although the much-hated Treaty of Versailles had placed huge restrictions on the development of weapons, space travel had been excluded. This played into the hands of the German military who quickly realised that liquid-fuelled rockets, launched from fairly simple, makeshift platforms, could travel further and faster than any artillery weapon, delivering their payloads into every major city in Europe.

Keller was thirty-six when he met the man in charge of the German space programme: the rocket engineer (and SS-Sturmbannführer) Wernher von Braun. The son of a Prussian baron, von Braun came from a family that had been fighting battles since the thirteenth century and he had never lost his aristocratic streak. He strutted into rooms, snapped at anyone who argued with him and could be coldly dismissive when he was in a certain mood. At the same time, he was utterly dedicated to his work, demanding the best of himself and everyone around him. Keller feared and admired him in equal measure.

Of course, by this time, a certain Austrian corporal had come to power and Germany was at war. But none of this particularly interested Keller. Like many of the academics and physicists who were his only friends, he had little interest in the world around him and if Hitler was going to plough funds – eleven million Deutschmarks appropriated from the Luftwaffe and the army – into rocket-powered interceptors and ballistic missiles, he could happily turn a blind eye to the Nazis' other, less savoury preoccupations. Indeed, when he finally stood at Peenemünde, with the first V-2 rockets being launched in the summer of 1944, he never considered the death and devastation that they would bring with their one-ton payloads. He was an artist and this was his canvas. Watching the launches was for him a moment of pure ecstasy: the clouds of white smoke filled with tiny sparks from the igniter that suddenly rushed together into a brilliant red flame, the cables falling away and the sleek, elegant creature being released into the sky. The vibrations coursed through him. His entire skin seemed to come alive and he felt the thrill of knowing that he was one of the handful of technicians who had helped in its creation, that the motors would produce an astonishing 800,000 horsepower and that the rocket would soon achieve five times the speed of sound. The citizens of London would have no idea of the perfection, the sheer genius of the weapon that killed them. Often, Keller couldn't help himself. He wept tears of pure joy.

The war ended and for a brief time Keller wondered if he might have to face up to certain repercussions. He had actually been present when von Braun surrendered to the Americans and had subsequently been interrogated by them as part of the famous Black List, the code name for German scientists and engineers of special importance. But he wasn't too worried. What von Braun and his team had created would be too valuable to the Allies and he was confident that somehow their work would continue. He was right. The two men were released from custody on the same day. Along with another dozen scientists and technicians, they were flown out of Germany on the same plane, finally arriving at Fort Bliss, an American army base near El Paso where, with new masters and – in a few cases – new identities, they continued their work exactly where they had stopped before they were so rudely interrupted.

Keller was fifty-four now and nearing the end of his career. He had lived in the United States for twelve years but nobody would ever have mistaken him for an American. He had the build and the physique of a foreigner, slow and cumbersome. His ponderous speaking manner and thick accent gave away his origins the moment he spoke. It didn't matter. The war was far enough away. People no longer cared. And anyway, in his own mind he had assimilated in ways that mattered more – and which gave him complete satisfaction. Three years after he had arrived he had married an American cocktail waitress he had met in El Paso and the two of them had moved to an all-American home in Salisbury, Maryland. Keller had been employed as a general supervisor for the Naval Research Laboratory (NRL) at its rocket launch site on Wallops Island. He had left his office there less than an hour ago.

And now he had arrived.

He stepped into the diner and at once felt the chill of the air conditioning just as the jukebox struck up another tune by the Everly Brothers.

Bye bye love
Bye bye happiness . . .

Keller had no interest in American music but it had been impossible to escape the tune for several months. It seemed to him that the words were strangely inopportune, for he had driven here in the hope and the expectation of the exact opposite.

The man he had come to meet was waiting for him exactly where he had said he would be, in the table at the corner window. He was wearing a Brooks Brothers suit, a button-down shirt and penny loafers, the same clothes he always wore. He had got there early. There was a newspaper on the table in front of him and he had partly filled in the crossword. Keller knew him as Harry Johnson but he was fairly certain that was not his real name. Slightly awkwardly, he raised a hand in greeting, then crossed the red and white tiled floor and squeezed himself in on the other side of the table. At the last moment, he realised he had forgotten to put on his jacket. Well, it was too late now. He was determined not to do anything that might look fumbling or ill-prepared. He laid the jacket on the banquette beside him.

'How are you, Mr Keller?' Johnson spoke with a flat, Manhattan accent.

'I'm all right. Thank you.'

Harry Johnson was ten or fifteen years younger than him but somehow seemed older with a long, drawn-out face, creases in his cheeks and closely cropped grey hair. He was rotating a ballpoint pen between his fingers. On one of them he wore a gold signet ring.

'What's the capital of Venezuela?' he asked.

'I'm sorry?' Keller was taken aback.

'Nine down, the capital of Venezuela. It's a seven-letter word beginning with C.'

'I don't know,' Keller said, irritably. 'I don't do crosswords.'

'Hey – it's all right. I was just asking.' Johnson glanced away from the grid. 'So is it done?'

This time, Keller knew what he meant.

It was the fourth time they had met. Keller remembered the first occasion, a seemingly chance meeting at a bar in downtown Salisbury. Johnson had somehow just been there, on the next stool. It was impossible to say when he had walked in. They had got talking. Johnson said he was a businessman, which was probably true but actually meant almost nothing at all. He seemed fascinated to hear that Keller was a rocket scientist and over a second round of drinks – Johnson insisted on paying – he asked a series of interested but innocuous questions, nothing to ring any alarm bells. Of course, it had all been arranged. He'd known everything about Keller before they'd exchanged a single word. At the end of the evening, the two men arranged to see each other again. Why not? Johnson was good company and, as he left, he casually mentioned that he might have a proposition to make. 'Could make you a bit of money. Just a thought. Let's talk about it next time.'

But next time he held back. They compared wives, families, pay packets, aspirations. It was all man-talk although it was Keller who did most of the talking. It was only on the third occasion, when they knew each other a little better, that Johnson came out with his proposition. That was when Keller should have gone to the police or, better still, to the Naval Security office on the southern perimeter of Wallops Island.

Of course he hadn't. Johnson, or the people behind him, had chosen Keller because they knew that he wouldn't. They had probably been sizing him up for months. And who exactly were they? Keller didn't care. It was exactly the same myopia that had seen him through the war. He didn't need to see the bigger picture. It wasn't important. He simply focused on the proposition being put to him and the two hundred and fifty thousand dollars, tax-free, that he would be paid if he complied. He agreed almost immediately and there was just one more meeting to discuss details. It was all very straightforward. What he was being asked to do wasn't easy. It would demand a thorough understanding of solid mechanics and tensile stress – but these were his areas of expertise. And once he had worked out the precise calibrations, there was still the question of the work itself. At best, he would have four or five minutes alone. There was considerable risk – but there was also the reward. This had been his first calculation.

'So is it done?'

'Yes.' Keller nodded. 'The task was in the end much easier than I had anticipated. I was able to enter the assembly hangar during a fire drill.' He paused. He had allowed his enthusiasm to get the better of him and he was in danger of underselling what he had achieved. 'Of course, I had to work quickly. They always increase the security in the run-up to a launch. And it had to be done with considerable care. There was the chance, you understand, of a last-minute inspection. My work had to be … *unsichtbar*.' He searched for the word in English. 'Invisible.'

'The engine will fail?'

'No. But it will not be effective. The quantity of propellant being pumped into the combustion chamber will be insufficient. It is as I explained to you. The result will be exactly what you wish for.'

The two men fell silent as a waitress approached with coffee and iced water. Two menus lay unopened in front of them. They did not intend to eat.

'What about the timing of the launch?' Johnson asked.

Keller shrugged. He did not like coffee. How many gallons of the stuff had he consumed since he had come to America, smoking and working through the night? He pushed the cup away. 'It is still timed twelve days from now. I have looked at the forecasts. The weather is good. But you can never be certain. The wind shear is all-important and if conditions are not right...' He let his voice trail away. 'But that is not my concern. I have done what you asked me. Do you have the money?'

The other man did not speak. His eyes were fixed on the German. Then he reached out and unclipped a pair of sunglasses that had been hanging from his front pocket. It was a sign that their business was concluded. 'There is an attaché case under the table.'

'And the money?'

'It's all there.'

Johnson was about to leave but Keller stopped him. 'I must tell you something,' he said. 'It is important.' He had rehearsed what he was about to say. He was rather proud of the formulation he had come up with, how carefully he had thought things through. 'I will not count the money. I will assume it is all present. But at the same time, I must warn you. I do not know who employed you and I do not care. You are clearly working for serious people. But a quarter of a million dollars is a lot of money. The stakes are high. And it is possible that for your own security, you may choose to silence me. It would not be so difficult, *nein*? For all I know, there could be an explosive device in this attaché case of yours and

I could be dead before I even reach my car. Or there could be an accident on the freeway.

'So what I want you to know is that I have written down everything that has taken place between us and everything that I have been asked to do. Not only have I described you, I have taken your photograph. I hope you will forgive me for this small deceit, but you will, I am sure, understand my position. I have also made a note of the car you drive and its registration plate. All this is lodged with a friend of mine and he has been instructed to hand it all to the authorities if anything suspicious should happen to me. Do you understand what I am saying? There will be no rocket failure. And although it may take the police some time to find you, they will know of your existence and they will forever be on your tail.'

Johnson had heard all this in silence. Keller finished and Johnson gazed at him with incredulity. It was the first time he had shown any real emotion at all. 'What sort of people do you think we are?' he asked. 'Do you think we're gangsters? I have to tell you, Tom, you've been reading the wrong sort of books. We have asked you to do us a service. You have rendered us this service and you have been paid. You are wrong, by the way. A quarter of a million dollars is not a great deal of money in the scheme of things. You will hear from us again only if it turns out that you have not done as we have agreed – and it is true that, in that instance, your life may well be at stake. But although you do not trust us, we have absolute faith in you.' He threw a few coins down on the table to pay for the coffee, rolled up his newspaper and got to his feet. 'Goodbye.'

'Wait...' Keller felt embarrassed. 'Caracas,' he said.

'Caracas?'

'Your crossword clue. The capital of Venezuela.'

Johnson nodded. 'Of course. Thank you.'

Keller watched him leave. It was true that his speech had been a little melodramatic, inspired by some of the movies he had seen with his wife. It was also, as it happened, untrue. There was no record of what had happened, no photograph, no friend waiting to go to the police. He had merely thought that the threat of it would be enough to protect him should the need arise. Had he been wrong? Had he made a fool of himself? Then he remembered the money. He scrabbled under the table and felt his knuckles rap against something that stood against the wall. The briefcase! He pulled it up and flicked the locks, opening it just enough for him to peek inside. It seemed to be all there: bundles of fifty-dollar notes, banded together in neat piles. He closed the case, pulled on his jacket and hurried out. There was no sign of Harry Johnson in the parking lot. He went over to his own car, threw the attaché case onto the front seat and climbed in.

It took him another twenty minutes to drive home where he knew Gloria would be waiting for him. The thought of Gloria made him smile and relax a little behind the wheel. At the end of the day, this had all been for her.

She was fifteen years younger than him, short and a little plump but in a way that excited him, her breasts and hips always fighting against the fabric of her clothes. She had been in her mid-twenties when the two of them met and when he had told her about himself she had been thrilled. Here was a man who had been smuggled into the country from Europe and who worked in a top-secret research facility building space rockets. It was like something out of the cheap paperbacks she liked to read, and the fact that he was

German, unattractive, and that he sometimes made painful demands of her didn't seem to matter. They had been happy enough when they married and had both taken the decision to move north, choosing Salisbury because of its proximity to Wallops Island. They had bought a house and chosen the furniture together. But since then, things had not gone so well between them. They were unable to have children and she was bored in the house and bored at her job which was managing a local restaurant that barely came to life until the weekend. She didn't want to hear anything more about rockets and these days she only reluctantly came to the launches. And yet Keller still loved her. He was certainly attracted to her. In a way he looked upon her as the ultimate status symbol, the validation of a lifetime's work. She was his American wife. He deserved her.

He had told her about his new friend, Harry Johnson, and what he had been asked to do. He wouldn't have dreamed of going ahead without her approval. He was glad he had done so. The stakes were incredibly high. He was about to commit a crime which, if discovered, might see him charged with treason. But from the very start Gloria had been even more determined than him, urging him on when his courage failed. For weeks now, the two of them had been talking about the future they would make for themselves together, what they would do with the money, how careful they would have to be not to spend too much of it too soon. It seemed to Keller that his wife had transformed. He remembered now how she had been when he first set eyes on her. All her energy and *lebensfreude* had returned. And she had a renewed appetite in bed, giving herself to him with the same abandonment as their wedding night.

She was waiting at the front door of their wood-boarded bungalow with its single picture window and pull-up garage. It was a house straight out of a sales catalogue with its neat front garden and white picket fence. Keller parked up in the drive and went to her, carrying the attaché case. They kissed in the doorway. She was wearing a flower-patterned day dress, tied tight at the waist. Her blonde hair fell in curls to her shoulders. At that moment, Keller wanted her more than ever.

'You've got it,' she said.

'Yes.'

'Did you count it?'

'It's all here. There's no need.'

'You should have counted it.'

'We can do that inside.'

They went in together, to the neat living room with its sofa, coffee table and flip-top TV. They opened the case and they counted the money, Gloria standing with her shoulders and buttocks pressing against him, his arms around her. When they were sure that it was all there, she twisted round and kissed him on the cheek. 'I put some champagne in the fridge,' she said.

He followed her into the kitchen and stood there while she fumbled in the drawer. 'I can't find the damn corkscrew,' she said.

He went over to her, and it was only as he reached her that he remembered that you didn't actually need a corkscrew to open a bottle of champagne and that was the same moment that she turned and he felt something pressing into him. He looked down and saw, impossibly, the handle of a knife jutting out of his stomach. It had to be a mistake. This couldn't have happened. But then he looked up and met her eyes and knew that it was true. He tried to speak but the blood was already rushing out of him and it took his breath and his life with it. Still holding her, he fell to his knees, then, as she stepped aside, he pitched forward onto the floor. Gloria looked down at him and shuddered. It wasn't the sight of his blood spreading over the linoleum that disgusted her. It was the memory of his hands on her body, the sour smell of his breath.

There was little left to do.

She had already bought the gasoline. She sprinkled it over her dead husband, over the kitchen, the living room, the stairs. Then she picked up the suitcase packed with the few things she intended to take with her and emptied the money into it. Finally, she lit a match.

She took her husband's Crosley station wagon, although it was a horrible car. At least she could rely on it to make it all the way across to California where she intended to begin her new life. She reached the end of the drive and turned into the road without looking back. And so she didn't see the first flames as they leapt up behind her or the smoke weaving its way into the evening air.

PART ONE:

WHAT GOES UP...

1

Back to Work

James Bond opened his eyes. It was seven o'clock exactly. He knew without having to look at the alarm clock beside the bed. The morning sun was already seeping into the room, feeling its way through the cracks in the curtains. There was a sour taste in his mouth, a sure sign of one whisky too many the night before. What time had he gone to bed? Well after midnight. And bed had not meant sleep.

'What time is it?' The woman lying next to him had woken up. Her voice was soft and drowsy.

'Seven.' Bond reached out and stroked the black hair, cut short above the neck, then gently trailed his finger down.

'Come on, James. I need my shut-eye. It's way too early.'

'Not for me.'

Bond swung out of bed and padded into the bathroom. It was one of the peculiarities of the flat in the converted Regency house where he lived, just off the King's Road in Chelsea, that the brightly lit, white-tiled master bathroom was exactly the same size as the bedroom. Perhaps one was too small and one too large but Bond had got used to it and there was absolutely no point knocking the place about, wasting time with architects and builders simply for the sake of convention. He stepped into the glass shower cabinet and turned on the water, very hot and then icy cold for five minutes, the same way he started every day.

He got out, wrapping a towel around himself, and went over to the basin. In a life where nothing was predictable, when even life itself could be threatened or terminated without warning, this morning ritual was important to him. It was good to start each day with a sense that everything was in its right place. He shaved, using the orange and bergamot shaving cream that he bought from Floris in Jermyn Street, then rinsed off. The mirror had steamed up and he ran a hand across the glass to expose blue-grey eyes that were quietly assessing him as they always did, a lean face and thin lips that could so easily be cruel. He turned his head to examine the burn on his right cheek, caused by a bullet fired at close range in a Stratocruiser high above the Atlantic Ocean. Fortunately, it had almost faded. Bond already had a permanent scar on his face and it occurred to him that one injury might be dismissed as a misfortune but two would most definitely invite comment – far from desirable, given his profession.

He pulled on a pair of Sea Island cotton shorts, then walked back into the bedroom. The bed was empty, the sheets still warm with the memory of the night before. He went over to the wardrobe and took out a dark suit, a white silk shirt and a thin, double-ended grey satin tie. He dressed quickly, at the same time noticing, with approval, the smell of coffee coming from the kitchen. Finally, he drew on a pair of black leather moccasins, then slipped his gunmetal cigarette case into his inside pocket, and made his way out. It was a little after seven-thirty.

Pussy Galore was waiting for him in the kitchen, wearing an oversized man's shirt and nothing else. As he came in, she turned and looked at him with the extraordinary violet eyes that had first attracted him when he'd met her at the warehouse in Jersey City barely more than two weeks ago. Then she had been the head of a lesbian organisation, The Cement Mixers, brought in by Auric Goldfinger to help him pull off the heist of the century. As things had turned out, the two of them had become allies and then, inevitably, lovers. The conquest had been particularly satisfying to Bond who had instantly recognised in her that untouchable quality, a refusal to be loved. He had desired her the moment he saw her, walking towards him in a well-cut suit, holding her own in a room full of mobsters. He examined her now; the black hair carelessly cut, the full lips, the decisive cheekbones. It was hard to believe that this was a girl who had felt nothing but suspicion and hatred towards men until he had come into her life.

She poured two cups of coffee – the extra-strong De Bry blend that Bond favoured – then brought a single boiled egg to the table.

'Here you go,' she said. 'Boiled for three and a third minutes, just how you like it.'

She didn't eat anything herself. She'd already made herself a Bloody Mary with a large slug of Smirnoff White Label vodka and enough Tabasco sauce to set the lining of her stomach on fire. She sat with it in front of her, absent-mindedly stirring it with a stick of celery. 'So what are you getting up to today, Bond?' she asked. 'You get to work at eight thirty. In my line of business, I never got out of bed before ten. I could think of plenty of things to do before breakfast, depending on who I was with. I used to stay in these swanky joints in New York and, I'm telling you, I gave "maid service" a whole new meaning. But you're different, right? Saving the country three times before lunch…'

In fact, Bond was booked in for a one-hour session in the shooting range located in the basement of his office. He would spend the rest of the day sorting through the paperwork that had piled up in his absence, perhaps breaking off for lunch with Bill Tanner, the Chief of Staff and his closest friend within the service. But he didn't tell her any of this. What happened behind the walls of the nine-storey building near Regent's Park was its own business, not to be discussed with anyone outside the profession. At the end of the day, it was easiest not to say anything at all.

'What about you?' he asked.

'I haven't decided.' The stick of celery made another circuit round the side of the glass. 'I love this town of yours. Really, I do. Everything you've shown me – the Tower, the Palace, the Houses of Whatever-they-were… I never figured I'd come to London and now I understand why you Brits are so pleased with yourselves. Maybe I could live here. I could start looking for an apartment. Whaddya think?'

'It's a thought.'

'A bad one. They'd never allow it. Who'd want a crook like me? Except you, and for all the wrong reasons.' She sighed. 'I don't know. I'm not in the mood for more sightseeing. Not on my own.'

'I can't take any more time off work.'

'OK. I'll go shopping. That's what a gal's meant to do in London, isn't it?' I'll buy a hat.'

'You'd look ridiculous in a hat.'

'Who says it's for me?'

'I won't be late. We can go out tonight. I can get a table at Scott's.'

'Yeah. Sure.' She sounded bored. 'Just so long as you don't make me eat any more oysters. I reckon I can get through the evening without a mouthful of slime.'

She waited until Bond had finished his egg, then lit two cigarettes – not the Morlands brand which were specially made for him and which he preferred, but one of her own Chesterfields. She passed it across and Bond inhaled deeply, reflecting that the first cigarette of the day definitely tasted better when it came from the lips of a beautiful woman.

They didn't speak for a while. It was an uneasy silence full of dark thoughts and words unsaid. Bond drank his coffee and glanced at the front page of *The Times* which she had brought in from the front door. Nothing about the ructions in America. Those had slipped out of the front pages. A story about apartheid. The Medical Research Council was insisting that they had found a link between smoking and lung cancer. Bond glanced at the glowing tip in his left hand. Well, he had never smoked because he thought it was good for him and, if cancer had any fancy ideas about killing him, it would just have to take its place in the queue. Across the table Pussy finished her Bloody Mary. Bond slid the paper aside, stood up and kissed her briefly on the lips. 'I'll see you later.'

Suddenly she was holding onto him and there was a hardness in her eyes. 'You know – if you want me to leave, you only have to say.'

'I don't want you to leave.'

'No? Well remember – you were the one who invited me here. I got by perfectly well without you and don't think I need you now.'

21

'Put away those claws, Pussy. I'm glad you're here.'

But was he? Sitting behind the wheel of his 4½ litre Bentley, cruising silently up towards Hyde Park, Bond thought about what he had said and wondered if he had meant it.

What had begun with a routine enquiry about gold smuggling had turned into one of the most dangerous – and most fantastical – assignments of Bond's career. Somehow he had found himself at the heart of a conspiracy that had brought together the elite of American crime syndicates including The Machine, The Cement Mixers and the Unione Siciliano. That was when he had met Pussy Galore and she had been with him at the end when Bond had confronted Goldfinger and forced his Stratocruiser out of the sky. In truth, she had done little to help him, but he had to acknowledge that knowing she was there, having a friend in the enemy camp, had spurred him on to make his hair-raising escape.

It was only afterwards that the question had come – what was he to do with her? He had left America in a storm with the press demanding to know more. The FBI and the Pentagon were on full alert. The fact that Goldfinger had come close to using a chemical weapon on American soil had caused shock and outrage in the highest circles. Goldfinger had told Bond that he had killed the four main gang leaders but this still had to be confirmed and meanwhile their associates were being harried up and down the country with more arrests being made. Pussy Galore had played her part in the conspiracy. She was a known criminal who had graduated from cat burglary to organised crime. She had colluded in the murder of Mr Helmut M. Springer of the Purple Gang. It had all been a close-run thing and the Americans were in no mood to make exceptions. If she fell into their hands, she would go down.

In the circumstances, Bond felt he had no alternative. He had taken her with him, justifying his actions by reporting (falsely) that she had agreed to co-operate and might have information that could help the Bank of England track down its missing gold. Pussy Galore had never been to London. She had nowhere to stay. It seemed only reasonable to install her in his own flat... at least until things had quietened down and they had decided what they were going to do...

He was already regretting it. Pussy needed him. But there was something in his make-up that didn't want to be needed, that resented the very idea. And the fact was that she was a fish out of water away from the streets of Harlem. Already the relationship was beginning to lose its appeal, like a favourite suit that has been worn one too many times.

Bond knew he was being unfair but he never felt completely comfortable sharing his life with a woman. He remembered his time with Tiffany Case, how it had ended with pointless arguments, the two of them snapping at each other before she moved into a hotel and then, finally, left altogether. He still desired Pussy Galore but he did not want her. Even the boiled egg she had given him for breakfast had somehow irritated him. Yes, he had his fads. He liked things done a certain way. But he didn't like to be reminded of it and he certainly resented the slight mocking quality in her voice.

He didn't know what to do with her. They'd had a wonderful few days together, visiting some of the tourist sights of London, and she'd loved everything with that sense of childish abandonment that comes of finally being out of danger. She'd insisted on taking a boat down the river and, sitting on the deck together, watching the various bridges glide past, they could have been any couple, just two ordinary people enjoying each other's company and then, later on, each other. And yet it couldn't go on for ever. Bond was already feeling uncomfortable. Only the night before he had bumped into an acquaintance at the Savoy and had been quietly pleased to see the other man's eyes gliding over the beautiful woman on his arm. But then she had spoiled it by introducing herself. Pussy Galore. The name, which had seemed both challenging and appropriate when he had first met her at the hoods' congress in Jersey City, became jejeune, almost puerile, in a serious London hotel.

He was just glad that May, his elderly housekeeper, was away for a month, nursing her sister who was ill in Arbroath. What would she have had to say about the new arrival? Bond could almost hear her voice as he joined the traffic at Hyde Park Corner and swept into Park Lane. It was as if she were sitting next to him. 'It's all right for you, Mr James. Ye must do what ye want and it's no' my place to say otherwise. But if y'ask me, I'd say you'd do better with a nice young English lassie looking after ye. Or better still a Scottish one. And you know what they say. Choose yer wife with her nightcap on! You should take heed of that...'

Two hours later, with the smell of cordite clinging to him, Bond stepped out of the lift on the fifth floor of the Secret Service headquarters and made his way along to the door on the far right. It led into a small anteroom where a young woman was sitting, sorting through the mail. She didn't get up as he came in, which told Bond at once that she was displeased with him. Loelia Ponsonby was in every respect the perfect secretary. Discreet, loyal, efficient, she also happened to be strikingly beautiful – he simply could not imagine working with a woman who was plain or unattractive. Normally she would have fussed over him, taking his coat and filling him in on the latest office gossip. But she had overseen his travel arrangements, returning from America. She had typed up his reports. Doubtless she had noted that Bond had not returned alone and that one P. Galore was now ensconced in Chelsea. Loelia Ponsonby was not jealous. Such a trait would not have been part of her emotional make-up. But spending so long in a world made up, quite literally, of secrets and service, some of its austerity had rubbed off on her and she disapproved of an agent – particularly from the Double O section – cavorting with someone who might be at best a distraction and at worst a security risk.

'Any messages?'

'Mr Dickson called. He said he's coming in next week and wants to see you at Swinley.'

Bond smiled to himself. Dickson was just one of the names used by Agent 279 who operated out of Station H in Hong Kong. Every year he came back to England for a fortnight, escaping from his cramped, windowless office on the water-front. 'Thank God – two weeks' respite from the Fragrant Harbour,' he would say. It was part of the ritual that he would invite Bond to a round of golf even though he was one of the worst players on the planet, topping the ball and hitting slices and pulls with a stream of filthy invective. But there was only one golf club in Hong Kong '…and the grass came from Africa, would you believe it?' He liked the change of scene. It made him feel at home.

'Anything else?' Bond asked.

'Only paperwork.' There was a hint of apology in her voice. She knew what he thought of paperwork.

Bond walked into his office with its three desks – two of them, as always, unoccupied – and sat down. Loelia Ponsonby had stacked up the brown folders and he knew that she would have placed the most urgent ones at the top. He took out his cigarette case and lit his fifth cigarette of the day, inhaled deeply and reached for the file.

His hand had barely pulled it towards him when the telephone rang, the bell almost indecently loud in the room with its wood panels and high ceiling. It was M's Chief of Staff. 'Can you come up?' he asked. 'M wants a word.'

And that was it. Eight words that might mean anything: a change of duty, an invitation, the need for an immediate death. Bond sucked once more on his cigarette, then ground it out and went to meet his fate.

2

Racing Uncertainty

The Communications Room of the Secret Service occupies the seventh floor of the building, although it used to be in the basement. It was forced to relocate as a result of one of the first directives sent by M in the week after he had taken over as Head of Intelligence. It was M's desire to bring at least some aspects of the physical training of his agents into the building and he had twisted Civil Service arms to find funds for a sophisticated, modern shooting range and full-time staff. When it had been pointed out to him that the Communications Room occupied the space that he required, he had sent one of the terse signals that were soon to become his benchmark: *Move it*. And so it had gone.

Perhaps as a nod to the past, the Communications Room still retains much of its subterranean nature though. The blinds are always drawn and although there is some overhead lighting, it is kept almost deliberately low as if this will somehow lend itself to the secrecy of the work that is done here. The operators – they are predominantly female – prefer the more concentrated glare of the Artek flexible metal tube lights which are clamped to their desks. The only constant sound in the room comes from the banks of chattering teleprinters round the walls. A circular table stands at the far end and it is here that the Communications Duty Officer sits and reads through incoming traffic before having it sent out to the relative sections. Beside him, there is a bank of pneumatic tubes leading to the section offices and every now and then, as the signals reach him, he gives the instructions for them to be rolled up, put in a cylinder and for the cylinder to be placed in one of the pneumatic tubes which opens and closes with a hiss. A spare copy of each signal remains on his table.

The evening before, as Bond was leaving the building, one of the girls had come over to the Duty Officer and given him a signal that she had just decoded.

'It's Station P again, sir,' she said.

The Duty Officer was called Henry Fraser, a darkly handsome man with the broad shoulders and solid features of a rugby player. He'd actually got his first cap at nineteen and he'd been a prized member of the Double O section until an assignment in Lisbon had gone badly wrong and he'd come home with a bullet in his spine. Now he was in a wheelchair. The British Secret Service is not good at looking after its wounded officers and the first inclination of the top brass had been to pension him off, somewhere out of sight. M had insisted otherwise – and once again he'd got his way. Now Fraser was an invaluable member of the team, a man of huge resource who had lost none of his good looks. All the girls wanted to mother him ... although several of them had rather less wholesome thoughts.

Fraser read the signal and his lips pursed in a whistle. He nodded and the girl rolled it up and placed it in a tube that was set slightly to one side. 'That'll put the cat among the pigeons,' he said.

Another hiss and the roll of information disappeared on

the next stage of its journey that took it, in seconds, to the ninth floor.

And now, a day later, Bond followed it, making his way down the long, anonymous corridor that led to the door of M's staff office. There was nobody else around and the soft carpet swallowed up the sound of his approach. He reached the green door that stood one from the end, and opened it without knocking. It led into the office of Miss Moneypenny, M's private secretary. She was watering a potted plant – an aspidistra – that was a recent addition to her desk and she looked up and smiled. She liked Bond and she didn't mind that he knew it.

'You never told me you had green fingers, Penny,' Bond said.

'I wish I didn't.' She scowled. 'It was my birthday last week. I notice, incidentally, that I didn't get anything from you.'

'What do you give a girl who has everything?'

'Not a potted plant. Some of the other secretaries clubbed together and I put it here in case they look in but I keep hoping it'll die.'

'Then why are you watering it?'

'I'm overwatering it. I'm trying to drown the bloody thing. But it doesn't seem to care.' She put the watering can down. 'You're to go straight in.'

Bond went through the adjoining door, closing it behind him. M was sitting hunched over his desk, a pipe resting in one hand, the other holding a fountain pen, which scratched noisily across the bottom of a sheet of paper coloured pink for *Most Immediate* as he appended his signature. He was not alone. Bill Tanner, his Chief of Staff, was with him and nodded as Bond came in – a signal perhaps that this was not a life-and-death situation: war hadn't been declared. The atmosphere in the big, square room with its dark green carpet and desk, centrally placed, was relaxed, almost informal. Bond had known it otherwise.

'Come in 007,' M grunted. 'Take a seat. I'll be with you in a minute.' He signed a second document and slid both of them into his out tray. Then, noticing that his pipe had gone out, he tamped the tobacco with his thumb and lit it again. Finally he looked up with the clear grey eyes that demanded absolute loyalty and which would know, instantly, those who could not deliver it. 'I seem to recall you used to be interested in motor racing. Done any lately?'

Bond was taken unawares but he was careful not to show it. When M asked you a question, he expected an answer, not another question. 'Nothing serious, sir,' he said. 'But I like to keep an eye on the form.'

'Well, then, you know all about this Russian racer they've turned out. Understand they're running it for the first time on that German track – the Nürburgring – in the European championship.'

'The Krassny?' Bond had the gift of good recall, an essential part of his psychological armoury, and he dredged up what he'd read, at the same time wondering where this was going. 'It's a bit of a beast from what I've heard. The Red Rocket they like to call it. Sixteen cylinders in two banks of eight. Two-stage super-charger, disc brakes, all the latest gimmicks. Sounds as if it ought to go.'

'How would you fancy its chances at Nürburgring?'

'Well, it all comes down to the driver – particularly in a tough race like that with plenty of cornering. I'd say that we and the Italians, and perhaps the Germans, should see them off. But you can't tell with the Russians. They've got big sleeves and quite a lot up them.'

'Just so. And they don't like having failures in public.' M puffed at the pipe and Bond recognised the smell of Capstan Navy Flake, the same tobacco that M had always smoked since he'd picked up the habit as a young officer serving in the Dardanelles. The grey-white smoke curled around his head. 'Would it surprise you to know that SMERSH has been called in to try and improve the odds for the Russian cars?'

SMERSH. Smiert Spionam – or Death to Spies. It was a secret department of the Soviet government but one that Bond knew well. How many *konspiratsia* had started life on the second floor of the drab building on the Sretenka Ulitsa in Moscow? Everything they touched brought ruin and death. And yet it was almost impossible to imagine them getting involved in the bright, modern world of motor racing. It was a clash of cultures.

'Good heavens, sir!' Bond startled. 'What have SMERSH got to do with it? Are they going to sabotage all the opposition or what?'

'Well, it's an odd business,' M admitted. 'But apparently the Russian team's been practising in Czechoslovakia and the atmosphere in their camp is completely cloak and dagger. No journalists allowed anywhere near. Out on the track at the crack of dawn. Almost as if they're preparing for a war rather than a race.'

'We got word from one of the pit staff,' Bill Tanner chipped in. 'He fought with the RAF over here during the war and he became curious about what was going on. He kept in touch with Station P.'

'That's right. He found out the Russians are utterly determined to win. They've studied the field and they're pretty confident of beating everyone except our own chap, the British champion Lancy Smith in his Vanwall. Fair enough, and I suppose that's the usual gossip you'd get in the pits. But our source, this Czech, became interested in one driver in particular. Number Three. He isn't a regular member of the Russian team but he's the one who's been calling the shots and everyone seems to be afraid of him. With good reason.'

'Who is he?'

'Ivan Dimitrov.' Tanner took out a file. There was a photograph attached, taken with a concealed camera. It showed a gaunt, scowling man standing beside a racing car with one arm raised. His eyes were two black slashes that were staring straight at the lens. 'He was a first-class racer until he was banned from the circuit two years ago. He deliberately forced another driver off the track, pushing him off at a corner. He said it was an accident but the officials thought otherwise. The other man ended up in hospital in a critical condition. He was lucky to pull through. Dimitrov hasn't raced since.'

'So where's the link with SMERSH?'

'Moscow put pressure on the FIA to allow this man back,' M said. 'And they certainly wouldn't do that just for the hell of it. Anyway, there's something else. Our Czech friend sent in his last report three days ago. He said he'd seen Dimitrov staging crashes and that he was convinced they were planning to put Lancy Smith and the Vanwall out of the race – crash him. He wanted to get closer to this driver, Number Three, and find out more about him. I was inclined to dismiss the whole thing. I agree, it doesn't sound like SMERSH. But last night we got another signal. Our man is dead. He was killed in a car accident. The local police are saying it was a hit-and-run but it seems too much of a coincidence. I think we have to accept that Lancy Smith could be a target.' M fell silent for a moment. 'What do you think? Would it be possible to arrange an accident at those speeds? Could they do it and make it look innocent?'

Bond considered for a moment. 'There are quite a few ways they could do it, sir,' he said. 'But it wouldn't be easy. Smith won at Monaco last year – and Monza. He's not going to let himself be outmanoeuvred.'

'So what's the most likely bet?' Tanner asked.

'Well, I suppose Dimitrov could try and hedge him in on a corner but he's already tried that once and it's too obvious. It would be better to come up behind Smith just as he was starting to go into a middle-speed curve, say at eighty or ninety mph. My guess is he'd do it fairly early in the race when everyone is close together and fighting for position. If he nudged Smith's inside rear wheel just as he was starting into the turn, it would make Smith's car oversteer and he'd almost certainly be a goner.' Bond shook his head, imagining the impact, the spinning metal, the possibility of devastation.

M lowered his pipe, resting his fist on the surface of the desk. For a moment his eyes were fixed on the bowl as if he could somehow divine the future in the smoke and the glowing ash. His face gave nothing away but Bond knew that he would be weighing up every possibility. Would the Russians engineer a crash, possibly involving the death of a champion driver, not to mention any number of innocent bystanders – simply to demonstrate the superiority of Soviet engineering? Bond had no doubt of it. It was just one more example of the utter cold-bloodedness and contempt that seemed to be built into the Slavic race.

'And I suppose, 007,' M went on, 'that while Dimitrov is trying to do this to Smith, if we had the right man in the right car, he could do the same thing...'

'...crash him before he got to Smith,' Tanner added.

Bond saw at once where this was going. And this time, he didn't hesitate. 'Yes, it could be made to work that way. Given the right car and the right man.'

M and his Chief of Staff exchanged a look but they had both made up their minds. 'I seem to remember you used to race that old Bentley of yours,' Tanner said. 'Do you think you'd be any good in a modern car?'

'They run about twice as fast these days,' Bond replied. 'But if you're thinking of something like a Vanwall or a Ferrari, of course the safety factor's gone up with the speed. Better brakes, better steering, better alloys in the frame. Given a bit of practice, I suppose I could last some of the distance if I was lucky.'

'You're going to need more than luck,' M rasped. 'The race is a week away and I want you to put in some serious training. We've got someone who's agreed to help. A professional racer, name of Logan Fairfax, works at a track near Devizes.'

'You can get three or four days' hands-on experience,' Tanner went on. 'Nowhere near enough but better than nothing – and if, as you say, Dimitrov tries something early on in the race, maybe you can come up with a trick or two that allows you to keep up with the pack. Anyway, the important thing is to protect Lancy Smith. The man's something of a national hero and the press like him too. He's got something of the dash of those Battle of Britain pilots we all remember so well and, frankly, these days we need our heroes alive and well.' He smiled. 'Girls swarm all over him too.'

The last remark was a cue for M to weigh in. 'I understand you still have that young woman staying with you,' he said, not disguising the gruffness in his voice. For M, the private lives of his agents were their own affair – until the moment they became entangled with the reports that crossed his desk.

'Miss Galore?' Bond feigned innocence. 'I felt I had to put her up for a while until she sorted herself out, sir. She was quite useful to me.'

'I read the report. But the Americans aren't happy about it. I had two men from the embassy in this office only yesterday. Well, that's what they said. Central Intelligence Agency, obviously. They have some questions for her and I'm not sure we can protect her if they want to bring her in.'

'I can speak to her.'

'I think you should, 007. The girl's a paid-up member of a criminal gang, let's not forget. It might not be a bad idea for her to make alternative arrangements.'

'Yes, sir.'

Bond was annoyed. But as he made his way back down to his office he had to admit the wisdom of what M had said and rather cursed himself for agreeing to let Pussy Galore travel with him. Incredibly, Loelia Ponsonby already seemed to know which way the wind was blowing. Perhaps she had picked it up on the powder-vine, the illegal conduit for information that began in the girls' restroom. At any event, she was more than usually attentive and as the day wore on Bond got a sense of everything being in its right place. This was his world. It was everything that mattered to him and anything else – friendship, even love – was extraneous. By the time he got into his car to drive back through London that evening, his mind was made up. He had a job to do and the girl had to go. It was time.

And yet, almost as soon as he arrived home he changed his mind. Pussy Galore was waiting for him when he walked in, dressed in a tightly cut jacket and short skirt. She looked just the way she had when he'd first set eyes on her in America. She had fixed two whisky sodas with plenty of ice and brought them over.

'I won't even ask about your day,' she said. 'Because I know you won't tell me. So here's mine. I went to Fortnum & Mason, then I had lunch at the Ritz. In the afternoon I went to that exhibition that's been in all the newspapers; that man, Klein. I didn't get it, if you want the truth. He seems to like blue an awful lot and slapping paint on a canvas – anyone can do that. Anyway, I hung around maybe an hour and then I left.' She took out a cigarette and lit it. 'There's something you should know…'

'What's that?'

'Well, maybe there's nothing to it, but there were two men outside the gallery. I spotted them at once. You get used to keeping an eye out in my line of work, and these two apes stuck out a mile. Cheap suits, tough-looking, American. They were waiting for me, no doubt about it. They straightened up the moment I came out and one of them dropped his cigarette and ground it out.'

'What did you do?'

'For a minute, I thought of dealing with them myself. It wouldn't have been too difficult, even without a gun. But I didn't think you'd be too pleased if I left you two stiffs on the London sidewalk. Sorry – pavement.' She smiled scornfully.

'So I pretended I'd forgotten something. I looked in my bag, then I turned round and went back into the museum. Hell, I'd spent enough time there already, but I'd noticed an exit on the other side and I just slipped away. But if they knew I was there, they could probably find me here.'

'Who do you think they were?'

'The Machine? The Mob? You tell me. We left behind quite a few unhappy people when we skipped New York, and quite a big heap of dead gangsters too. My girls will be wondering why I ran out on them and they won't be alone. They're gonna want answers to some questions and maybe they've sent over some muscle to get them.'

'I don't think you've got anything to worry about,' Bond said. He was remembering what M had told him. He'd had two men from the CIA in his office only the day before. The same two men? 'Nobody's going to try anything here in London and there's probably a perfectly innocent explanation for it. But I'll have a word with my people and make sure they keep an eye on you.' He drew a breath. 'I have to leave London for a couple of days.'

'Oh yeah?' There was a flash of anger in her eyes.

'It's a job. It's not very far away and I'll leave you the name and number of my hotel. I'm sorry. But that's how it is.'

She was going to argue, then thought better of it. She shrugged and managed to smile. 'Sure. I get it. Waving the flag for Britain while the little woman stays behind. Is that it?' She blew out smoke and crumpled the cigarette in an ashtray. 'Well, you promised me dinner and I've got an appetite like a horse. And maybe you can order those oysters of yours after all. I just remembered they're an aphrodisiac so tonight I want to see you swallow a plateful.'

A little while later they left together and, maybe because Bond had other things on his mind, he didn't notice the two men sitting in the grey Austin, parked in the shadows. But they saw him. They saw the girl. They were prepared to wait. Their moment, they knew, would come.

3

Back to School

Bond watched the needle touch 100 mph, enjoying the sudden emptiness of a long, straight road that had invited him to put his car through its paces, speeding across the Hampshire Downs. He had bought the Bentley Mark VI just days after he had lost his old model, crushed beneath fourteen tons of newsprint – a parting shot from Hugo Drax as Bond pursued him through the Weald of Kent.

He hadn't yet had time to add the Amherst Villiers supercharger that he favoured but that had certainly pleased Cranwell, the former Bentley mechanic who tended Bond's cars with an almost proprietorial care and who didn't approve of blowers. 'Forget all the twiddly bits, Mr Bond. These superchargers! All they do is suck, squeeze, bang and blow. Who needs it?' Bond couldn't help smiling as he remembered the mechanic's aphorism. Who indeed?

And yet, just after he had bought the car he had been forced to surrender it for a week to Q Branch who had added a few accessories of their own. That was typical of M. If a piece of equipment ever failed one of his agents, he would take a long, hard look at what had happened and would try to make sure it never happened again. It was the reason Bond had been forced to give up his much loved Beretta .25 after it had jammed just once.

Q Branch had put in an alarm button – it would transmit his precise location at the same time as it called for help – run-flat tyres and a secret panel in the glove compartment to conceal a weapon, particularly useful if he was crossing international borders. He had opened it to discover a Walther PPK already waiting for him, doubtless provided by Major Boothroyd, the Secret Service armourer. The Bentley had other safety features but Bond ignored them. The car belonged to him, not to his work.

He came to a roundabout and changed down, the right-hand gearstick gliding smoothly in his hand. The journey had taken him just two hours from London, leaving at first light, down the motorway into a countryside that in the years following the war had become too complacent with its thatched cottages and croquet lawns, the homes of bankers, judges and retired brigadiers who weren't content just to live there but had to take the place over. Suddenly 'country' meant not just where you lived but how. He had been told to look out for a church, Norman of course, and there it was with its neat little graveyard, home to nine generations or more, all of them doubtless dying comfortably in their sleep. And beyond it, there was the sign, FOXTON HALL 2 MILES, poking out of a hedgerow still studded with poppies.

A narrow, twisting lane led down to a valley surrounded by woodland, a secret place almost hidden away from the modern world. If there had ever been a hall here, it had long since been pulled down and the Foxtons had gone with it. But their name had been attached to the airfield that had been constructed here in the years leading up to the first war and which had served three Hawker Typhoon fighter bomber squadrons during the second. After that it had been decommissioned, passing into private hands. It was now a training school for would-be racing drivers – more than that, it was a meeting place for enthusiasts, somewhere to fine-tune their vehicles and their own performance away from the pressure of the Grand Prix circuit.

Bond drove through a gate and into the airfield, noticing a row of hangars on one side and a low, brick building that might have been an officer's mess on the other. A couple of mechanics were working on a car which they had dragged into the sunshine and Bond instantly recognised the raised nose and the solid bodywork of the Cooper-Climax T43 which had made its debut on the racing circuit just a few months before. This one wouldn't be going anywhere. Its innards had been spread over the grass and the two men were smoking, chatting to each other, clearly in no hurry to put it back together. Bond parked the Bentley and got out, languidly lighting a cigarette, his first since he had left London.

At the same time he heard the familiar, angry buzz of an engine and saw a car hurtling around the perimeter track that wound its way all round the airfield. It was a bright red Maserati 250F, a car born to be a classic, and it was being handled by an expert; he knew that at once. Bales of hay and oil drums had been arranged to exaggerate the corners and to provide chicanes and the driver was taking them aggressively, barely slowing down as she put the car through its paces. How did Bond know it was a woman behind the wheel? There was no way he could make her out at this distance – and anyway he was unable to see very much of her, seated in the cockpit with its wraparound Perspex screen, her face concealed by a leather cap and goggles – but there was a lightness of touch about her driving. As she swung round the corner, she barely touched the apex. It was as if she was flicking ash off the shoulder of a man's coat. Only a woman drove that way.

Bond walked slowly to the edge of the circuit and waited as the car slowed down and finally shuddered to a halt beside him. It really was a beautiful thing with its stretched-out bonnet, high tail and soft curves – not a single straight panel in sight. It was somehow instantly recognisable, the sort of car that every schoolboy would dream of driving. Even the sound it made was perfect, a vast sheet of calico endlessly torn. Bond loved its colour. He couldn't imagine the Maserati being anything but that flamboyant red, racy in every sense. Suddenly he was looking forward to this assignment. To hell with SMERSH and their endless malevolence. To hell with the Russians and their pathetic quest for world domination in every field of human activity. He would do what he had to do, but for once he would do it cheerfully. He was going to drive this car at Nürburgring and he was going to enjoy it.

The driver had turned off the engine and climbed out. Even before she took off the headgear, Bond had noticed the shape of her breasts, the full hips, the strong, rather muscular, arms and legs. Maybe it was the way she had handled the car, her affinity with that beautiful machine, but he found her instantly desirable, even before she had removed the helmet to release chestnut hair that fell carelessly down to her shoulders and taken off the goggles to reveal deep brown eyes that were all the more enticing because they looked at him with such scorn. She smelled of sweat and high-octane fuel and there were streaks across her cheekbones, left there by the sunshine and the wind. She had the hard edge and the self-confidence of a woman in a man's world. She must have been about thirty years old.

'Do you have a cigarette?' she asked.

Bond took out his cigarette case and offered her one but she didn't wait for a light, using a Zippo which she took out of her breast pocket.

'You're Bond?'

'Yes.'

'I'm Logan Fairfax. They told me you were coming. They said you were some sort of policeman.'

'That about sums it up.'

'And you're going to race at Nürburgring – for the first time. Is that right?'

'Yes.'

'A stupid sort of policeman, then. Quite possibly a dead one.'

She began to walk towards the hangar and, suppressing a smile, Bond followed her. Everything about her body language spelled trouble, the way she had casually turned away from him, the way she was walking now, the uncaring sway of her hips. They passed the two mechanics, who glanced up briefly, then entered the hangar where a makeshift office had been set up behind two more racing cars – an old 8CTF and an Aston Martin which immediately caught Bond's eye – along with stripped-down engines, tyres, pieces of bodywork and all the other detritus of the racing world. She pulled off her jacket to reveal a faded denim shirt, unbuttoned at the neck. She wore no jewellery but Bond noticed an Omega Gold Seamaster automatic on a brown leather strap. It was exactly the sort of brand he'd expect a professional racing driver to have, but he was surprised to see it on her wrist. It was a man's watch.

She sat down in an old-fashioned swivel chair and examined Bond coolly. 'So where have you raced?' she asked.

'Goodwood and Silverstone,' Bond replied. 'Also at Albi in south-west France—'

'Albi? You mean the *Circuit des Planques*. That's strictly for beginners. Do you have any idea what you're letting yourself in for? Has anyone told you about Nürburgring?' She blew smoke into the air and it hung between them so Bond had to look through it to meet her eyes. 'I've heard it called the green hell. It's 22.8 kilometres. Twenty-two laps. One hundred and seventy-four bends and it's only twenty-six feet wide. Nürburgring never lets go of you. It never lets you rest. You think you can do a few laps in a Maserati down here and prepare yourself for that? You have to know every bump, every curve, every rise, every blind brow – and that still won't prepare you. The Eifel Mountains have their own weather pattern. You can start with the sun in your eyes, turn a corner and find yourself fighting through mist or drizzle. Dry road, wet road – either way, Goodwood's a billiard table compared to Nürburgring. Fangio, Behra, Schell ... they've all let it get the better of them and Fangio is the current race-lap champion. Nobody can expect to go round twenty-two times perfectly. You're airborne one second too long? You drop into the Carousel one second too late? You scratch your nose and for half a second you forget to concentrate? You're finished – and the best thing you can hope for is that you won't end up wrapped around a tree. Nürburgring will kill you, Mr Bond. But that's not what worries me. It's the thought of the people you'll take with you.'

Bond lit a cigarette of his own. 'First of all,' he said, 'you can call me James. And secondly, you seem to have got it into your head that I'm here because this is some kind of lark. The people I work for are very serious about this and there's a good chance that someone is going to be killed – at least, they will be if I'm not there to stop it happening. So why don't you be a good girl and stop lecturing me? If you don't want to help me, fine. But you might as well tell me straight away because I've driven a long way to be here and if you're not interested I need to find somebody else.'

She blushed slightly. 'Of course I'll help you,' she said. 'I agreed to help the moment I was asked. I was just trying to make you see what you're letting yourself in for. If this was Silverstone or Monza or anywhere, really, I'd just let you go ahead. But as it is, you have to *understand*.' Suddenly she was severe again. She swivelled round and opened a drawer, taking out a thick bundle of photographs and files. 'I want you to study these,' she said. 'Every night while you're here. Where are you staying?'

'I'm booked into a hotel outside Upavon.'

'These are photographs of Nürburgring. They show every detail, every curve, and I've got some moving film too. An entire lap. It was taken with a camera mounted on the front of a BRM. I want you to watch it again and again until it's printed on your mind – and even that won't be the same as driving it yourself. I want you to promise me you'll do at least a dozen circuits before you take part in any race. When you get out there, I can arrange for someone to show you round.'

'Hand on heart,' Bond assured her, matching the action to his words. 'And for what it's worth, in my line of work I try to look after myself. It's very much in my interest to make sure I'm prepared. Maybe you could go through some of these notes with me over dinner?'

The soft brown eyes considered the proposal for a moment, then dismissed it. She stubbed out the cigarette. 'Let's see if you can drive.'

A few minutes later, now wearing goggles and a leather cap of his own, Bond climbed into the Maserati. Logan Fairfax watched as he familiarised himself with various instruments in the cockpit. 'Comfortable?' she asked.

'Yes.' Bond was surprised by the amount of space. He had plenty of elbow room and he felt good being so low down.

Quickly, Logan took him through the practicalities of the car; the five-speed gearbox, the air vent, the all important gauges: revs, fuel pressure, water temperature. As she leant over him, her loose hair brushing against his cheek, he had to force himself to concentrate. 'Take it easy to begin with,' she was saying. 'The Maserati is one of the most perfectly balanced cars you'll ever drive. Get the feel of it and it will never bite you. All right? Let's see how you do...'

The car had no starter motor. The two mechanics from the hangar had come over and together they rolled the car forward. Bond slipped the gear lever into second then lifted the clutch. He heard the engine fire and at once the Maserati seemed to come alive, the energy flowing through it with a life of its own. He remembered something that Fangio had once said: 'You should never think of a car as a piece of metal. It's a living being with a heart that beats. It can feel happy or sad. It all depends on how you treat it.' This was the car that would come with him to Nürburgring. The two of them were in this together.

Bond pressed down on the throttle and felt the world fall away behind him, the slipstream rushing over his shoulders.

He changed up and pushed the gear lever effortlessly into place. It connected with barely a click. He had swung himself onto the perimeter track – he liked the oversized steering wheel – and knew at once that he would need all the strength of his shoulders and biceps to control the Maserati, particularly over a distance, but that if he played fair with this car, it would reward him with total obedience.

Logan Fairfax watched him speed into the distance. She saw him take the first corner in fourth gear, finding exactly the right slip angle and controlling the direction of travel. He was a good driver. There was no doubt of that. But Nürburgring? She shook her head and slowly walked away.

4

The Devil's Own

Two days later, Bond would have known everything there was to know about Nürburgring blindfolded – not that he would ever have suggested as much to Logan Fairfax. He had spent six hours a day driving the Maserati and another six going over the films, photographs and written descriptions she had provided: Brünnchen down to Pflanzgarten and then the vicious right bend to Schwalbenschwanz, the sudden change of surface at the Tiergarten brow. By now, the perimeter ring at Foxton Hall felt very short and tame. But at least he had begun to get a real feel for the car, that strange sense of being plugged in, of controlling everything through the lower part of his body, reading the signals without even having to glance at the gauges. The sound of the engine told him exactly how fast he was going and at how many revs per minute. He had calculated the right angle for the next corner long before he had reached it. He understood the car so well, he was beginning to think like it.

Logan would be waiting for him after every circuit and no matter how well he drove, no matter how far away he was when he made an occasional error, she didn't miss a thing. 'You need to work on the double-declutch. I want to see less wheel spin, and you overstrained the gearbox on that fourth bend. Do you want to rip out the linings?' The criticism never stopped, delivered with the air of a doctor admonishing a particularly wayward patient. There didn't seem to be any words of praise in her vocabulary. 'You're still braking too heavily. Just jab it gently and give it time to respond.'

But a woman's eyes never lie and Bond could tell that she was secretly pleased with his progress. Slowly, some of the ice seemed to have melted between them and tonight, for the first time, she had accepted his invitation to dinner and had even picked him up at the hotel, driving him in her Aston Martin to a little place she knew in Devizes where, she said, the food would prove there was some hope for English cooking after all. Without saying as much, they knew they had come to the end of the training and Bond had already worked out his route down through the Continent. The Maserati would travel ahead of him on a low-loader and it would be souped up and ready for him once he arrived.

Bond had a particular dislike of English country restaurants with their lace curtains, patterned plates, the napkins folded into shapes and the food which managed to be over-fussy and at the same time overcooked. The napkins at the Star and Garter had been shaped into swans, but it was run by a cheerful young husband-and-wife team. The room was welcoming with flagstones and Georgian windows and Bond was pleased to find a Petrus on the wine menu, a 1950 vintage no less – one of the great years for claret.

The two of them ordered smoked salmon, which was good, if cut a little too close to the skin, followed by excellent lamb cutlets from a local farm, cooked to a perfect pink. Vegetables – also from the area – were served *al dente* in a huge tureen. The wine, with its deep, ruby colour and scent of blackberries, set the meat off perfectly, and for the first time since he had left London, Bond felt completely relaxed.

'I've spoken to one of the drivers at Nürburgring,' Logan told him. 'He's agreed to look after you when you get there. You've probably heard of him. He's quite famous. His name is Lancy Smith.' Bond had to conceal a smile. Smith was the man he was supposed to be protecting – although of course he hadn't told Logan that. It was ironic that he should be the one who had agreed to help. 'He'll show you the circuit and introduce you to everyone else,' she went on. 'I haven't told him anything about you. He just thinks you're a rich playboy trying to buy your way into the racing circuit. There are a few people like that out there so no one will ask any questions.'

'How long have you known him?' Bond asked.

'All my life, pretty much. Everyone knows everyone in the racing circuit. They're all competing against each other but they're still friends. Lancy was a friend of my father's.'

'Alan Fairfax?' Bond was annoyed with himself. The connection should have been obvious from the start. 'I saw him race once at Silverstone. That would have been '52.'

She nodded. 'The World Driver's Championship. It was one of his last races.' Logan picked up her wine glass and held it close, breathing in the aroma. 'Dad bought Foxton just after I was born,' she said. 'He ran it as a business when he wasn't racing and I always loved it there. He'd have liked me to join the circuit. He had me sitting in a car before I was six months old. You saw that old 8CTF back at the office? That was his. I used to come back from school and help him strip it down. But my mother couldn't stand the idea of me racing and she simply put her foot down. She said it was too dangerous and in the end, of course, she was proved right.

'My father died at Le Mans two years ago. He wasn't even driving. He was there as a spectator and it was just his bad luck to be sitting in the grandstand when Pierre Levegh and Lance Macklin had their collision at 125 mph. I'm sure you'll have read about it in the papers and of course there were all those newsreels. The bonnet of Levegh's Mercedes came off and sliced through the crowd, killing a whole row of spectators, one after the other. It literally cut them in half. And that was just the start of it. There were pieces of smashed-up engines and brakes – then a fireball of burning petrol. Eighty-three people died that day. There were a hundred more with terrible injuries. He was one of them. He was taken to hospital in Angers but they couldn't do anything for him. He died the next day.'

'I'm sorry.' What else could Bond say?

'I was meant to be with him but I was here, working. And after he'd gone I just carried on. My mother never comes here any more. She can't stand the sight of racing cars.' Logan set her glass down. 'Is there really a chance that someone might get killed at Nürburgring?'

'It's possible.'

'Don't let it happen, James. These drivers are so brave . . . you'll see. Take care – and look after yourself too.'

Suddenly Bond wanted to be closer to this girl. She was smart, attractive and adventurous, but above all she had the quality that always acted as a magnet for him. The need to be loved. He wondered why she was so alone. He reached out and put his hand on hers. 'Thank you, Logan,' he said. 'You've done a great job looking after me. But why don't we take the night off? We weren't going to talk about motor racing. There must be other things you like.'

She drew her hand away. 'Yes, there are plenty of things. I like long walks and good food and the smell of mown grass and sunsets. But that's not what you're talking about, is it? Nearly all the people in my world are men and they're all after the same thing. You'll find that out soon enough when you get to Germany. There are plenty of girls who throw themselves at racing drivers. You'll see them in the stands. Peroxide blondes in short jackets and tight dresses. The saddest ones even travel from circuit to circuit hoping they can latch on to someone new. But I'm not like that.'

'And I'm not a professional racing driver,' Bond replied. 'Remember? I'm meant to be a rich playboy with more money than sense. All I'm saying is that in a couple of days I'll be out of your life. But that doesn't mean we can't enjoy tonight.'

'I am enjoying it.' She produced her first genuine smile and it changed her face, lighting up her eyes and bringing a warmth that Bond hadn't noticed before. 'I don't know anything about you either. Except you can handle a car, I'll say that for you. And you're obviously not afraid of danger. Where did you get that scar, for instance? There are all sorts of things I'd like to ask about you but I'm sure you won't tell me.'

'That depends how hard you try.'

The rest of the meal passed pleasantly enough and the two of them were touching shoulders as they returned to the car. Logan had insisted on driving and he was secretly glad that it meant she had to come with him to the hotel. It was a fairly ordinary place with solid beams and an inglenook fireplace in the reception, uneven walls and stairs that creaked. He had asked for the best room and had been amused to find himself in the honeymoon suite. Tonight he would be sleeping in a four-poster bed that sagged in the middle. And Logan?

He could sense that she wanted to stay with him but that something was holding her back.

And then, as they drove into the gravel path that swept round to the front door, everything changed. A grey Austin four-door saloon was pulling away and the driver was in a hurry. The wheels skidded, spitting up some of the surface, and the car leapt forward with an angry start. There was nobody in the front passenger seat but two people in the back. One of them was a woman with black hair and violet eyes that flashed briefly in the window – and at that moment Bond knew that he had seen the car before, outside his house in London, and that the woman was Pussy Galore.

Logan Fairfax came to a halt and Bond threw open the door. 'Stay here,' he commanded. 'Keep the engine running.'

'What is it?' She had heard the urgency in his voice and had seen him become, quite suddenly, a different man: colder, harder, single-minded.

'I'll be right back.'

Bond ran into the hotel. He still wasn't sure what was happening. Why had Pussy decided to come here? Why had she suddenly gone? He had given her the name and the telephone number of the hotel when he left London but he wouldn't have expected her to drive down without calling him first. In fact (he admitted it ruefully now), there had been a part of him that had been hoping she would simply pack her bags and fly home, that she would be gone when he returned. Then he remembered what she had told him. She had said there were two men following her. He had just seen two men in the Austin. The CIA? Bond had made the assumption too quickly. Suddenly he had his doubts.

He went straight to the reception desk where there was

a young man sitting uncomfortably in the bellboy uniform that his employers forced him to wear. 'That woman who just left—' he began.

'Did you miss her, sir?' The boy was annoyingly cheerful. 'That was your wife.'

'What?'

'Mrs Bond arrived earlier this evening, sir. She had dinner alone in the dining room. She said she was expecting you soon.'

'And those men?'

'They must have been waiting for her when she came out. I didn't actually see them meet her, to be honest with you. I just caught a glimpse of them leaving a moment ago. Is there anything wrong?'

But Bond was already on his way out of the hotel, back to the car. Logan Fairfax was waiting for him, concerned. She had left the engine running as he had asked.

He pulled open the door. 'The car that just left. Did you see which way it went?'

'Yes.'

'We have to follow it.'

She didn't argue. Of course she was the sort of girl who would know when to ask questions, and when simply to get on with the matter in hand. She was away at once, moving off as quickly as the Austin, but with much more control. The gravel stayed where it was.

They hit the main road. Already Bond was cursing himself. He had wasted time going into the hotel. He should have followed his first instincts and set off at once. There was no sign of the other car and it was a pitch-dark night. If the driver turned off into one of the many lanes that snaked through the countryside they would plunge almost immediately into thick woodland and disappear from sight. Logan seemed to have picked up his thought. 'There isn't a turn-off for a couple of miles,' she said. 'With a bit of luck, we should be able to see their tail lights.'

But there was nothing ahead of them ... just thick Wiltshire woodland and sprawling undergrowth on either side. No cars came the other way. Logan was utterly focused on her driving and Bond saw the speedometer touching sixty. With anyone else he would have been nervous. The road was narrow, twisting and unlit. But she was completely relaxed behind the wheel of the Aston Martin, pushing it through the darkness, and with every minute that passed Bond was certain they must be closing in on the Austin.

And yet still there was no sign of it. They reached the brow of a hill and Logan brought the car to a halt, gazing ahead of her.

'I don't understand it,' she said. 'They must have turned off. We should have caught up with them by now and if they were ahead of us, I'm sure I'd see their lights.'

'We haven't passed any turn-offs.'

'There aren't any.' She frowned. 'Wait a minute ... There's a track going into the woods. It must be a couple of miles back.'

'Where does it go?'

'It doesn't go anywhere, really. There's a clearing in the forest and a stone circle. There's not much of it left but it's a bit of a local tourist attraction. It's probably not its real name but people call it The Devil's Own.'

The Devil's Own. Bond digested the three words. Pussy Galore had been in fear of her life and she had come to him. Quite possibly she had fallen into the hands of the two men she had seen in London. But who were they? What did they want with her? And how would an old stone circle lend itself to their cause? There were no answers to those questions and time was running out. Right now, Bond had to decide. Did he continue along this road or did he turn round and go back? The wrong choice might well lead to her death.

'Let's try it,' he said. 'Unless you can think of anywhere else they may have gone.'

'They could have driven up to Walbury Hill, I suppose. Or they could have just pulled in and turned off their lights. They could be half a mile ahead of us now and we wouldn't see them. But they had no idea we were following them so why would they do that? I think you're right. I think we should go back.'

The decision was made. Logan turned the car and they drove back the way they had come, more slowly this time, staring into the darkness for the giveaway glow of a rear light. She hadn't even asked him who Pussy Galore was, although surely she must suspect the truth ... or at least, some of it. Bond gritted his teeth as they crawled along the road. He had a feeling that this was all his fault – and it looked very much as if it was going to end badly.

And then he saw it, so brief that he might have imagined it, except that Bond had never allowed the dark worm of imagination to get in the way of his work. There had been the briefest glimmer of light between the trees. It was white, not red, and too small for a headlight. A torch!

'There!' he said.

Logan was already accelerating. They reached a rough track they had passed a few minutes before but ignored because it had no signpost and hardly went anywhere. But this must have been the way the men had taken. She drove more carefully, not wanting the purr of her engine to give them away, knowing that any sound might travel all too easily in the still of the night. And the car played its part too, the tyres crunching almost silently over clumps of gorse and pine cones.

'What do you think they're doing?' she whispered.

'I don't know. How far does this track go?'

'I haven't been down here for years. Not very far, I think.'

'When we get to the end, turn off the engine and wait for me here. Whatever you do, don't get out.'

'What are you going to do?'

It was a good question. Bond thought of the Walther PPK tucked uselessly in the secret compartment of his Bentley. The Bentley was still parked at the hotel. How he wished now that he had been the one who had driven tonight. He put the thought out of his mind. Instead, as they rolled forward through the wood, he twisted round, wondering if there was anything in the car he might use as a makeshift weapon. Creeping up on two men, unarmed, in unfamiliar terrain was not an option – and to make matters worse, the moon had finally slid out from behind the clouds, lighting everything with a silvery-white glow. But the back seat was not promising: an umbrella, a paper bag with shopping supplies, a newspaper and a couple of books. What about the boot?

The track ended and they drew in close to the grey Austin, which sat there, dark and empty. The standing stones must be somewhere up ahead. Bond searched through the trees and was rewarded by a second flash of light. Was there going to be an execution? Was this what this was about? Bond braced himself for the terse rap of bullets in the dark but there was nothing.

'Wait for me here,' he said.

'Good luck.' Logan didn't seem to be afraid but her eyes were wide in the moonlight.

Bond took what he needed. A minute later, he was slipping through the forest, his rope-soled shoes making no sound whatsoever on the soft mosses beneath his feet. There was a footpath winding through trees that were suddenly huge and primeval beneath the moon and he could feel the ancient magic that might have drawn the druids or whoever it was who had come here to build their stone circle. The undergrowth brushed against his legs as he hurried forward, carrying the two items he had brought from the car. The night whispered to him, warning him to go back.

He came to a clearing and Bond knew that, even with all the extraordinary things that he had experienced in his line of work, he would never forget the sight, bathed in moonlight, that presented itself to him now.

The Devil's Own consisted of seven huge stones, broken fingers worn away by time and the elements. The ground on which they stood, forming an irregular circle, was flat with patches of wild grass and the surrounding trees seemed to lean in – as if they were complicit with what was going on. Pussy Galore was standing, stark naked, the moon accentuating her shoulders, her outstretched arms, the curves of her breasts. Ropes led away from her wrists, disappearing behind two of the stones. She was swearing, her body writhing, but the men were ignoring her as they continued with their work.

They were killing her. With gold paint.

Bond watched them in disbelief. Each of the men had a paintbrush and a tin of paint, which they were slapping onto her body so that it covered every inch of her flesh. Her arms and stomach were already coated. There was gold paint in her hair and it was trickling down the insides of her legs and dripping from the inverted V beneath her pudendum. Pussy rasped something particularly filthy and one of the men slapped paint across her face, half-covering her nose and lips. She choked and fell silent. The other man said something and they both laughed.

Bond knew exactly what was happening. He remembered what had been done to Jill Masterton, the girl who had helped him when he had first met Auric Goldfinger at a hotel in Miami. As revenge, Goldfinger had had her painted gold, clogging up the pores of her skin and causing her to die of suffocation. Bond was grateful he hadn't seen the obscenity for himself. He had been told about it later, by Tilly Masterton, Jill's sister. So the two men in the grey Austin must be in some way connected to Goldfinger. Someone, somewhere, blamed Pussy Galore for her part in his downfall and the failure of Operation Grand Slam and they had come for revenge. This was a hideous death in a public place that even had a suitably lurid name (the two men had surely chosen it deliberately) and would make the front pages of every newspaper in the world. And the message would be clear, the link to Goldfinger obvious. She was the betrayer. This was the price.

If Bond had not followed her from the hotel she would have been dead before morning. As it was, he had very little time. Her body was almost entirely covered with gold. He wouldn't be able to clean it off himself and the nearest hospital must be at least an hour away. He had to act now.

The two men had their backs to him. They had no idea he was there, about fifty feet away at the edge of the clearing. Bond had two cartons with him, which he had taken from Logan's shopping: Fry's cocoa and Cerebos salt. Had two such innocent items ever been put to more deadly use? He had emptied the contents and then filled the containers with petrol from a spare jerrycan that Logan kept in the boot. He'd also made two fuses out of strips of torn newspaper. There was every chance that they would blow up in his hand but it was too late to worry about that. Bond waited for the right moment. Now. The two men had stepped back as if to admire their handiwork. Pussy Galore was slumped between them, glistening gold, her head hanging down, the muscles in her arms straining to support her body weight. Bond took out his lighter, lit the fuses and threw his two makeshift bombs.

One fell short. The other hit the ground right next to the nearest of the two men and exploded, the flames leaping up, instantly devouring his legs and stomach. The man screamed. His companion had been splashed by some of the burning petrol – not enough to put him out of action but as Bond raced forward, covering the short distance between them, at least his attention had been well and truly diverted. He turned as Bond approached but too late. The heel of Bond's palm, lent extra force by his own momentum, slammed into the underside of the man's chin, rocketing his head back and almost certainly breaking his neck. Bond was already turning his attention to his partner who had seen what was happening and was caught between a set of contradictions that might almost have been comical: trying to scrabble for his gun with hands that were also fighting the flames. Bond didn't want to burn his own fists so used a judo move, twisting round and lashing out with the flat of his right foot. The man went down but even before he hit the ground the fire had half done Bond's work for him. He was dying or dead, a crumpled figure with the flames licking his back.

Bond ran over to Pussy Galore and released her. She fell against him and he felt the gold paint sticking against his clothes. He was sickened by what she had just been through and wished that he had listened more carefully when she had described the two men following her in London. CIA indeed! She didn't speak as he laid her gently on the ground and took off his jacket to cover her lower body. Using his bare hands he rubbed off as much paint as he could, exposing the flesh and, hopefully, allowing it to breathe.

'What have they done to her?'

Logan Fairfax was suddenly there beside him, and Bond glanced up at her angrily. 'I thought I told you to wait in the car.'

'That's right, James. And I decided to ignore you. Why don't you tell me what's going on here? Who is she?'

'A friend.' The two words sounded feeble, the stale admission of a suburban husband found cheating by his wife. While he had been trying to seduce Logan over roast lamb and a classic Bordeaux, Pussy Galore had been walking into this. 'We have to get her into hospital,' he went on. 'I can carry her to your car.'

'Do it quickly. We'll take her to Marlborough.'

'James?' It was the first word Pussy had spoken since he had reached her and it seemed to Bond that she spoke it with hostility. She couldn't open her eyes. The paint had sealed the lids shut.

'Don't talk,' he said to her. 'We're going to get you some help.'

The flames were still flickering on the grass and around the dead bodies as Bond carried her back to the car.

5

No Regrets

Marlborough had a cottage hospital – it looked more like a private house – and Bond was relieved to see a doctor and two nurses come hurrying towards them, alerted by the speed of Logan's approach and the scything of the tyres as she stopped. Pussy Galore was lying on the back seat, half covered by Bond's jacket, her breathing rapid, her eyes closed. Bond stood back as the medics helped her out onto a stretcher.

'What on earth happened?' the doctor asked. He was young, only recently out of medical school, with his white coat flapping around him. He seemed more offended than shocked. He had never seen anything like this before.

'I'll explain later.'

'Who did this to her?'

'It doesn't matter right now. Can you just look after her. Please?'

The doctor nodded. 'All right. You need to clean yourself up.'

Bond had gold paint smeared on his arms and across his chest. He could feel it sticking to his hands. He watched as Pussy was carried into the building. Logan was standing beside him. She looked at him curiously and Bond wondered if she thought this was his fault.

He cleaned himself as best he could in a downstairs bathroom and was waiting when, an hour later, the doctor returned. It was well after midnight and there was a sort of tiredness in the air, a sense of respite that only a hospital can have.

'She's all right. She wasn't hurt too badly and I've given her a shot of Pentothal to calm her down. We managed to get the paint off with turpentine and baby oil. The worst of it was around her eyelids, nose and mouth. I'm afraid there's going to be some irritation there and she's going to have to stay in for at least twenty-four hours. Do you live nearby?'

'I have a house here,' Logan said.

'Well, she's lucky she wasn't blinded. I can't imagine who would do such a thing to a woman. It's disgusting. Have you spoken to the police?'

'They're on their way.'

Bond had used the payphone in the hospital reception but he hadn't called the police. He had spoken to the duty section officer in London and told him everything that had happened, knowing – with a sinking feeling – that it meant opening the whole can of worms about Pussy Galore. M had told him to get rid of her – 'alternative arrangements' as he'd put it – and although Bond had fully intended to do something eventually, he had certainly been slow off the mark. God knows how the old man would respond when he read the signals on his desk the following morning. Meanwhile, Bond could imagine all the phone calls and the *MOST URGENT*s making their way between the Secret Service and Scotland Yard throughout the night. There were two dead men to be explained; Bond himself; and an American woman who had been the victim of a bizarre attack. This sort of thing didn't usually happen in quiet Wiltshire towns. The local press would be onto it like carrion crows and they'd have to be dealt with too. Meanwhile, the race at Nürburgring was just four days away and Bond knew that even if Logan was right and he was responsible for what had happened, he couldn't afford to hang around.

He spent the night crumpled on an armchair and he was there in the ward soon after Pussy woke up. Logan Fairfax had stayed in the room with her while she slept but now she had gone home to get some things – 'women's things,' she'd said – and Bond and Pussy were on their own. The hospital had just twelve rooms and she had been put at the far end of a corridor, as far away from the other patients as possible. They'd had to shave off some of her hair. She was pale and her voice was hoarse. But as she sat, propped up on pillows, those amazing eyes of hers were full of fight and in every other way she seemed her old self.

'Well, whaddya know,' she began. 'For once, Mr James Wonderful Bond got it wrong. I seem to recollect you said I had nothing to worry about. Just a figment of my imagination. Was that what you said? And before you say anything else, who's that girl you've been hanging out with? Pretty as a peach with those chocolate-brown eyes. I can't remember you mentioning anything about dinner *à deux* in some swanky pad as part of your mission to save the world.'

'Don't be ridiculous, Pussy,' Bond replied. 'She's just been helping me with my work. That's all. Now tell me what happened. How did you get here?'

'OK.' She took a breath. 'After you left, I didn't know what to do. Don't get the idea that I was a little-girl-lost without you! I was bored – that's all. I hung around the house for a while. I did a bit of shopping. I saw a movie. To be honest with you, I was beginning to think of heading back stateside. I'm not quite used to being Mrs Stay-at-Home – know what I mean? Anyway, I was walking down that King's Road of yours when I saw them again – two guys in a grey automobile. The same two guys I'd seen outside that gallery I went to. That was when I knew I had a problem. I thought of calling you but I'm not the sort to jump on the phone when I'm in trouble. Jeezus – when I was in Harlem, I took out plenty of hired muscle myself. It's amazing what you can do with a broken bottle and a little determination. A gal has to look after herself, and sitting there with my knees trembling, you know, I began to wonder what exactly had happened to me since I came to London with you.

'In the end, I decided to come down here. I thought I'd surprise you and let you handle it your own way. It's like I said the first time this happened, I didn't want to embarrass you. I was sure your bosses wouldn't be too pleased with you if I muscled in on your operation and there were dead bodies turning up on your doorstep.' (Well, that's true enough, Bond thought). 'I hired a car and drove down. It was good to get out of London anyway. I don't know how they followed me. Trust me, I took care but maybe it's because you people drive on the wrong side of the road and you've got so many twists and turns and traffic circles … I don't know. Maybe they already knew where you were staying and they got here ahead of me. They certainly knew all about that stone circle place.'

She broke off as a large, matronly type suddenly entered the room, carrying a cup of tea and two coconut fingers on a tray. Pussy Galore looked down disdainfully. 'Thanks all the same,' she said. 'But I don't suppose you could get me a tomato juice with a large slug of vodka?'

'Certainly not!' The nurse set down the tray and left.

Bond waited until the door had closed. 'So what happened when you got here?' he asked.

'I found the hotel and checked into your room. I told them I was your wife. It seemed the easiest thing to do. So I was waiting for you to turn up – I see you've been taking your work very seriously, by the way – and then I got hungry and went down for dinner. Horrible food too. So while I was eating, the waiter came in and told me there was someone asking for me in the reception and naturally I assumed it was you. I came out only to find Abbott and Costello and before I could do anything, one of them had pulled out a gun, keeping it low so only I could see. There was nothing I could do. They were pros – I could see that from the start. They made me walk out with them and bundled me into a car – and the rest of it, I guess you know.

'So tell me about Miss Fairfax. How does she fit into all this? Are you really here on a secret mission or did you just tell me that so you could skip town?'

'She's a racing instructor.'

'I know.'

'It's complicated, Pussy. I can't really tell you about my work but it looks like I'm going to have to drive in a race and she's been helping me.'

'She was nice to me too. She was here all night and when I woke up she stayed, talking to me. I'm getting out of here later today and she says I can move into her place.'

'Is that what you want to do?'

'Well, I'm not going back to London on my own, that's for sure. And you can keep your hotel. It's not my style. I don't know what I want to do, really. I need a bit of thinking time. Can you give me that?'

'Of course.'

In fact, Bond didn't see her for the next twenty-four hours. First he had to look into the local police station where he was kept waiting in a blankly empty interrogation room by a scowling detective inspector determined to show that he wasn't going to be pushed around – and certainly not by some hotshot from the city. Fortunately (as Bond found out later), a call came in from Ronnie Vallance, the head of Special Branch, and after that, Bond was rushed through paperwork and hurried out of the building as if he had contracted some particularly contagious disease.

Next, he drove back to London for meetings with Bill Tanner and a wasted afternoon in the Records Department. The two men who had taken Pussy were American – that is, their clothes, their haircuts and their dental work were American but they had carried absolutely nothing that might identify them; the mark of true professionals. One of them had a teardrop tattoo on his shoulder, made not with ink but with melted rubber, probably from a shoe. That suggested prison time. Photographs and fingerprints had been sent to New York but it would be days before any results came in.

'M isn't too pleased,' Tanner said, over lunch in the officers' canteen. 'He told you to get rid of that girl. He certainly didn't expect her to turn up in the middle of Wiltshire.'

'That makes two of us,' Bond agreed.

'How are you getting on with the Maserati?'

For the next few minutes Bond talked about the skills he'd learned and the pleasures of putting the car through its paces and the Chief of Staff had to smile. 'Girls and fast cars. Perhaps you're in the wrong job.'

That night, Bond stayed in his own flat. He realised that it was the first time he had been alone for quite a few weeks – and it also occurred to him that he preferred it that way. Steadily, without really enjoying it, he drank his way through half a bottle of Old Grand-Dad, then threw himself into bed. He slept badly, snapshot images of Pussy, Logan and – absurdly – M flickering through his mind. But of course that was what had caused his malaise. Bond liked to keep his life – and his women – in separate compartments, something which, for once, he had signally failed to do.

He woke up with a nagging hangover and the sense of disgust that comes with drinking alone, showered, and after three strong coffees, drove back to Marlborough. But by the time he got to the hospital, Pussy Galore had gone. According to the matron, she had checked out at lunchtime and she hadn't turned up at the hotel either. He wondered if she was staying with Logan. Perhaps she was angry with him. Both women must have known what was in his mind, the way he had toyed with them. So much for separate compartments. With nothing else to do he went through the Nürburgring photographs one last time. He suddenly had an urge to be out of the country.

He was sitting, smoking, in the lounge, when she walked in. She was wearing a loose-fitting raincoat and sunglasses that he hadn't seen before. It was possible that they were covering the damage that had been done to her eyes but it occurred to him that she was dressed for travelling. She sat down opposite him.

'I've come to say goodbye,' she said.

Somehow he wasn't surprised. He waited for her to continue.

'I'm heading back to Harlem. Seems to me I'm a sitting duck if I stay here and I need to get my gang back together – what's left of it – and pick up where I left off. One thing's for sure. I've seen enough of the British countryside to last a lifetime.' She reached for Bond's cigarette. He handed it over and she inhaled, her eyes never leaving his. 'You and me got it wrong, Bond. You made a mistake inviting me and I made a mistake coming. But you know what I always say. There are two types of mistake; bad ones and good ones. You were definitely one of the good ones. We had fun, didn't we? That Goldfinger thing was crazy and I'm glad that in the end we were together just so I could find out what it was like. But there's no future in it. You know it and I know it and we might as well pack it in before it all goes sour.'

'Whatever you want, Pussy.'

'Don't say that to me, you bastard! It's what you want too – don't think I don't see it. You know what the big difference is between us? You can't live with a woman in your life.'

She took another drag on the cigarette and handed it back.

'When are you leaving?' Bond asked.

'There's a flight out of Heathrow this evening.'

'Let me at least give you a lift to the airport.'

'You don't need to. I'm not going alone.'

Her eyes flickered to the doorway and Bond saw Logan Fairfax standing there. There was a gleam in her eyes that he recognised and understood at once. She had never looked happier.

'Yeah. I know it's insane,' Pussy continued. 'We've only known each other five minutes. But you gotta remember how we met and we had a whole night being next to each other and talking and somehow we both knew... something had clicked. We're going to take it one day at a time but – what the hell? If you don't live dangerously, why bother to live at all?' She got up and held out a hand. 'No regrets?' she asked.

Bond took it. 'No regrets,' he said.

She walked over to Logan and Bond watched as the two women disappeared together.

After they had gone, he went and paid his bill. A few minutes later, he drove away.

6

Nürburgring

Twelve years after the war, it was still too soon to be back in Germany. Bond wondered if he would ever be comfortable there. The ghosts were still present – the dead and the living. Driving through what was left of old Cologne, he reflected on the sickness that had seized hold of a nation and propelled it down the path to almost total destruction. He couldn't avoid it. The evidence was all around him in the gaping holes that still remained in the city and the cathedral – grim in that peculiarly Teutonic way – that had only been left intact so that the RAF could use it as a direction finder. All the rebuilding – the new park, the lakes, the cable car, the strikingly ugly blocks of flats that were going up on all sides – could not disguise it.

Bond's attitude to the war had always been simple. It was a cataclysmic struggle between good and evil, starker and more straightforward than any war that had ever been fought. As a teenager, in the thirties, he had been taken skiing and climbing in Kitzbühel, a medieval town in the Tyrol, and on his return to London, acting on his own initiative, he had sat down and painstakingly compiled a report on what he had seen – planes, troop movements, political activity and so on – which he had then sent with a covering letter to the Foreign Office. A few years later, even before the actual outbreak of hostilities, he had lied about his age to enter the Royal Naval Volunteer Reserve as a lieutenant and had been delighted to see a copy of that letter in the file before him. His enemies might be different now but, for Bond, the moral certainties remained the same.

Nürburg was two hours south, surrounded by fields and woodland that stretched out luxuriantly, ignorant of recent history. It would have remained an anonymous little town, neither ugly nor particularly attractive with an assortment of very ordinary houses, a local shop and a dilapidated fortress high up on a hill, but for the decision made thirty years earlier by the Allgemeiner Deutscher Automobil-Club. It was they who had agreed to the construction of the fourteen-mile circuit, which had at last given the place a reason to exist. More than a reason. Racing had become its heart and its soul and the high-pitched scream of engines tore across the countryside long before you drew near.

After his long journey, Bond was glad to slow down and cruise gently past the hotels and guest houses that had recently sprung up and which were almost shamed by the astonishing assortment of prestige cars haphazardly parked outside them. Shops and garages advertised a hundred brands of tyres, lubricants, gaskets, dry liners and motor accessories. There were people of every nationality parading in the streets and it amused Bond to identify them: the Italians self-consciously stylish, the French cocksure and casual, the Germans on their own, the English superior and the Russians ... Yes. He spotted them soon enough, walking together with that pinched look that comes from a poor diet and their dead-fish eyes. They made up a quartet, all dressed in clothes that were cheap and far too formal. He looked for Ivan Dimitrov. Did his teammates have any idea who he was? Not just another racer but an operative working for SMERSH? For the moment there was no sign of him and Bond drove on.

He checked into his hotel and changed into the clothes that would be both comfortable and practical on the circuit – a woollen jersey with waterproof patches on the shoulders and arms, trousers with pockets on top of the thighs and above the knees. He was wearing boots, light lace-ups lined with asbestos to shield him from the heat that would be transferred through the pedals, and an elastic body belt to protect his kidneys from road-shock. He carried with him a helmet, goggles, gloves, earplugs and, with so many gear changes ahead of him, a good supply of sticking plasters for his hands. He had arranged to meet Lancy Smith at the pit area and after a quick lunch of *Ahle Wurst*, rye bread and salad and a bottle of Gerolsteiner – the local mineral water – he strolled down to present himself.

He had seen Lancy Smith on newsreels and in the press and knew something of what to expect. Late twenties, fair hair, an easy smile and even a schoolboy scattering of freckles – if someone had designed a pin-up for the sport, this is what they might have come up with. On first sight, as he walked across the pit area through a crowd of mechanics and machines, he carried himself with the easy confidence and charisma of someone who had grown up surrounded by wealth. Bond recalled that his parents were titled with an ancestral pile somewhere in Berkshire. Well, this was a rich man's sport. No surprise there. There was something inside Bond that was prepared to dislike him but it vanished the moment they shook hands. Smith exuded warmth and good nature, something that the films hadn't been able to capture.

'Welcome to Nürburgring. Good journey down?'

'Yes, thanks.'

'I think I saw you in that Bentley of yours. Lovely car. Must have been fun bringing it down the Continent. Anyway, let's get you started...'

As far as Smith was concerned, Bond was an amateur, an interloper, but his greeting had been genuine, his enthusiasm and desire to help unforced. And if, like Logan Fairfax, he had his doubts about an inexperienced driver taking on Nürburgring, at least he expressed them less aggressively.

'I understand you've been around the block a few times,' he went on, as he walked with Bond to his car. 'Goodwood and Silverstone, Logan said. How is she, by the way? Great girl, don't you think? I knew her father – brilliant racer. Nerves of steel.' His voice trailed off and just for a moment Bond saw the doubt in his eyes, the recognition that he, Bond, was just an amateur by comparison. But then it had gone. 'Anyway, we'll drive round together in my old MG and I'll try and show you some of the horrors. Then you can do as many practice circuits as you can manage. I'd suggest nine or ten at the very least because there are the time trials tomorrow. See if you can get a feel for it, and if you have any questions you can catch me later. We usually have a pint at the Blaue Ecke. There's quite a crowd there. OK? In you get...'

Smith drove a beautiful little MG A Roadster, English white with red leather seats. A boy's toy, Bond thought as he climbed in. Once again, he was glad he had been given this job. Someone in Moscow had decided, quite casually, to kill or at the very least maim this young Englishman simply because they wanted to show off their own engineering. Forget the fact that he had friends, lovers, a life that he enjoyed living. It was a job to be done. And if fifty or a hundred spectators went with him, to hell with them too. That was the extraordinary thing about SMERSH, the way they reduced everything to ideology. They had once targeted Bond himself, turning his very existence into some sort of chess game with his destruction simply the final move. Well, it wouldn't happen this time. He would take a very personal pleasure, once again crossing their path, in keeping this young man alive.

'All set?' Smith asked. 'Then off we go.'

Twelve and a half minutes and one circuit later, Bond understood something of the challenge that lay ahead of him. Nürburgring was a brute from start to finish, cruel and unforgiving. The MG couldn't rival the speed of a racing car but the view from the passenger seat made the photographs and 8 mm films he had studied at Foxton Hall seem almost irrelevant. It was a long, green scream that would test every fibre of his being – physically, mentally, to the very depths of his soul – with a series of terrifying challenges that would demand an exact response within microseconds. Bond was reminded of the shooting gallery in the basement at Regent's Park where he practised against a tricky little device that effectively shot back at him. The circuit would test him in the same way, only this time *he* was the bullet and when the race began, he would be fired down a passageway as dangerous in its own way as the barrel of a gun.

Smith drove expertly, taking the corners at about seventy miles an hour, and Bond felt some of the centrifugal forces that would be five times worse when he was behind the wheel of the Maserati. There were moments when they left the road and hung in space, still hurtling towards the next obstacle. This was nothing like Goodwood or Silverstone. Bond had driven along country roads in Scotland and it seemed to him that Nürburgring had the same wildness, the same sense of magnitude. It was the road, not the car, which was the master here. And he would be up against real professionals; people who spent their whole lives taking on challenges just like this. As they accelerated down the long straight that led to the finishing line, Bond wondered for the first time if he – and M – hadn't bitten off more than they could chew.

Smith took him round twice, the second time more slowly, adding a commentary that described the journey in almost mystifying detail. There were fast corners and descents, humped kinks and blind spots, each one demanding a different set of calculations. Finally, he returned to the pits where they had begun.

'Well, that's about it,' he said, cheerfully. 'Good luck. I hope you enjoy yourself. You're driving a Maz, aren't you? Bloody nice car, absolutely made for racing – not cobbled together like some of the crates you see out here. I like what they've done with the chassis and you've got a real advantage being so low. Anyway, I'll see you tonight? We normally gather around six – then early to bed before the big start. Nice meeting you.'

And that was it. The man who was at the centre of a SMERSH conspiracy, and whom Bond had been sent to protect, drove off without a care in the world. Left on his own, Bond walked over to the pits, listening to the throaty roar of different engines as they were warmed up and fine-tuned by the mechanics. The air smelled of oil and methanol. Some of the drivers were crouching down by their cars. Others were standing in small groups, smoking. There was a sense of camaraderie that Bond knew would disappear the moment the chequered flag came down but right now, on the eve of battle, everyone was relaxed.

No. There was one man standing apart. Bond saw the car first, a black Krassny with a single figure – number three – painted on its belly-pan fairing. The car had none of the elegance or classic curves of the Maserati and quickly betrayed its origins; half a dozen production Soviet cars bastardised to produce this one ugly creature. The driver had also lit a cigarette and it seemed to Bond that his face was exactly the same colour as the smoke he was exhaling, with hooded eyes and thin strands of hair that hung loosely over a high forehead. His mouth was a narrow slash, a wound made with a blunt knife. For a brief moment he looked up and his snake eyes locked onto Bond's. He said nothing and showed no emotion but Bond knew that the connection had been made. The Russian had clocked him, made his assessment of this new contender, and filed the information away to be considered later.

Well, Bond had done the same and it helped him to have seen his enemy and, for that matter, the car he would be driving. The two of them would meet soon enough but for now Bond turned his back and went off to find his own car.

The Maserati had been unloaded that morning and sat waiting for him like an old friend. There was a man already working on the engine and he looked up as Bond approached. He was in his late fifties with greying hair and strangely aristocratic features given that he was wearing coveralls, spattered with oil. 'You're James Bond?' he asked.

'Yes.'

'My name is Bernardo Hertogs.' He spoke with a slight South American accent. 'Logan called me a few days ago. She asked me to look after you – or at least, to look after the car, which is the same thing.'

'You know her?'

'I raced with her father. We did the Panamericana together, back in '51. That was my last race. These days I like to work with the mechanics in the pit – just to be close to the cars.' He wiped his hands with a rag and then gestured at the Maserati. 'We've warmed the engine. Now you must let it cool for a few minutes and after that it will be ready for you. This is your first time at Nürburgring?'

Bond admitted that it was.

'We've just had the weather reports in and it looks as if it's going to be fine for tomorrow. But I will give you some advice. Watch out for the adhesion factor on the road surface. That's the whole secret. You don't want your wheels spinning too wildly. Other than that, take it easy at first.' He smiled crookedly. 'If you give the impression that you're not comfortable with the car, the rest of them will write you off. And then, when you put your foot down, they won't see you coming!'

Bond waited until the car was ready, then he put on his helmet, goggles and earplugs and climbed in. Bernardo and another mechanic pushed him off and suddenly he was away, just he and the Maserati, plunging into the green hell...

At the end of the day, with his second medium dry Martini in front of him, Bond lit a cigarette and contemplated his chances of success. Nürburgring was every bit as brutal as he had been warned and against the likes of Lancy Smith, the

Italian Luca Franchitti, the German Klausman, and even the Russian Number 3, he wouldn't stand a chance – certainly not over twenty-two laps. His only hope was that Dimitrov would make his move early, in the first or second lap, and everything he had learned made this the most likely scenario. Leave it too late, when the pack would have separated, and he might not get a chance. And that being the case, Bond had a few tricks of his own up his sleeve. If he got off to a decent start and kept his focus on the more vicious turns, he might just get away with it.

The Blaue Ecke was a pretty, old-fashioned place on a corner, as its name suggested, and, with the warmth of the evening, the drinkers had spilled out onto the cobbled street. There were about thirty of them but the number had been almost doubled by the girls who swarmed around like brightly coloured flies. Fast guys, fast cars, fast girls. Bond was an unknown, so they left him alone but he noticed that the racers seemed to be on easy terms with them and there was plenty of banter and lewd jokes. He felt a sense of complicity in the air and could easily imagine a game of musical beds that went from country to country. There was a stir as Lancy Smith arrived. He didn't need to buy himself a drink. A flute of pink champagne had appeared at exactly the same moment and found its way into his hand before he had even stopped.

He saw Bond and came over to him. 'How did you get on?'

'I was grateful for your help,' Bond said, non-committally.

'All set for tomorrow?'

'I hope so.'

Bond raised his glass midway to his lips – then stopped.

Three more men had gathered together across the road. They were directly in his eye line and even if he hadn't immediately and shockingly recognised two of them, his attention would certainly have been captured by the third.

Ivan Dimitrov was the first. The second man was also Russian and had presumably travelled all the way from Moscow to be here. Bond had never met him but had seen his photograph enough times in the files to know him as Vladimir Gaspanov, a high-ranking member of SMERSH and a possible successor to Colonel General Grubozaboy-schikov – 'G' – whose whereabouts were still unknown following the disastrous failure of his last operation a few years ago. Well, there it was. The link with SMERSH was proved. But what the hell was the general doing here? There was no way that such a senior officer would break cover, quite possibly putting himself in harm's way, simply to watch two cars collide.

And then Bond turned his attention to the third member of the group and knew at once that this wasn't just about the Krassny, that there was something else going on in Nürburg and that he had stumbled onto it quite by chance. This other man was angry. He was speaking rapidly to the general in a way that would have been a death sentence if the man didn't have some sort of power or protection of his own. Bond's every instinct screamed at him. Get a photograph. File a description. Find out more.

He was a Korean. Bond's first thought had been that he was Chinese but he had quickly corrected himself. His eyes were too small and didn't have the double eyelid, the famous epicanthic fold that he associated with the majority of that race. He was also too tall, very slender, with the long, delicate fingers of a concert pianist. His skin was olive-coloured, smooth but very pale and completely without blemish, like a china doll, and this – along with his slightly effeminate features – made it almost impossible to tell his age. Bond guessed that he must be around thirty but he could have been much younger, perhaps even in his late teens. Apart from the very faintest suggestion of eyebrows, he had no facial hair and the hair on his head was cut short with a dead straight fringe. Beneath this, he wore wire-framed spectacles that were almost cartoon-like, as if they had been drawn onto his face. The glass was unusually thick, suggesting poor or even damaged eyesight. As he spoke, he showed childlike teeth, as white as pearls and somehow inappropriate between the grey, half-suggested lips. The last Korean Bond had encountered had been squat and ugly, the sort of man who could only have been improved by being sucked through the window of a Stratocruiser, but this one was at least passably good-looking with the confident, easygoing aura that often comes with considerable wealth. He was immaculately dressed in a grey silk suit that had been made to measure, a white shirt open at the neck and well-polished Italian black leather shoes. He spoke at length, gesticulating with one hand. Ivan Dimitrov hung back, nervous.

Lancy Smith had noticed them too.

'Do you know who he is?' Bond asked. He gestured at the Korean.

'As a matter of fact, I do. He's got an interest in Grand Prix – strictly as a spectator sport. I've met him in Monaco and Paris. Interesting chap, by all accounts. His name is Sin Jai-Seong but that's not what people call him. On the racing circuit and in the fashion magazines they've inverted his name and Westernised it to Jason Sin. It's become a bit of a joke. Sin by name, sin by nature. And it works for him. Makes him seem racy, a bit of an adventurer, when actually his business is rather dull.'

'What does he do?'

'He has a recruitment agency and he's involved in construction. Based in America. They say he's one of the richest Koreans in the country. He certainly has a glamorous lifestyle, houses all over the world, including one not far from here. You can see it if you like. He always throws a big party after the race and all the drivers are invited.'

'Are you going?'

'I'll say! Cristal champagne, *foie gras* and caviar flown in from Paris, and plenty of girls. Just try not to break your neck, James, and I'll see you there.'

Lancy Smith moved away and Bond stood watching as the three men exchanged a few words and then went in separate directions. Bond thought of following one of them but decided against it. He had enough on his plate already and there was nothing to be gained by trudging through the streets at night. Even so ... Two Russians and a Korean meet in a small German town. It was like the start of a bad joke but Bond was certain he'd stumbled onto something. Dimitrov and Gaspanov were obviously connected. Was it just a coincidence that the two of them had been in conversation with Sin?

That night, Bond wrote a cable using the customary transposition code based on the day of the month and addressed it to the Chairman, Universal Export, London. It occurred to him that he might be jumping the gun but it never hurt to be ahead of the game, and if anything happened to him the following day, at least London would know where to start. He requested a full background check on Sin Jai-Seong, also known as Jason Sin, with particular reference to any connection with SMERSH.

7

Murder on Wheels

The grandstand was packed, the sun beating down.

Not just hundreds, but thousands of people had descended on the little German town, coming from all over Europe to be present at the race. Bond was aware of the strange atmosphere of excitement and anticipation that accompanied the growl of the engines and the rising scent of petrol fumes. Yes, they were here for the glamour of a major international event but there was something else that he detected in their eyes and in the way they smiled. It was the possibility of sudden death. He remembered the words of the Italian racer Umberto Maglioli, who had driven in ten World Championship Grand Prix: 'Road racers are like roulette players.' Bond had been in enough casinos to know the greed and the fear at three in the morning, the tightening stomach as the ball slowed down just before it dropped into its pocket, the horror of losing everything but being compelled to try one more time.

But this was different. It was often said the young racers who had gathered here had about as much chance of surviving as if they had been fighting a war – a one in eight chance, according to some estimates. When you're reaching speeds of 160 mph, sometimes inches away from the next competitor, you have about one fifth of a second to react, to make the decision that might save your life. Every season, racers make mistakes. Every season there are deaths. Nürburgring alone had been responsible for seventeen fatalities. But still the crowds came and took their seats and chattered and waited for the chequered flag to fall. Was Jason Sin among them? Bond looked for the Korean but couldn't see him. It might well be that he had chosen a more private vantage point somewhere along the track. Was he sitting somewhere, watching the race with Colonel Gaspanov? Bond remembered the argument he had briefly witnessed and wondered how he could get closer to the two men. Was the SMERSH man even in the area?

Bond was one of twenty-four drivers. The race would begin with a three-two-three formation and – following a poor time trial that morning – he was starting five rows back. He had known almost straight away that he'd fluffed it, fumbling a gear change and causing the crankshaft to whirl. He'd been very lucky not to blow the engine and when he'd returned to the pits he hadn't been surprised to see Bernardo shaking his head in dismay. Bond had already put the error behind him. Anyone can have a good circuit just as they can have a bad one, and perhaps it was as well to have got it out of the way. This was his moment of truth, the reason he had come to Nürburgring – and there was something that none of the other drivers knew or could possibly guess. He alone had no interest in winning the race. He wouldn't even finish it. He was going to do this his own way.

He saw Lancy Smith striding towards his car, at the same time waving to the crowd who in turn rose to their feet, cheering him on. And there was Dimitrov, surrounded by his teammates, fixing a red silk scarf around his neck. The Russian hadn't shaved that morning and his cheeks were covered with grey stubble. His eyes were fixed on Smith, following him as he walked over to his Vanwall, and if Bond had ever had any doubts about his intentions, they were dispelled at that moment. He knew exactly what he was seeing. Dimitrov had the same eyes, the same intensity as an assassin behind a sniperscope. Bond himself had lain in position with the wooden stock of a rifle against his cheek and his entire being focused on the cross hairs as they settled on his target. There is no relationship in the world quite like the one between the man who intends to kill and the man who is about to die. The snake and the rabbit. That was what he was seeing now.

Bernardo was waiting for Bond at his Maserati, and if the other racers were puzzled that a former champion was devoting so much attention to a completely unknown driver – and worse than that, a playboy who had bought his way into this simply for the fun of it – none of them had dared say so. Bernardo smiled ruefully as Bond approached. 'You really loused it up this morning.'

'Yes. Don't worry about it. I won't make the same mistake again.' It was time for Bond to play his ace of spades. 'I want you to empty the tank,' he said. 'Preferably without anyone else seeing.'

'Empty? What do you mean?'

'I want to start with a quarter of a tank.'

'Are you serious?' Bernardo looked unhappy. 'It means you'll have to stop at the pits very early on for a refuel. And you may find it hard to recover.'

'Just leave me enough for two or three circuits. That's all I need.'

'Whatever you say.' Evidently Logan hadn't told him anything about Bond's mission and, as far as he could see, Bond was already throwing in the towel. But there was no time to argue. He called another mechanic over and the two of them went off to do the work.

Bond was gambling. He was convinced that Dimitrov would make his move early in the race, when the cars were still close together. It made sense. After a couple of laps, Lancy Smith could pull ahead and the Russian wouldn't get another chance.

At the same time, Bond was giving himself a huge advantage. With so little fuel in the tank, the Maserati would be the lightest vehicle on the track – and what it lost in weight, it would gain in speed. The only problem was that he was crippling himself when it came to distance. If Dimitrov didn't make his move very quickly, Bond would have to pull in to refuel and after that the only way to catch up would be to drop an entire lap. That would not only be very difficult, it would draw attention to himself: something he most certainly didn't want to do. But Bond knew he would never keep up with professional racers if he played on their terms. For him, it was all or nothing. If this really was a game of roulette, he had just put all his chips on one number.

He watched as Bernardo set about his task, drawing a screen around the Maserati so that none of the other drivers would see what he was doing. At the same time, Bond got himself ready. He pulled on the gloves, screwed in the earplugs (he'd forgotten them that morning and the shriek of the exhausts had almost shattered his eardrums) and lowered the goggles. He had worked out what he had to do, and, in his mind, there was no longer any possibility of failure. He saw Dimitrov snapping at a mechanic who had been leaning over his vehicle. The Krassny was already snarling, warning the other cars to stay away. There was a poisonous cloud of black smoke spitting out of its exhaust. The other cars were starting up all around and Bond felt the roar of the pack envelop him. He glanced at his watch. Four minutes until the start. It would be a while before he next had the leisure to check the time.

The screen had been withdrawn. Bond saw one of the mechanics hurrying away with two jerrycans. Bernardo called him over and he slipped into the Maserati, already ticking off a mental checklist. Get comfortable. Goggles adjusted, seatbelt and shoulder straps locked. Sit close to the wheel with your arms well bent. How many times had Logan Fairfax told him? The maximum force and the maximum precision come from your arms. Get that wrong and you won't get anywhere. He was aware of two more mechanics approaching him, one on either side. They rolled him forward and suddenly he was there, on the starting line, one eye on the flag but already plotting how to weave through the other drivers. Smith was in the front row. Dimitrov was just behind Smith and over to the left. The other contestants – Germans, Italians, Czechs, French, Americans and, of course, the English – were lined up in formation. He was alone in the middle of them, the sun warming his shoulders, his senses already assaulted by the noise and the petrol fumes, waiting for the sudden scream that would tell him it had begun. A bead of sweat trickled down the side of his face. For a moment, Bond thought of the perimeter track at Foxton Hall. It was a kindergarten compared to this. Briefly he remembered his interview with M in the office overlooking Regent's Park. 'Done any racing lately?' Well, he had never done anything quite like this. He was definitely in big school now.

The flag came down.

And at that moment time disappeared, sucked into itself,

as twenty-four racing cars simultaneously exploded into life with a deafening roar and Bond found his thoughts being torn between the first gear change, the road surface, the wheels, the steering, the weight transfer and the possibility of finding a way past the other drivers without causing a pile-up at the very start. Part of him wanted to check his rev counter. He should be holding the engine at about half the rev capacity (when the clutch is home, that's when you accelerate – but make sure you avoid wheelspin and for God's sake don't break something in transmission) but was he already overdoing it? Surely the needle had already crept past the little red line? He didn't dare look down. His eyes were in front of him, behind him. He was aware of everything around him – everything and nothing. The spectators had disappeared, a vague blur, no heads and no bodies and – God almighty – he was already on the downhill section with the first hairpin right in front of him and the road surface turning to pavé. He wrenched the wheel – no, that was too much! Keep it subtle – and found himself edging past a Porsche and a couple of Coopers. The Maserati was doing half the work for him, and with the lighter load nothing could hold it back.

He'd reached the first corner and he was already silently shouting at himself. Come on, you bastard. You've already been round this a dozen times and you've studied every inch. Find the right line. That's good – as close to the verge as you can. All the diagrams and photographs he had studied in Wiltshire were gone, scattered like leaves in a storm. He was driving by instinct, fighting the centrifugal forces that threatened to push him into oblivion, countering them with the force of adhesion that kept him on the road. It was all in his legs, his stomach, that extraordinary feeling of being one with the car. And – goddammit – he was edging ahead! He slipped past two of the Italians in Ferraris. *Addio, signori*! Now where was he? And, more to the point, where were Lancy Smith and Dimitrov? They had both started ahead of him. He had to find them, quickly, and then do what had to be done.

He risked a quick glance at the speedometer and cursed as that single microsecond, the lack of attention, caused him to mistime his next move. The car had come off the crest of a hill and he was in the air. He should already have been straightening up, preparing for the next corner. Instead, he came down with a bone-shaking crash and almost lost control. He was doing 120 mph. He didn't need to know that. Not if it was going to kill him. Bond only just made it out of the corner. Go in slow, come out fast. It was one of the oldest dictums in the racing book and he had managed to do the exact opposite. Once again he screwed himself down. Into the next curve, touch the brakes, slide – but not too much – now more throttle. What's that ahead? A pool of oil. Get round it, you idiot! He did.

One after another the various sections of the Nürburgring flashed past. The Peak, the Mine, the Carousel, the Little Fountain. The innocent names didn't do justice to the horrors each one contained. A tight right-hand corner, then a sharp left-hander, then a sudden drop-off, one after another, testing him over and over again. The last section welcomed him with a blind corner followed by a stomach-churning drop that Bond didn't see until the last half-second because it was concealed behind a bridge. The Planting Garden that followed almost did for him altogether. Once again Bond found himself in the air and as he came plummeting down into the next switchback he felt the hideous lurch that told him he had gone into a deadly slide. If he had touched the brake at that moment, it would all have been over. Somehow he managed to correct himself with his steering, and brought the car under control. But it had cost him several seconds and both Lancy Smith and Dimitrov were out of sight.

Bond knew now that he would never have managed to keep up for the entire twenty-two kilometres. His arm and leg muscles were already aching as he fought to keep each turn under control and he could feel the blisters on his hands and feet. His whole body had been pummelled by the different G-forces and the constant centrifugal pull made him sick to the stomach. God! These drivers had to be fit to put themselves through this week after week. But he still had his one big advantage over them. They were driving carefully. They had to protect their cars. But Bond didn't care how badly he drove, how much damage he did to his engine in the long term. He was over-revving. He was braking hard and late, overheating the drums. None of it mattered provided this was over soon. A couple of laps. That was all he needed. Where were they? Yes – just ahead of him. Despite everything, he was managing to keep up.

And then the Maserati coughed. Bond felt that the sweat on his chest and forehead was suddenly cold against his skin. He couldn't be out of fuel ... could he? It was impossible! Had he punished the racing car too much and too quickly or had the almost-empty tank somehow caused a blockage in the fuel-injection system? It coughed a second time. He felt the wheel shudder in his hands. A huge poster flashed past with words in red paint: SPRICH ZUERST MIT FORD. He had already seen it once, surely to God. Either the Ford Motor Company had paid for two identical advertisements or he had completed an entire circuit and begun another. But that wasn't possible. The record lap time on Nürburgring was nine minutes and forty-one seconds. Surely he'd only been driving for two or three minutes since the flag had gone down? That was what it felt like. But in fact it had been much, much longer. He had misjudged everything. What a fool he had been! He could already see himself grinding to a halt and while he was being refuelled, the Russian would take out Lancy Smith.

With his concentration momentarily broken, Bond took the next corner in a straight line, putting two wheels onto the grass – and for one horrible second he had no grip at all. But the manoeuvre saved him a few precious microseconds, and with a new sense of determination he put the near-empty tank out of his mind and pressed on. Where exactly was he? Green trees and green bushes were rushing past, a green tunnel. There were no barriers, nothing other than a painted line to show the edge of a road. Now he came to a straight, which allowed him to rest his arm muscles, to check his oil pressure, water temperature and revs. Everything shipshape. He stamped down on the throttle. The Maserati, as light as it could possibly be, surged forward, overtaking another car, and with a huge sense of relief he saw the pulsating black profile of the Krassny. Somehow, despite everything, he had made it to the very front of the pack.

Lancy Smith was in front. Then it was Dimitrov. Then Bond. For a few moments the three of them were separated from the other racers, if only by a matter of yards. Bond crept into Dimitrov's slipstream and got the benefit of its tow. The two of them were incredibly close. He gritted his teeth – 110 mph. That was 160 feet per second. Thirty-two feet in one fifth of a second. At this speed, one tiny miscalculation and he would kill both the Russian and himself. Smith would be saved but not the way he'd planned.

Bond saw Dimitrov's hand reach over his shoulder, as if he were adjusting his seatbelt, and the next moment he was blind. Something had hit him in the face. He felt his goggles break and at the same time the Maserati swerved left and right, the tyres screaming, almost escaping from his control. What had happened? Bond fought with the steering wheel and somehow managed to right himself. He put his hand to his face and felt blood. It was incredible! The Russian had thrown something, stones or grit, and it had been carried by the slipstream and had hit Bond full in the face. His eyesight was partly obscured. One of the lenses was cracked.

Dimitrov and Smith had leapt ahead and Bond knew with a sick feeling that this was where the murder was to take place. It was why the Russian wanted him out of the way. There were no spectators in sight. The track was hemmed in on both sides by thick trees. Inch by inch, Dimitrov was closing in on Smith, the Krassny howling, a black beast out of Hell, and Bond had been left behind, running on fumes. He pressed his foot down on the accelerator, hoping there was enough precious juice left in his tank to propel him forward. There was nothing else he could do.

The Russian was closing in on Smith, halving the distance between them, ignoring any safety margins, performing exactly the manoeuvre that Bond had described to M. There could be absolutely no doubt of his intentions. He wasn't going to overtake. He was going to give the other car the fatal nudge that would send it spinning off the road and Bond was too far back to stop him. But then, at the last second, Smith became aware of the Russian creeping up on him. He touched his wheel, skewing over to one side, and Dimitrov found himself too far ahead, out of line. He was forced to reposition himself and that gave Bond the chance he needed. He pushed down on the throttle and, for one last time, the Maserati responded, leaping forward.

This was it. This was the moment. Bond pulled out as if to overtake and for two, maybe three seconds, he was right next to the Russian, the nose of the Maserati about halfway along the Krassny. Bond saw Dimitrov turn, as if aware of the catastrophe that was about to befall him. It was too late. Bond tugged at the steering wheel so that his car edged over and suddenly his front left tyre was right next to the chassis of the Krassny, inches away from where Dimitrov was sitting. It was actually *between* the front and back right tyres of the Russian's car. Grimly, Bond pressed down on the brake. His front tyre and Russian's back tyre made contact.

The whole world was jerked out of his vision. He had never felt anything like it. His own car fishtailed away, and if he hadn't been ready for it he would have been smashed. He felt his neck and spine being twisted out of shape as different forces wrenched at him and his eyes seemed to pull back in their sockets, his mouth opening in a rictus grin. He was turning, twisting, out of control, and other cars were whipping past him, brightly coloured bullets fired from an invisible machine gun and, miraculously, none of them had hit him. He heard an almighty bang. His feet were scrabbling at the pedals. He was aware of grass under his tyres and trees looming up. Was he going to hit them? No. Somehow he had come to a halt at the side of the track. His engine stalled. The race was over.

Feeling sick and dazed, Bond pulled off his helmet and goggles and climbed out of the Maserati. The world came back into focus, and after the incredible speed of the last fourteen or fifteen minutes, everything was very slow, as if he was walking in a dream. He was alone. The other cars had rushed past, disappearing around the next corner. If there had been an accident, it wasn't their problem, not now. Had Dimitrov managed to keep his car on the road? Had he gone with them? Then Bond remembered the sound of the impact that he had heard. He turned his head – slowly. His neck was stiff and hurt like hell. Finally he saw a sight so extraordinary that at first it was hard to make sense of it.

The Krassny was facing upwards, at ninety degrees to the ground, as if it was trying to take off. It was wedged against a thick oak tree, the bonnet with its bright number 3 crumpled beneath an overhanging branch. How was that possible? As Bond walked unsteadily towards it, he realised what had happened. Dimitrov had come off the track at a point where a bank of grass formed a steep curve and it had acted as a launch pad, forcing the Krassny onto its back wheels and catapulting its front into the upper reaches of the tree. The Russian was still trapped behind what was left of the steering wheel. It had crumpled on impact. His arms were writhing and he was shouting but it was only now that Bond realised he couldn't hear anything. The pandemonium of the race, the howl of the engines, the intensity of the experience had deafened him. Then he remembered that he was still wearing the earplugs. He wrenched them out. Dimitrov was screaming. He could hear him now all right. The screams weren't entirely human.

Bond took another step closer and took in the full horror of the collision. The Krassny's fuel tank had ruptured, and because of the bizarre way it had come to rest, engine oil – close to boiling point – had come gushing out, a deadly cascade that had splashed directly onto the driver's face and hands. Dimitrov was unrecognisable, twisting in agony beneath the hideous black mess. Smoke and steam were rising into the air. What if the car caught fire? It might have already, for one of the true nightmares of methanol was that it burned invisibly and it was quite possible to watch a man die a horrible death without knowing what was killing him.

Even so, Bond couldn't stand idly by. It hadn't been his intention to murder the Russian and certainly not in such a gruesome way. The Krassny didn't seem to be alight. As Bond reached the slope at the side of the road, he could feel the heat from the engine but there were no flames, invisible or otherwise. Even so, that could change in seconds. One spark and the leaking petrol could ignite and that would be the end of both of them.

Dimitrov was slightly above him, trapped, jerking crazily in his seat. Bond was wearing gloves and he wasn't going to take them off, not with the scalding oil splashing down. But the thick fabric made it difficult to unfasten the belts. The locking device seemed to have caught, and as he struggled to release it he could feel the acrid fumes entering his nostrils and stinging his eyes. The whole thing was going to blow. It was going to happen any second now. The Russian must have been aware of it too. He was screaming, his arms flailing in terror. At last, Bond felt the mechanism click and the belt came free. He grabbed Dimitrov under his armpits and, using all his strength, dragged him out and away from the car, back down the slope and away along the side of the track. He had taken no more than five or six steps when the explosion came. Bond felt a blast of heat across his neck and shoulders and threw himself down, protecting the Russian with his own body. Burning leaves and pieces of debris rained down. Turning back he saw that the Krassny was now ablaze, along with many of the trees around it.

Two cars had pulled up on the side of the track and there were people running towards him, some of them carrying fire extinguishers. Further along the circuit he knew that they would be holding out a yellow flag: serious danger, slow down. But the race would continue. Ivan Dimitrov had passed out. He might well be dying. What did it matter? Somebody else would win.

8

Castle Sin

A white moon, a castle and a black lake. It could have been a perfect setting for one of those German folktales, or so it seemed to Bond, standing in evening dress in the darkness. But what sort of creature would have made his home here? An Erl King, or perhaps a less welcoming Grendel.

The Schloss Bronsart was about half an hour from Nürburg, in the thick woodland south of Bad Münstereifel. It was a water castle, one of the many *wasserburgs* scattered across the German lowlands, buildings that had begun life as ordinary homes but which had grown in scale and splendour in direct proportion to their owners' fears of marauding bandits or Hussites. This one was situated in the middle of a huge, artificial lake with a single causeway leading to a front entrance complete with drawbridge and portcullis. The main accommodation was three storeys high with the mullioned windows and crow-stepped gables that characterises so much of old Europe. There was a second structure standing next to it, a single tower, topped with a weathervane and steel grey tiles reminiscent of a First World War helmet. The two buildings were connected by a short bridge, just over the water, and, higher up, by a narrow corridor to which brick and thatch that had been added almost as an afterthought. A miniature jetty invited visitors to ignore the road and arrive by boat. It was both impressive and absurd at the same time, the vain recreation of something that had been vain and extravagant to begin with.

James Bond was standing at the far end of the driveway, examining the scene before him. He had left his Bentley in a parking area hidden among the trees. Guests were expected to leave the twentieth century behind them as they walked the last hundred yards across the lake. Blazing torches had been set at intervals, reflecting in the dark water, and two bronze cauldrons burned on either side of the main door. Jason Sin certainly seemed to have a liking for the dramatic. The moon was full, forming a perfect circle in the night sky. A band was playing 'La Vie en Rose' – Bond knew the song well – the notes drifting out over the water. It was about nine o'clock and most of the guests had already arrived, the men in black tie, the women in silk and fur with jewellery that was surely borrowed or fake. Bond made his way forward, following them.

The warmth, the light, and the music at full volume hit him at the same time, drawing him in. At the door, a waiter handed him a flute of champagne and he took a sip, noting that it was not Cristal, as Lancy Smith had promised, but an equally acceptable Dom Pérignon '53 – still young but a remarkable vintage. He found himself in a hallway, tall and spacious, with a wide marble staircase climbing to the upper floors. But he could already see that these were off-limits to the guests. There was a German standing there, bald, thickset, his arms folded, dressed as if for the party but definitely not a guest. He was as stiff and unmoving as the suits of armour that stood on either side – in fact, he wouldn't have looked completely ridiculous with a halberd in his hand. Bond smiled at him and raised his glass. The man didn't even blink.

There was a doorway to the left and Bond passed through it into a reception room, which in turn led to a great hall, the principal scene of the party. The band was playing up above in a minstrels' gallery. About two or three hundred people were milling around on the flagstones and it was easy to spot who had taken part in the day's race: each one of them was surrounded by their own small crowd of admirers. In fact, Bond had never seen so many pretty girls fighting for attention. There was something almost animal about their desire to be noticed and if you had raced the Nürburgring and survived, you could reach out and they would be yours – for tonight, for several nights or, if you cared enough, until you left for the next circuit. Presumably the same would be true for Bond and yet, as he moved into the room, he felt uneasy. Almost every woman he had ever known had put up at least some measure of resistance, challenging him to win her round. This display of soft acquiescence didn't appeal. All those wide eyes and pouting lips. No. Not for him.

And one of the two dozen racers who had set off that afternoon was still in hospital, alive but horribly burned. Well, nobody had much sympathy for Ivan Dimitrov among the champagne and the canapés. Even his teammates had turned out, the three of them looking darkly guilty in their cheap dinner jackets. In the end, Lancy Smith had romped home in his Vanwall, a full twenty seconds ahead of the nearest competitor. Bond had achieved what he had been sent here for but he had already put it out of his mind. He had seen Colonel Gaspanov, a SMERSH commander, arguing with the Korean and he wanted to know more. There was no sign of the old fox here. He was probably on his way back to Moscow, working out how to explain that yet another SMERSH operation had failed. And that left Sin Jai-Seong – or Jason Sin. Bond had received a brief and largely unhelpful call from the Head of Records in London.

'There's not a lot I can tell you. He keeps himself to himself as much as he can… hardly ever in the news. He seems to have emigrated from South Korea at the start of the war – the Korean War, that is. He turns up in Hawaii and then in New York State, which is where he's based. He's the head of a recruitment company – Blue Diamond – which specialises in low-paid workers, particularly in transit, construction and sanitation. In fact he's rather cornered the market. There are no estimates to his wealth but he's said to be the wealthiest Korean in the country. In some respects, he's a bit of a playboy. You'll find him around the Grand Prix circuit… also tennis, horses, sailing. Pretty much what you'd expect. But at the same time, he has no known vices. He's not married and doesn't seem to have any interest in women. He's not homosexual either. No political affiliations although he turned up at a couple of Republican dinners at the last election and may have given them a donation. But that's common practice for a businessman wanting to hedge his bets and anyway, in America, bribing a politician is part of the etiquette. Are you looking for some sort of affiliation with SMERSH?'

'I don't know, Records. I just wondered why he was here.'

'Probably the same as everyone else. To watch the race.'

But not everyone had been talking to Colonel Gaspanov. When Bond had hung up the phone he had decided that he would, most certainly, come here tonight.

And now there was a stir, a ripple in the crowd, as Sin

appeared in a doorway beneath the minstrels' gallery and moved into the room, accompanied by another man who managed to be both close to him and yet apart with the blank watchfulness of the professional bodyguard. And he was armed. Bond saw at once the telltale outline of a hard leather shoulder holster beneath his jacket. (Bond had always preferred chamois which, though less practical when it came to the draw, had one main advantage: it didn't spoil the line of his jacket.) For a moment, the bodyguard's eyes – ice blue and unforgiving – settled on him, then slid away. Bond turned his attention to the party's host, the wealthiest Korean in the USA.

Sin Jai-Seong was wearing a beautifully tailored Brioni Roman dinner jacket, not black but midnight blue, and holding a glass of what looked like iced water. Like many very wealthy people that Bond had met he had a sort of magnetism that was hard to define. He was not larger, better-looking or louder than anyone else in the room but he seemed to move in a void of his own making and no matter where he stood he was at the epicentre of everything around him. He was more lithe, more delicate than Bond remembered but that strange aloofness was still present. When he smiled, it was without warmth. His eyes, shielded by the thick, almost opaque spectacles, sucked in every last detail of those around him but gave away nothing. It was as if this party – the silver platters of food, the champagne, the music, the chandeliers, the great hall with its tapestries and antique mirrors – had all sprung from his imagination. He moved through it like a sleepwalker.

He had seen Bond and came over to him. The crowd parted to let him pass, the bodyguard close behind. Finally, the two men stood face to face and at that moment Bond heard the first whispers of dangers still to come. He was not superstitious, at least, not in the crudest sense. He would not step out of the way to avoid walking under a ladder. But he did believe absolutely in the physicality of a 'sixth sense' operating in some secret corner of his consciousness. Think of it as an animal instinct. Nobody teaches you that spiders are ugly or that snakes are dangerous. You're simply born with the knowledge. So it was here. Sin was smiling. He seemed relaxed, friendly. But even as Bond reached out and shook his hand, part of him was recoiling, warning him to stay away.

'Mr Bond?' Sin's voice was soft, monotonous. 'I saw you at the race today, although only briefly. I understand you were the other driver involved in the accident.'

'Yes. It was very unfortunate. I've spoken to the racing stewards. It was nobody's fault.'

'From my experience, these accidents are always somebody's fault – the driver, his mechanic or . . .' the dark brown eyes settled on Bond, 'another competitor. It's a shame that, in this instance, the accident occurred at a point where there were no witnesses. And surprising too. Mr Dimitrov is a superb racer. I saw him drive on many circuits.'

'That would be before he was banned.'

Sin ignored Bond's remark. 'I have not seen you race before,' he continued. 'I find that very strange.'

'Not really.' Bond tried to sound nonchalant. 'Only got into it fairly recently. To be honest with you, I may think twice about the whole thing after what happened. I hope that Russian chap's going to be all right.'

'He has been severely burned.'

'Well, I'm glad you haven't let it spoil the party. Quite a place you have here, Mr Sin.'

'You may call me Jason.' The invitation should have been friendly but somehow it was vaguely menacing. 'Sin Jai-Seong is the name that I was born with but people seem to find these things difficult in the West and, anyway, I have left my past life behind. As to this building, I own properties close to many of the world's racing circuits. It gives me the opportunity to provide hospitality as I am doing tonight. The Schloss Bronsart was constructed by the von Schleiden family, the same people responsible for the fortress above Nürburg. I stay and work here often when I am in Europe.'

'Have you had it long?'

'I purchased it from the last owner a few years ago. He drowned.'

'Really?'

'Yes. The lake is very cold and very deep. I would advise you to take care when you return to your car.' He nodded. 'I will wish you a pleasant evening, Mr Bond.'

'Thank you. And please give my best wishes to the Russians.'

Sin had been about to leave. But the last remark had been targeted, the words carefully chosen. He turned back to Bond and although the face was still empty, the eyes had narrowed. 'I'm sorry?'

'You are talking to the Russians?' Bond said, innocently.

'Who do you mean?'

'Dimitrov. His teammates. And his family.'

Sin nodded again, more slowly this time. 'I have already ascertained that Mr Dimitrov is comfortable. It is not my responsibility to look after his welfare or that of his com-patriots.'

'Well, if you do see any of them, do pass on my good wishes.'

Sin drifted away and the crowd surged in to fill the space. Bond thought back on the conversation. The barb about the Russians had hit home. Sin might not be talking to any griev-ing relatives but he was certainly talking to SMERSH. And he had given away more than he had intended. He not only lived part of the year at the castle, he also worked here. That meant he must have an office somewhere in the building – and where there was an office, there would be files, letters, memos ... all manner of information. Bond glanced upwards. As far as he could tell, the whole ground floor of the Schloss Bronsart was given over to reception rooms, ballrooms and lounges. Bond would find what he was looking for somewhere above.

Sipping his champagne, he looked around the room. The four-piece band was playing Cole Porter now and a few people were dancing. He noticed Lancy Smith in a corner, surrounded by women. The driver nodded without coming across. The two of them had not spoken to each other since the race and Bond was glad to keep it that way. It was quite possible that the English champion would know something of what had really happened and Bond's own appearance at Nürburgring might now seem suspicious, given the circum-stances. All in all, it was better not to meet again. He slipped out the way he had come and hovered on the edge of the hallway. The guard was still there, standing implacably in front of the stairs.

Bond was wondering what to do next when a woman appeared, coming out of a room on the other side. His first thought was that she couldn't be with one of the racing drivers – she wasn't glamorous enough. Her evening dress was a little too formal, the midnight blue grosgrain well tailored without actually showing her body off to full effect. Bond would have preferred a lower cut and a little less fabric around the bodice. If you're given that shape you might as well flaunt it, and although she was shorter than he liked, and slightly boyish (the close-cropped blonde hair was another mistake), she had a gamine quality that put him in mind of the French actress, Jean Seberg. In fact, looking at her a second time, he decided he had been unfair to her. She wasn't beautiful in a conventional way but she was attractive all the same, with an intelligence in those off-blue eyes that was somehow challenging. Her lips, though a little too small, were still desirable. This was a girl who was too serious for her own good. She was wearing hardly any make-up and her only jewellery was a pair of diamond ear-studs. She might have made more effort, especially at a party like this. But actually the French had a good word for it: *jolie-laide*. It translates as ugly-pretty but it's always used as a compliment. That was what this girl was.

As Bond watched, she went right up to the security guard who automatically adjusted himself to block her way. 'Excuse me, I need to go upstairs.' She spoke loudly. She had an American accent.

'I'm sorry, Fräulein. Upstairs it is private. The way is *verboten*.'

'I just wanted to lie down for a minute. I have a headache. Can't I use a bedroom?'

'I'm sorry, Fräulein.' The man spoke slowly, repetitively, with a heavy German accent. 'Nobody is allowed upstairs.'

'Not even for a minute?'

'I'm sorry, Fräulein...'

The woman gave up and as she moved back towards the great hall she almost bumped into Bond and glowered at him. 'Can you get out of the way?' The accent was Manhattan; but not the smart end.

'My aunt always used to recommend a houseleek for a headache,' Bond said.

'I don't even know what that is.'

'It's a herb that grows in Scotland. Failing that, a head massage might do the trick.' He smiled at her. 'I'm James Bond.'

'I know. You had the crash with the Russian in his Krassny.'

'That's right.' She tried to get past but he stopped her. 'Did you see the race?'

'Of course. I'm a writer – a journalist. I've been sent here to do a report.'

'Oh really? Who by?'

'*Motor Sport.*'

It made sense. She certainly didn't look like a hanger-on: she had the air of intelligence that might well belong to a journalist. 'Well, if you write about my accident, go easy on me, will you? I heard something blow in the engine just before it happened. You'd have thought Maserati would have learned by now. These eight-cylinder configurations are far too complicated.'

'I wasn't going to write about you at all, Mr Bond,' she said, coolly. 'My readers are more interested in the winners.'

She slipped past him and continued on her way. Bond watched her, amused, as she passed through the outer reception room. It was clear to him that whatever she might be doing here, she most certainly wasn't writing for *Motor Sport*. Even the most ill-informed journalist would know that Maserati had always favoured six-cylinder engines which were more than adequate for the sort of speed they needed.

He put her out of his mind. He was fairly sure she had nothing to do with him and he had other things to think about. He needed to find a way upstairs.

9

A Leap in the Dark

As far as Bond could see there was only one set of stairs leading up to the first floor and it was right in front of him now. There might be another way up through the minstrels' gallery or perhaps a second staircase somewhere out of sight, but he had no reason to doubt that Sin would have taken the same security measures throughout the castle. This was a man with something to hide.

Bond slipped out into the cool evening air and examined the castle walls. There was a little ivy, but certainly not enough to bear a man's weight, and anyway the windows above were firmly closed. He glanced down at the moon in the black mirror of the lake and next to it the tower, shimmering slightly in the breeze. Despite the bridge running from one structure to the other and the narrow corridor higher up, there was no obvious way into the tower, even assuming he could somehow double back. It was approaching midnight, and although the party would continue through to the small hours, Sin himself might soon retire. If he was going to make a move, it would have to be soon.

There was a movement at the door and instinctively Bond pressed himself into the shadows. Even before he knew there was any danger, he was taking care to avoid it. A lifetime in the service had programmed him this way. Standing in the shadows, he saw the bodyguard who had been with Sin in the great hall. He smiled. Such was the power of tobacco! He needed to smoke and he had come outside so he wouldn't be seen abandoning his duties. He had taken out a packet of Nil – Bond recognised the plain blue packet with the German eagle, a brand that had been around before the war. The bodyguard leant down to pluck a cigarette out using his lips, then, holding it in place, he lit it with a silver lighter that only caught on the third strike. Bond was reminded of that old wartime superstition. The enemy notices the first spark, aims on the second and fires when he sees the flame. It's why no soldier will ever light three cigarettes from one match and it occurred to him that the same had to be true of a lighter.

Like a snake, Bond slid out of the darkness, coming up behind the man just as he exhaled his first cloud of smoke. He had already chosen his tactic, a straightforward Japanese Strangle, straight out of training school. Without breaking pace, his right fist shot out, slamming into the man's kidney. The bodyguard grunted and tilted backwards, the cigarette falling from his lips. Bond followed with his left forearm, whipping it round the man's neck and slamming into his Adam's apple with such force that he was probably unconscious from that moment. But Bond had to be sure. He placed his hand flat on the back of the man's head, formed a lock in the crook of his own arm, and squeezed. Too hard and he would break the man's neck. Too long and he would asphyxiate him. For once, Bond wasn't out to kill. A dead body would cause problems with the German police and anyway, he needed this man unconscious but alive.

The bodyguard had collapsed heavily against Bond, his jacket falling open to reveal a holster with a pistol – a Sauer 38H, an old Luftwaffe weapon. This one had an ivory inlay along the barrel and an ivory grip, which told Bond that it must have once belonged to a high-ranking officer. He clasped his hands around the man's chest and dragged him back into the front hall, his heels making parallel tracks in the gravel. Once he was inside, Bond allowed him to spill onto the carpet, noticing with satisfaction that he was barely breathing and that his face was an unpleasant shade of grey.

'Can anyone help me?' he called out. 'Is there a doctor in the house?'

Already a small crowd had appeared, partygoers with champagne flutes, looking down at the unconscious figure with a mixture of awkwardness and alarm. Out of the corner of his eye, Bond saw the man who had been guarding the stairs start forward. Good. This was his colleague, or quite possibly his boss. How could he stand by and do nothing?

'He was standing outside and he just collapsed,' Bond went on. 'I think it may have been his heart.'

More people arrived. The bodyguard lay sprawled. He might have been dead apart from the rise and fall of his chest. The man from the stairs was crouching over him, feeling for a pulse. Carefully, Bond edged away. Yes. It had worked perfectly. Not only was everyone's attention diverted, the crowd had created a screen. Bond slipped through it and, without hesitating, continued up the stairs, taking them three at a time. In seconds he had turned a corner and was out of sight. It could hardly have been easier.

Sin had to have an office or something of value upstairs – at least, that was what Bond had assumed. Why else would the way have been barred? But as he made his way along the corridor, he began to wonder. The lower and upper parts of the Schloss Bronsart seemed to bear no relation to one another. The party was taking place in rooms that were sumptuously furnished, an evocation of *fin de siècle* Germany with no expense spared. This part of the castle seemed almost derelict, the wallpaper damp and peeling, the carpets threadbare. Sin had said he lived here, but if so he hadn't tried to make the place habitable. It was very odd. This area of the castle was off-limits, private, and a guard had been posted to keep it that way. And now this! Bond was being given an insight into the mind of the Korean millionaire. But it was empty. There was nothing there.

He continued round a corner. Now he came to a series of oil paintings, hanging at intervals in gold frames, and somehow he got the impression that they must have been here when Sin bought the castle, that they hadn't been added for his enjoyment. They were eighteenth or nineteenth century, mainly portraits of people – archdukes and margravines – who had been rich enough to commission them during their lifetimes but who had been forgotten very soon after. With all his senses alert to the slightest sound or movement, it took Bond a few moments to realise that something was wrong. What was it? Then, with a sick feeling in his stomach, he looked at the eyes. In every single picture, the eyes had been neatly burned out with a cigarette, leaving lifeless black holes. It was an extraordinary act of vandalism and one that would have cost many thousands of pounds. Bond had no doubt that it must have been Sin himself who was responsible. Why else would he have allowed the ruined and sinister portraits to remain in place? But what did it mean? What sort of man vandalised artworks that hung in his own home?

There were plenty of doors that might lead to an office, some of them missing handles, all of them with paintwork that was scratched or smeared. He opened one of them and found himself looking into a bedroom, uncarpeted, empty but for a narrow, iron bed, soiled sheets, a few clothes thrown carelessly on the floor. Bond was sure the clothes were Sin's. They were certainly expensive enough and they were similar to what he had been wearing at the race track. So this might be where he slept. But why the squalor? It was more a prison than a bedroom and the single bed told its own story. Curiouser and curiouser, Bond thought to himself, although he doubted he was going to bump into any white rabbits. Much more likely a mad hatter. This was where Sin lived, but where did he work? Bond found the answer behind the next door; a large, square room looking out over the front of the castle with the causeway and the car park beyond.

There was no need to turn on the light. The curtains were open and the room was flooded with moonlight, slanting down onto an ugly mahogany table with thick legs and a polished surface, the sort of table from which wars are planned. A single, curved chair stood behind it. There was a chandelier, missing many of its crystals, and an antique mirror, cracked and splintered. A rug covered a large area of the floor. It looked new. But it was the contents of the table that drew Bond's attention. If this was his office, then Sin had been busy. The surface was strewn with documents and photographs, handwritten notes, files. Bond closed the door behind him and took a step forward. His foot was still in the air, a few inches above the rug, when he stopped and drew it deliberately back. Why the rug? It seemed out of keeping with everything he had seen on this floor, as if it had been placed there as an afterthought – and by someone else. Keeping to the edge of the room, Bond followed the rug round. Yes. There it was. A thin wire curled out from beneath the fringes and disappeared into a hole in the wood. The rug concealed some sort of pressure alarm. If Bond had continued straight to the desk, he would have set the damn thing off.

He edged round, then eased himself into the chair. From here he surveyed the evidence laid out on the table. Virtually all the documents were in Korean. Bond was annoyed with himself. He should have asked Q Branch for a camera before he came out – the lightweight Minox A 111 with its close-focusing lens would have been perfect, particularly in this poor light. Well, it was too late now. Bond examined a few of the sheets then selected some at random, folded them and slid them into his pocket. You never knew what they might contain. Then he turned his attention to the photographs.

Bond didn't know what he was looking for. At the end of the day it was idle curiosity – along with the instincts that guide every secret agent – that had brought him here. Jason Sin was connected to SMERSH and that was a good enough reason to search his office. What Bond hadn't expected was the series of photographs that he now spread before him. In fact, could there have been anything less appropriate on the first floor of a fairy-tale castle in the middle of a German wood?

They showed a three-stage space rocket. Not a missile. That had been Bond's first thought, but there were several images of satellites, seemingly for communications, attached.

The rocket had been photographed from different angles, preparatory to a launch. Where? The sky and the metal gantry gave nothing away. Quickly, Bond turned the photographs. He was aware that the moment the bodyguard recovered and explained what had happened, they would come looking for him. Perhaps it would have been safer to kill the man after all. Several different rockets had been photographed and at different stages: pre-launch, mid-launch, disappearing into the sky. However, it seemed that Sin was interested in only one rocket type. Each one had that slim, sexual quality that made the whole world of rocket science so attractive to scientists and schoolboys alike. Bond came across a picture of a group of men, engineers surrounding a metal square, a movable firing structure. They were dressed in overalls and hard hats but one, standing apart, wore a lumberjack shirt. They were Americans, Bond was sure of it.

He examined another photograph. Yes. This was American engineering. If he had been looking at a Sputnik or a Semyorka, it would have had the telltale heaviness, the ungainliness of all Soviet design. And yet Bond was aware that there was something strange, something that didn't add up about the image he was examining. He was looking at half a rocket – the nose cone and the metal housing that contained the spin mechanism, the roll jets, the third-stage motor. It was lying flat in some sort of warehouse, presumably in the final stages of construction before it was connected to the second and first stages and transported to the gantry. What was it that had caught his attention? There were three men at the very back of the shot, all wearing white coats, one of them holding a clipboard. That was it! They were slightly out of focus but even so Bond could see that all three of them were Koreans. And that made no sense at all, particularly if, as Bond suspected, the photograph had been taken in America. Was it possible that Sin was building his own space rocket? If so, what was its purpose and what exactly were these pictures doing here? A Korean multimillionaire with a recruitment company in New York. Colonel Gaspanov. SMERSH. Nürburgring. Bond considered the four pieces of the puzzle but no matter how he looked at them, he couldn't get them to fit together.

One last photograph caught his attention. The same rocket, standing upright – but this time the shot had been taken from a distance and Bond was able to see a long strip of coastline, waves breaking on a stony shore, a scattering of buildings painted white, scrubland. There was water on both sides. He was looking at an island, a launch site. Somehow the landscape looked familiar but before he could work out where it was he heard footsteps outside in the corridor and, seconds later, the door handle turned.

Bond was already backing away, hiding in the one obvious place that the room afforded: behind the curtains. For a moment, he was reminded of his own childhood. He had an image of a little boy who already had fantasies of being a spy, caught in his father's study, rifling through incomprehensible letters from Vickers Aviation in search of super-weapons. When his father had caught him he had simply laughed, but Bond didn't think he'd get the same reception this time. He heard the door open and close. He was aware that someone else had come into the room.

Bond looked round the edge of the curtain. He was expecting Sin or one of his men. Instead, it was the girl with the headache who had come in. The journalist who wasn't a journalist had slipped through the door without completely opening it and had closed it softly behind her. She hadn't turned on the lights. She stood for a moment, checking that she was alone, then moved forward to the desk. The photographs and other documents were still spread out. She began to rifle through them just as Bond had a few moments before.

But she hadn't gone round the rug! Bond realised it with a jolt in his stomach. She had walked right over the pressure pad, presumably setting off alarms somewhere within the building. They had minutes – perhaps less – to get out.

He had no choice. Bond pushed back the curtain and stepped out. The girl started when she saw him, standing there like a criminal caught at the scene of the crime, one of the photographs already in her hands. Bond saw a flash of fear in her eyes, replaced a moment later by angry defiance.

'What are you doing here?' she demanded.

'I don't have time to explain,' Bond replied. 'You've set off an alarm.'

She looked around her, saw nothing.

'You're standing on it,' he said. 'We have to move now. We can talk about this later.'

He snatched half a dozen photographs at random and shoved them into his inside pocket. He didn't have to cover his tracks. Thanks to this girl, Sin would know he had been here and would guess that some of the pictures had been taken. His only chance was to get out of the Schloss Bronsart, or at least back into the party. Surely Sin wouldn't try anything in a crowded room filled with racing drivers from the international circuit, local officials, journalists (real ones) and friends? No. Bond knew half a dozen ways to disable someone surreptitiously in a crowd. There were sleeper holds, strangle holds, silenced weapons, injections. He had only met Sin for a few moments but he was already wary of him. He thought of the empty bedroom, the portraits in the corridor with their burned-out eyes. Suddenly he wanted to be not just out of the castle but as far away as possible.

Fortunately, the girl wasn't arguing with him. She was angry with herself and somehow – the wrong thought at the wrong time – it made her more desirable. Bond hurried past her and opened the door. There was nobody in the corridor but already he could hear footsteps on the stairs.

'This way,' he said.

The two of them hurried out and went in the opposite direction. Already Bond was considering his options. The moment security had been breached Sin would throw a protective cordon around the castle. It would be easy to do. There was effectively only one way out: the narrow cause-way that connected the island with the edge of the lake. There would be guards at the front door, on the stairs and more outside. It was in Sin's interests to keep any intrud-ers separate from his guests but that wouldn't be hard to achieve either. Maybe he was already taking steps. 'Ladies and gentlemen. A brief speech. This way, please ...' He could address them beneath the minstrels' gallery in the great hall while Bond and the girl were hunted down elsewhere. Was there a second staircase in the building? Bond hadn't been able to find it but it had to be there. Would it be guarded? Almost certainly.

They passed more portraits, more closed doors, arriving at a passageway that ran left and right. Even as they turned the corner, Bond heard Sin's men arriving behind them, throwing open the door of the study. Somebody shouted something in German. The girl was close behind him. She had kicked off her shoes, getting rid of the high heels so that she could move more quietly, and more quickly, too. There was a slash in the side of her dress, exposing her leg as she ran forward. Who was she? What was she doing here? Part of Bond cursed her for her clumsiness. She had given them both away.

They were still on their own but that would change the moment Sin's men discovered that the study was empty and decided to fan out. Now they had reached a narrow corridor with windows on both sides and Bond remembered the bridge that he had seen, connecting the main building with the tower. He came to a spiral staircase, a corkscrew that offered him a simple choice: up or down. He tried to remember the layout of the castle. If he went down, might he be able to reach the jetty? And if so, was there a chance he might find some sort of boat?

It was a hopeless thought, and anyway, the choice was snatched away seconds later as he heard a door open somewhere below him and knew that the way was already guarded. The corridor behind him was still empty but there was no question of going back that way. That just left one option and it occurred to Bond that he should have chosen it from the start. What was the basic rule? When you're cornered, choose the least obvious course of action.

Up. He didn't ask the girl what she wanted to do. There was no time for a discussion and anyway, he wasn't responsible for her. Whoever she was, she could presumably look after herself. In fact, she followed. She must have come to the same conclusion as him. There was no other way.

The spiral staircase occupied most of the space within the

tower with just a few alcoves and storage spaces on the sides. The walls were bare brick with tiny, slit-like windows that provided a glimpse of the night sky. There was no route back into the main castle from here. They might find somewhere to hide but it would do them no good. Sin's men would systematically search every inch of the place and it was inevitable that they would be found. They climbed past the third floor and continued, curving round on themselves. At last they came to a solid wooden door, locked. Bond positioned himself a few steps away. He lashed out with his foot. The lock shattered on the second blow. They stepped out into the night breeze.

They were at the very top of the tower, trapped in a circular space with a low wall and the lake three floors or about fifty yards below. It was a long way but Bond was remembering what Sin had told him. 'The lake is very cold and very deep.' Well, the second part of that equation would be useful to him now. He already knew he was going to have to jump. If the tower were a clock face, then from midnight until four o'clock was clear, with the water directly below. From where he was standing, he could see the jetty and the main entrance. Just as he had expected, several guards had taken up their positions outside but there were two elements in his favour. First of all, they were gazing into the castle, waiting to challenge anyone who came out. None of them was looking up or out towards the lake. And the band was still playing. Bond could hear the music seeping out into the darkness. That was a mistake on Sin's part. Provided he could enter the water without making too much of a splash, there was every chance that he wouldn't be heard.

He stepped closer to the edge. Next to him, the girl understood what he intended.

'I can't do this,' she said, simply. 'It's too high.'

'What's your name?' Bond demanded.

The girl hesitated. Then she answered. 'It's Jeopardy. Jeopardy Lane.'

Bond took this in. He knew that, this time, she was telling the truth. 'All right, Jeopardy,' he said. 'It's a simple choice. You can come with me. Or you're on your own.'

'You can't leave me here.'

'I can and I will. It's been nice meeting you. I hope you get a good story for your magazine – although it might help if you learn a thing or two about racing cars.'

Bond turned his back on her and went over to the wall. The girl was right. It was a hell of a long way down and in the moonlight the surface of the water looked like polished steel.

'Wait for me, you bastard!' Jeopardy said.

Bond looked back. She was already walking over to him. The two stood together on the edge. If she was afraid, she wasn't showing it. If anything, she was angry, as if this was his fault.

'After you,' Bond said.

'Hell with that,' Jeopardy growled.

They leapt together. Bond was aware of the rush of air, the great expanse of the lake filling his vision as he plunged towards it. He was going to enter feet first. There had been no question of attempting a dive. But he tried to make himself as streamlined as he could, stretching his legs and clutching his hands above his head, so as to enter the water more cleanly, like a knife. Only now, when it was far too late, did the thought flash through his mind that Sin could have been wrong, the lake might be much shallower than he had suggested. There could be rocks, debris of some sort hidden beneath the surface. This adventure could end with Bond shattering his legs – or worse. How long can three seconds last? A whole world of pain and different possibilities suggested itself to Bond as he fell and then came the shock of impact, his feet smashing the black mirror, cleaving a hole for the rest of his body to follow. Down and down he went into a darkness that was absolute and unyielding and a coldness that was not so very different from death. He had been holding his breath but it was almost punched out of him. The lake might actually be a thousand feet deep, fed with the meltwater of glaciers a million years old. Its grip was lethal. Bond's entire body went into shock, heart palpitating, lungs shrinking, every nerve screaming in outrage. Was he rising or falling? He could feel nothing. He could not even be certain he was still conscious.

He felt he had stopped moving, hanging in the water as if suspended there, and kicked out with his arms and legs, his jacket and shirt ballooning around him. He needed to breathe. A few more seconds and he would suck in water involuntarily. He kicked again and then, somehow, he had re-emerged. He was breathing air, shards of water falling off his face, the blinding light of the moon in his eyes. He had to remind himself not to thrash around, not to make any noise. If any of Sin's men had heard them, they could be picked off from the castle – fish in a barrel indeed. He twisted round. Jeopardy had made it. Water was streaming out of her fair hair, which was plastered across her skull like a bathing cap. Her eyes seemed abnormally large. He could hear the short, uneven rasps of her breathing, but otherwise she was silent.

Had anyone heard? Had anyone seen? For a few seconds, Bond trod water, aware of the dreadful cavern beneath him. There was nothing. He signalled to Jeopardy and slowly they began to swim away from the main entrance, away from the causeway. That was where Sin's people would be looking for them, but with every stroke Bond put a little more distance between himself and the castle and that thought alone spurred him on.

The cold was numbing, sucking all his strength. It was as if the lake, having failed to kill him one way, was determined to do it another. He couldn't feel his fingers or his hands and his teeth were chattering so loudly they sounded like castanets. At first it seemed that the shoreline refused to get any nearer. Jeopardy was struggling to keep up and it occurred to Bond that she should have taken off her dress before she jumped. The fabric was dragging her down. But there was nothing he could do to help her. He concentrated on what he was doing. At this temperature, he might survive five or six minutes. Any longer and he would be finished.

After what seemed like an eternity they reached the edge of the lake behind the castle and dragged themselves out. Bond looked back and saw the glow of the chandeliers behind the windows and imagined the guests, still partying with their champagne and canapés, oblivious to the events taking place around them. Just a short while ago Bond had been one of them. Now he stood, shivering, beside the woodland. He held out a hand for Jeopardy and pulled her to her feet. Beads of water, like mercury in the moonlight, clung to her face and neck. She was shivering uncontrollably.

'How did you get here?' Bond asked. 'Do you have a car?'

She shook her head. 'Cab. My bag, cash ...' She jerked

round in the direction of the castle. The music was still drifting out across the lake, taunting them.

'It doesn't matter. We can take mine.' Bond's keys were lodged on the front wheel of his car, a precaution he had taken without even thinking about it. The photographs were still in his jacket. Hopefully, they wouldn't be too damaged. He would look at them later. 'We'll go through the trees,' he said. 'I don't suppose anyone will be looking for us there. With a bit of luck, they'll think we're still hiding somewhere inside.'

Together, they skirted through the wood and reached the parking area. Bond waited until a couple had climbed into their car and left, then sidled up to the Bentley, found the key and unlocked it. Jeopardy slid into the front seat and closed the door. Bond climbed in next to her and turned the heating on full. Water dripped onto the blue upholstery.

'Where are you staying?' Bond asked.

'I was going back to Cologne. I had a taxi coming at midnight.'

'Well, I'm afraid you're going to miss your taxi and I don't think you'll be getting anywhere near Cologne looking like that.'

'I have no money. I've nowhere to go.'

'Then you'd better come back with me. I have a room in a hotel in Nürburg.'

She nodded but her face was blank. 'Who are you?' she asked. 'What were you doing in that room?'

'I was about to ask you the same.' She turned away and Bond took pity on her. 'We can deal with all that in the morning. It's only a half-hour drive. You'll feel better after a hot bath. And we can get a couple of brandies from the concierge.'

He reversed the car. The Schloss Bronsart appeared one last time in the mirror. He was glad to see the back of it. He drove off into the night.

10

'Pick a card...'

Silence sat in the room, an uninvited guest.

Jason Sin, still in black tie, had been speaking on the telephone for several minutes. He put down the receiver and stared sullenly at the photographs strewn over the surface of the table. Three men, Germans, stood facing him with their faces purposefully blank, not speaking until they were spoken to. They were his personal bodyguards and knew very well what was about to happen. A fourth man was sitting, slumped in a chair in front of Sin, his eyes cast down. This was the bodyguard that Bond had attacked outside the schloss. His gun had been taken from him. His jacket hung loose.

'It is most unfortunate.' Sin seemed to have taken several minutes to find the right formulation of words. He took off his wire-framed glasses and laid them on the desk. The brown eyes in the olive-skinned face were neither angry nor disappointed. They gave nothing away. 'It would seem that half a dozen photographs have been taken. It is unclear whether the intruder knew what he was looking for but I would suspect that the theft was opportunistic. Certain documents are also missing but they were in Korean and were actually insignificant.' He was speaking in English not German and although the four men were listening intently, it was not clear how much they understood. It didn't matter. He was turning over the thoughts in his head, assessing the situation more for his benefit than theirs. 'There was a danger that my associates would consider that the entire operation was now compromised but, fortunately, I have managed to persuade them otherwise.' He paused. 'You have let me down very badly, Herr Luther. I have to say I am disappointed.'

Luther was the man in the chair. He nodded slowly. As a result of the damage that Bond had inflicted on him, it would have been difficult to do otherwise. There was a dark mauve bruise around his neck and he had one arm clasped across his stomach. Even so, a glimmer of defiance remained in the bright blue eyes. Bond had guessed correctly. Luther's pistol, the Sauer 38H, was a souvenir of the Luftwaffe. Luther had risen through the ranks, not as a flier but as a commander in one of the seven Feldregimenter. He had fought against the Soviets on the eastern front. He was a survivor. 'I understand you completely, *mein Herr*,' he said.

'I really don't know quite where to begin,' Sin continued. 'As Head of Security both at this castle and at my other businesses in Germany, it would have been your responsibility, at the very least, to check the names of the guests invited to this gathering tonight.'

'The invitations were informal. Many of the guests came with friends. I was never given a complete list of names.'

'That may be the case. But you should have demanded it. And as it happens, this man – Bond – was here under his own name.' The tiniest furrow of anger picked at the skin above Sin's eye but the rest of his face ignored it. 'It now turns out that James Bond is well known to my colleagues in Moscow. He is a highly respected member of the British

Secret Service. He was doubtless sent here to protect the racing driver Lancy Smith. It cannot be a coincidence that he was involved in the supposed accident at Nürburgring. We can only surmise what it was that drew him here tonight. My guess is that he probably saw me with Gaspanov.' Once again, Sin spoke to himself. 'I told him. I did tell him that he was making a mistake, forcing me to meet him here. But would he listen? The trouble is that his organisation has made too many mistakes and as a result he refuses to delegate. He has to go over everything face to face even though a telephone conversation would have more than sufficed. He must see for himself that everything is going according to plan. And what is the result? We draw attention to ourselves and now we have British intelligence on our backs.'

Sin's eyes flickered as he remembered the man in the chair. 'That is why we have to be so careful, Herr Luther. We cannot make mistakes at our end. And yet you have behaved in a manner which has been frankly amateurish.' He paused. 'What were you doing outside?'

'I went out just for a minute,' Luther said.

'A dereliction of duty. I never gave you permission to leave the building. Your place was beside me. I might have been attacked while you were enjoying yourself in the night air and anyway it allowed Bond to creep up on you, to knock you unconscious, to use you as a diversion.'

'I did not see the person. We cannot be sure it was Bond.'

'Please, Herr Luther. Do not insult my intelligence. Who else could it have been?' Sin ran a tongue along his lips. There was something slightly obscene about the gesture, the little grey knife cutting a slit through the flesh. 'Bond carried you

129

into the front hall and immediately, without any thought, the guard on the stairs abandoned his position.'

One of the three men stiffened but said nothing.

Luther was about to reply but Sin held up a hand. 'I have almost finished. There were no guards on the upper corridor. The door to this room was unlocked, despite the most sensitive material remaining in plain sight following my meeting with Colonel Gaspanov. *Shi bai kepu seck yi*!' Koreans do not often swear but Sin had used one of the filthiest expressions that existed in his language. 'There were no security measures taken at all.'

'The pressure alarm was activated.'

'Too little, too late. By the time your men reached the room – and it might have been sooner had they not been attending to you – Bond had gone. And just to conclude what had already been a disastrous series of events, they were unable to find him. Do you have any idea where he is now?'

'We do not believe he is in the building.'

'Lamentable. Truly lamentable.'

'This has never happened before, *mein Herr*.' The Head of Security knew that his words were futile but spoke them anyway. 'It will not happen again.'

'Of that much we can at least be certain.'

Jason Sin put his glasses back on, then reached into his inner pocket and took out a deck of playing cards. As soon as Luther saw them, he swallowed hard, the colour draining out of his face. Sin cleared a space on the table and then spread the cards out so that the backs were showing. They were very beautiful, each one decorated with images of birds, trees and flowers, painted in the Japanese style. 'You have heard me speak before of Hanafuda,' Sin continued. 'They are playing cards which are very popular in Korea and which I often used as a child. Hanafuda translates as flower cards. As you can see, there are forty-eight of them. The suits are represented by the twelve months of the year and each suit has four different flowers. In Korea we used to play Hwatu, which means, literally, "the battle of the flowers", but there were also other games such as Koi-Koi and Go-Stop.

'These cards are, however, different. I have had them customised to my needs and as you are very well aware, Herr Luther, I am not intending to play with you. These cards are going to decide the manner of your death.'

'Please—'

Before Luther could say any more, Sin raised a hand. 'Do not speak. Do not attempt anything rash. I am armed. There are three men, your former colleagues, standing behind you. Let us try to do this with dignity. It may go better for you.'

He composed himself, his hands crossed in front of him. The High Priest. The fortune teller.

'There is nothing more random nor more certain than death. I will die. You will die. The only questions – and they are very important ones – are when and how? I have had experience of death, Herr Luther. I have come face to face with it in a way that few people could describe and so these questions have become something of a preoccupation. When and how. That is the great power of death. It is what makes death so fearsome. And I have taken that power upon myself.

'Right now, in front of you, there are forty-five different ways to die. They are printed on the backs of these cards. Some of them demand your own co-operation. You may be asked to take poison or to slit your wrists. Some of them are fast and painless. There is a decapitation card – which is messy but dramatic – and there is also the option of a bullet to the head. A few are prolonged and unpleasant. A month ago, in America, we tortured a man to death, an experience that took several days. In your case, you might be electrocuted or drowned. Let me assure you that I have no particular preference. I have no malice towards you. I am punishing you because you need to be punished but, speaking for myself, I feel nothing.'

Luther sat there, breathing heavily. He was staring at the colourful backs of the cards with utter loathing, as if they were the ugliest things he had ever seen.

'Pick a card,' Sin commanded.

Luther didn't move. 'Please, sir, I have worked for you for two years. I have done everything you ever asked me.'

'Do not make me choose one for you, Herr Luther. Because if you do, you'll make me angry and I can assure you that I will choose something very nasty. But perhaps you have forgotten – I have permitted you a very small chance of escape. I said that there were forty-eight cards but only forty-five of them carry what you might call methods of execution. Three cards are blank. Should you happen to choose one of them, we will forget this whole unpleasant business and say no more about it. A one in sixteen chance. Not great odds, but better than no chance at all. You have thirty seconds to make your choice.'

Still Luther seemed to take an age to decide. His chest rose and fell as he stared at the row of brightly coloured illustrations, almost trying to see through them. Nobody spoke. There was no clock in the room. Time was measured by heartbeats. At the last moment, almost without thinking, Luther reached out and turned over a card near the centre of the spread. It was not blank. There were two words printed in capital letters, in English.

HANG YOURSELF

Luther threw himself forward, his hands reaching out for Sin, but the other three men had been waiting for this moment. As one they were onto him, pinning him down as Sin stood up and moved away from the table. 'We will need a rope,' he said.

Two men held their former colleague while the third left the room, going downstairs and out to the jetty. He returned a few minutes later carrying a thick coil of rope that had been used to tie the boats. Sin glanced up at the ceiling. A single beam ran the full width of the room, made from wood felled from a tree two hundred years before. He took hold of the chair on which he had been sitting and carried it round, placing it beneath the beam.

'I will not do this!' Luther hissed. His face was white. He was swaying slightly on his feet. 'It is madness!' He turned to the other men and spoke to them rapidly in German. The men looked away. It was as if they had not heard him. He turned back to Sin and now there were tears in his eyes. 'Herr Sin. This is not my fault – what happened tonight. It was the responsibility of all of us. Please, sir. I have a wife and two sons. I beg of you!'

'Do I look as if I'm about to change my mind?' Sin interrupted. 'It's late and I want to go to bed. I'd get on with it, if I were you. There are many worse cards you could have chosen and if you won't play by the rules, you will regret it. Come on, now. You've seen all this before. You need to make a noose.'

'No.'

'If you refuse me, I will bring your wife and children here. You will see them die first.'

Luther was shaking. 'I don't know how…'

'It is not difficult. Any knot will do. It just has to go around your neck.'

There is a moment when every fighter knows his time has come, when he is trapped in a situation from which there is no way out or when he has been wounded and knows that the blood will not be staunched. Luther had arrived at that moment and something went out of his face, as if a switch had been thrown. Sensing it, the two men eased their grip. At the same time, the third produced a gun, stepping aside to have a clear line of fire. Luther took the rope. It lay in his hand like something dead. He stared at it, then, with a series of short, jerky movements tied a knot, leaving a loop large enough to pass over his head. Finally he climbed onto the chair and attached the other end of the rope to the beam. The noose hung in front of him.

'Herr Sin, will you say to my wife and to my sons…' Luther addressed the Korean, his face framed by the rope that was about to kill him.

'I will tell them that you died in an accident, nothing more nothing less. How old are your children?'

'Nine and fourteen.'

'Very young to lose a father. But there you are…'

Luther put the rope around his neck. He searched for some last words to say but couldn't find them. Feebly, he rotated his legs, trying to topple the chair. It didn't move. He tried again. It toppled to one side. His body came crashing down.

Sin went back to the table and gathered up the cards. He

tapped the ends to straighten the pack and returned them to their box. Finally, he glanced at the German who had been holding the gun. He was the youngest of the three. His face was filled with horror. 'Your name?' Sin asked.

'Artmann, *mein Herr.*'

'All right, Artmann. I'm promoting you. You'll take over Herr Luther's responsibilities. Start by getting rid of the body in the lake. Make sure it's properly weighted down.'

'*Jawohl, mein Herr.*'

'Good night.' Sin slipped the cards back into his pocket and left the room.

11

Jeopardy

Jeopardy Lane came out of the bathroom wearing nothing but a towel, which she had wound under her arms. She had regained some of her colour but there was a wariness in her eyes.

'Do you have a cigarette?' she asked.

'Help yourself.'

There were cigarettes on the table. Also a bottle of Asbach Uralt brandy that Bond had persuaded the night porter to release from the bar. *Weinbrand*. At the end of the First World War, with more than ten million people dead and the world trying to sort itself out, the French had seized the moment to demand exclusive use of the word 'cognac'. These things obviously mattered. Bond had poured two large glasses and had drunk them both while Jeopardy was in the shower. He poured her another as she reached for the packet.

The room was in the eaves of the hotel, all slanting roofs and shuttered windows looking out to the sloping countryside and the Eifel Mountains. It had the snug, old-fashioned feel of a Tyrolean ski lodge and Bond couldn't wait to get out. He had already showered and changed. He intended to leave first thing after breakfast. His wet clothes were drying in the bathroom and his case was packed by the door. It was now two o'clock in the morning. A particularly nasty clock with a cow painted onto the face sat on the mantelpiece, showing the time. Bond and Jeopardy were going to have to spend what remained of the night together here. He had made that clear to her in the car, driving back. They were probably safe. It was unlikely that Sin would attempt to follow them to the village of Nürburg and even if he did it would be hard for him to find them. (Bond had given the night porter five hundred Deutschmarks and instructions to tell anyone who called that Bond was not at the hotel. And if anyone enquired, he would tell Bond at once.) It was still sensible for the two of them to stay close. Jeopardy had nowhere else to stay in Nürburg. She had no money, no clothes, nothing. There were, however, several questions Bond wanted to ask her and until he had the answers, he wasn't letting her out of his sight.

He didn't get a chance to start his interrogation. She lit her cigarette and snapped the lighter shut, then turned to him angrily. 'If you think I'm going to sleep with you, you can forget it.'

'The thought hadn't even crossed my mind,' Bond lied.

'I can't believe I let you talk me into that. I wasn't thinking straight. What the hell was going on in your head? Chasing off like that. And the tower! You nearly got me killed.'

'What are you talking about?'

'You know what I'm talking about, goddam you.' She emptied half the glass in one gulp. 'I don't know who you are, Mr Bond. You're obviously not a racing driver.'

'And you're obviously not a journalist.'

She ignored this. 'Maybe you're some kind of crook. That's what you look like, despite your fancy car. And I don't know what business you had with Jason Sin. But we could have easily talked our way out of that study. There were plenty of reasons we could have been there. We could have got lost. We could just have been snooping. So what? Even if he'd decided he didn't like it, what was the worst that could have happened? He would have called the police and I don't know about you but for me that would have been perfectly fine. Instead of which, we go haring off down those passageways. We make it up to the roof. And we risk breaking our goddam necks taking a night dive into the lake. If I'd had five seconds to think I'd have turned round and taken my chances, instead of which I've lost my purse and my cash. I've missed my cab. And now I'm stuck here with you.'

'You're not stuck with me, Jeopardy,' Bond returned. 'If you say one more word, I'll throw you out and you can see if you can find a room somewhere else.' He looked at her coldly. 'First of all, Sin wouldn't have asked questions. Nor would he have called the police. He's a seriously dangerous man. Did you notice the portraits with the burned-out eyes? That might have told you something. He was holed up in a castle in the middle of a lake and he was surrounded by armed security men. And you really wanted to trust yourself to him?'

'Sin's just a rich guy—'

'Don't give me that. You've got nothing to do with racing. I saw you trying to talk your way up the stairs. I suppose you must have followed me after I cleared the way. So maybe you should start by telling me why you were there and what you were looking for.'

'I'm not telling you anything.' She was still scowling. Bond thought it was the prettiest scowl he had ever seen. 'I need to make a phone call. To New York.'

'You're not going to get a line tonight.'

'Tomorrow morning then.' There was a long silence. She took another sip of the brandy. 'Are you?' she asked.

'What?'

'A crook?'

'No. I'm a sort of investigator. I'm working for people who might be interested in Sin.'

Bond's jacket, still sodden, was hanging in the bathroom. He had taken the photographs out of the pocket and laid them carefully on the radiator. Inevitably, the water had done some damage but as each one dried, he could still make out most of the image. He picked one up and looked once again at the strip of coastline, the white buildings, the rocket in its gantry. 'I don't suppose this means anything to you?' he asked.

'It's a rocket launch site.'

'I might have worked that out for myself. Do you know where it is?'

'No.'

This time, she was the one lying. Bond was sure of it. But how much was he going to tell her? How could he get her to trust him? Suddenly he was tired. He'd had enough of the evening and knew that the next day he would have an early start and a long drive. 'I need to get some sleep,' he said. 'You can have the bed. I'll take the sofa. And you don't have to have any worries. I won't pounce on you in the night.'

'I'm sure you won't. I can see you're not that sort.' They were the first words she had spoken that sounded conciliatory.

Bond drew a spare blanket out of the cupboard and made up the sofa. At the same time, Jeopardy slid discreetly out of the towel and into the bed. When he next looked at her, only her head and arms were showing. The covers, stretched tight across her chest, came all the way to her neck. She was pressing them down as if to close off the entrance. With her cropped hair, the slightly upturned nose and her skin so pale in the moonlight, she reminded Bond of a novice nun having her first night in a convent, terrified of the wandering hands of the mother superior.

Part of him recoiled. He had never slept like this before, certainly not with a girl as attractive as Jeopardy Lane a few feet away. A naked, attractive girl, he reminded himself. And he could feel the brandy warming his stomach, reanimating him. He threw himself on the sofa and pulled the blanket up. It was fortunate he was so tired. Sleep came at once.

In the morning, things were different.

Bond was woken by the sun streaming in through the window. Jeopardy was still asleep, her head on her arm and the sheet draped so perfectly across her that it could have been painted by a Renaissance artist. He slipped into the bathroom, showered and dressed. When he came out, she was awake.

'Are you all right?' he asked.

She nodded. 'I was a little hard on you last night,' she said. 'But I was tired and I was confused. Also, I don't like sharing a room with a man I've never met. Where I come from, there could only have been one consequence. But you've behaved like a gentleman, I'll say that for you. Maybe you're right about Sin. He's certainly a creep. And whether he's a gangster or whatever I'm glad we didn't hang around to have a chat.'

'Are you going to tell me why you're interested in him?'

She hesitated. 'It's personal...'

'You know him?' Bond took a guess. 'Did you work for him?'

'Something like that.' She sighed. 'Look. I'll tell you everything, I swear. But not until I'm dressed and that means you're going to have to go out and buy me some clothes. I also need breakfast. I want eggs and coffee and juice. I don't want to eat here. I want to go some place neutral... there's a Danny's coffee shop just outside town. That'll do. And I'm not telling you anything about me until I've heard about you. James Bond. Is that your real name?'

'Yes.'

'It sounds fake. You say you're an investigator and you're British. Are you from Scotland Yard?' She said it as if it was some sort of joke. 'You can tell me all that later. All I need is a jersey and jeans. And you should be able to find some court shoes or something. Nothing with high heels. I'll pay you back sometime although it's your fault I've got nothing to wear.'

'You don't need to worry about the money and I'll see what I can find. I've got quite a good eye for sizes but I can't promise I'll get much in the way of the latest fashion in a place like Nürburg.'

'I'm not interested in fashion.' She glanced at the clock with its cow face. 'It's half past eight. The shops probably won't open for a while. But don't worry about me. I'm going to take a long bath and then I might go back to sleep. Just make sure the door's locked on the way out and slip the key underneath.'

Bond did as she had asked. The night porter had been replaced by a new man who greeted him as he left the building, stepping out into a warm, pleasant day. He had parked the Bentley out of sight and down the road. If Sin had sent his men after him, he wouldn't have wanted the car to act as a signpost to the hotel. There was nobody around. Without the excitement of a race, the little town had gone back to sleep and Bond's instincts told him that the night's adventures were well behind him. He drove out to the main road and after a while he found a general store with a few items of women's clothing in the window, although he had to wait ten minutes until it opened. He picked out a short-sleeved double-knit (*100% Dacron – the fibre that knows all there is to know about winning form*) and a pair of pedal pushers. The store had sandals but no shoes. He wasn't sure that Jeopardy would thank him, but the outfit would have to do until she got to Cologne.

He drove back to the hotel, parked the car and went back to the room. The door was open. Suddenly Bond felt uneasy. Jeopardy had told him to lock it. It was the last thing she had said. Bond slipped the Walther PPK out of his pocket. He had taken it from the secret compartment at the back of the glovebox in his Bentley. Holding it in front of him, he softly pushed the door ajar and looked into the room. The bed was empty. The bathroom door was open. Jeopardy had gone.

It didn't take him long to piece it all together. There was a laundry room just down the corridor. One of the uniforms worn by the hotel maids – a blouse and pencil skirt – had been stolen. The receptionist had actually seen her leave. Bond didn't make any further enquiries. He assumed she had hitch-hiked out of town. Back to Cologne? There was no certainty that that part of her story had been any truer than anything else she had said. In a way he quite admired the way she had so coolly sent him off in pursuit of an outfit that she had known she wouldn't need.

But a few minutes later, when he had returned to the room, that admiration had turned to anger ... not with her but with himself. Jeopardy hadn't left empty-handed. The photographs had gone.

12

Rocket Science

'Unlike you, James, to let a girl get the better of you. And after a night on the sofa, too! You must be losing your touch.' Charles Henry Duggan let out a bellow of laughter and threw back the last of the Selbach-Oster Riesling which he had ordered with lunch and most of which he had consumed himself. Bond was not fond of German wine, particularly the Auslesen which were too sweet, too heavy – too *German* at the end of the day. Duggan had picked out the most expensive bottle on the menu. 'The food here's bloody awful so we might as well make up for it. Bloody Jerries! If I'd known I was going to be packed off here until I popped my clogs, I might have thought twice about joining the service.'

'Nonsense, Charlie. You love it here.'

'Bad Salzuflen? Even the name sounds like something you might catch in a brothel. All they've got are spas and salt springs. Most of the people are here for their health but the one thing they haven't got is a cure for terminal boredom.'

Bond had driven north-east to the famous health resort close to the Teutoburg Forest mountains. His first thought had been to return to London but he had a feeling he had no time to lose. There had to be a reason why Sin was examining photographs of an American rocket in his private office, just

144

as there had to be a reason for Jeopardy to steal them. Back in 1946, the SIS had set up a sub-section of the Intelligence Division whose primary role was to keep an eye on the buoyant economic and political scene in Germany with particular reference to any resurgence of Naziism on the one hand and to the ongoing activities of the communists on the other. Things had quietened down since then but the section – now known as Station G – was still a vital part of intelligence gathering, particularly with reference to Eastern Europe. It was housed in a nondescript office building close to the railway station. For the past ten years, it had been headed by Duggan and he had turned it into his own fiefdom with a staff that turned a blind eye to his idiosyncrasies. Bond was right. The post suited him well. And at the weekends there was always Berlin with darker backstreets and racier clubs than he would ever find at home.

Duggan had already given Bond a full debriefing. Together, they had sent a signal to London giving a detailed (if not comprehensive) account of what had occurred at the Schloss Bronsart. Bond had requested further information about Sin Jai-Seong, about a woman calling herself Jeopardy Lane and about all the imminent rocket launches in the USA. There was nothing more to do until a reply came in so the two men had gone to a local restaurant for lunch.

Duggan was a great many things that are unusual in the world of the secret service. He was fat – really fat – loud, bearded, frequently indiscreet and often, at least in appearance, drunk. He dressed badly in clothes that would have more suited a country squire – jackets and waistcoats in heavy checks and brightly coloured ties. He was also homosexual and didn't care if people knew it. He and Bond had almost come to blows late one night in a Montmartre bar on the only occasion when the topic had come up, Duggan damning him for his Protestant upbringing and his blinkered world view. 'The trouble with you, James, is you're basically a prude. I bet half the boys at that bloody public school of yours were buggering each other blind and you didn't even notice or looked the other way. Anyway, the service is crawling with sisters. You know it and I know it. Look at that dreadful man Burgess. It's a gift to the Soviets, letting them set up their honeytraps, snaring civil servants who are too young and too scared to know better. God knows how many secrets we've lost that way. Change the law and let people be what they want to be – that's what I say. And as for you, maybe you should try to be a bit less of a dinosaur. This is 1957, not the Middle Ages! The second half of the twentieth century!'

There were very few people who could talk to Bond in this way but the two of them had served together in the RNVR during the war and had even shared a flat for a short while in Victoria, sometimes travelling home together through the blackout. Fifteen years later, Bond couldn't help liking Duggan. The man was loyal to his friends, reliable in his judgement and ran a first-class operation. Immediately after the war, he had helped set up JUNK, an underground railway that ran agents into the satellite states of Russia. He had cheerfully sold cheap Swiss watches behind the Iron Curtain, using the money to entice wavering apparatchiks to defect. It was thanks to his efforts that a great many clues about the Soviet chemical and biological warfare capability had come to light. He was good company. He knew how to live.

He could also be discreet when he wanted to be and as he waved for the bill he lowered his voice. 'This business with the rockets,' he muttered. 'I have to say, I don't like it at all. If you ask me, the chickens are coming home to roost.'

'What do you mean?'

'After the war, you were too busy running around saving the world. But some of us were thinking ahead. It was obvious that rocket technology was going to shape the future – and I'm not just talking about ICBM's. I got drawn into it for a while. There was an operation called Backfire. We took a close look at any of the V2's we could get our hands on and saw just how very good they were. So then we tried to recruit some of the boys from Peenemünde. We even had Wernher von Braun in London for a while. Horrible man. Anyway, we didn't have any luck. There was that debacle with Colonel Tasoev who changed his bloody mind and then there was Professor Tank who disappeared to Argentina with all his plans hidden in his underpants, would you believe it! We managed to bag a few German engineers but none of the scientists were interested. They loathed the French. They were terrified of the Soviets, of course. But we couldn't afford what they wanted to be paid so the whole lot went off to America and they've been there ever since.

'I don't know how much you know about the space race, James. I know that old bastard M keeps you on more or less full-time active service. But right now you should be looking to the stars. Let me tell you, that's where the next war is going to be fought and that's where it's going to be won. Did you ever see that article in *Collier's* magazine? Written by Wernher von Braun, God rot him. A fully paid-up member of the Nazi party now working for the Yanks! Anyway, he claimed it was possible to establish an artificial satellite in outer space – he called it a space station. It would have people living and working outside the earth's atmosphere. Using tele-scopic cameras, they'd be able to see the face of every single human being on the planet. You light a cigarette in Leicester Square and they'd clock it. And they'd be able to launch guided missiles with pinpoint accuracy – this was written a few years back, remember – and von Braun concluded: "The first nation to do all this will control the earth."

'Since then the superpowers have been going at it hammer and tongs. Or maybe that should be hammer and sickle and tongs. The Americans have got Cape Canaveral. The Russians have got some sort of space city in a hellhole called Tyuratam in the middle of the Siberian desert, as far away from Western listening posts as they can get. They've built towers, bunkers ... they poured a million cubic feet of concrete into the launch platforms alone. We don't know very much, to be honest with you. As you can imagine, it's a hellish problem getting information out. But their aim is to get a thermonuclear device weighing five tons into outer space and they may get there eventually. If they don't, it certainly won't be for want of trying.'

The waiter came over and they paid the bill. It seemed to Bond that the effects of all the alcohol Duggan had consumed had vanished in an instant. As they walked back through the town, he was utterly serious.

'The thing about the space race is that it's a strange mixture. You've got the scientists on the one side and the military on the other. So it's all about exploring other planets, new frontiers and living together in peace and harmony. Or it's about blowing the hell out of your enemy, utterly destroying them and devastating their country. It just depends who you talk to. The scientists need the money. The money comes from the military. But at the same time there's something about space travel that's really caught hold of the public imagination. Wernher von Braun even made a television programme, for heaven's sake! Walt Disney's *Man in Space*, also known as Mickey Mouse on the moon! But it worked. Forget the fact that the Americans and the Russians actually want to wipe each other out. Forget the fact that the entire space race began with the Korean War and the Americans' ever-so pressing desire to drop a nuclear bomb on the Chinese. Suddenly it's all twinkle, twinkle little star. Satellites. Communications. Artificial stars circling the earth in just two hours. Passenger rockets. Trips to Mars! Of course, a lot of it is hogwash but it's still managed to weave its way into the dreams of ordinary people and suddenly it's all become about prestige. You don't even have to go to war. If you want to rule the earth, you've got to rule outer space. It's as simple as that.

'And this is a particularly interesting year, as it happens. They've even got a name for it. The International Geophysical Year. It's something to do with an eleven-year cycle. Sun spots are particularly active at the moment. I was never good at science at school and it's above my head in every sense but the point is that there's never been a better time to measure radiation in the upper atmosphere and around seventy countries have come together to get a slice of the action, including the USSR. They're all talking about mutual goals, a new spirit of co-operation and all the rest of it, but that's the scientific side. The military boys are as busy as ever.

'This is how Eisenhower sees it. The Americans put a civilian rocket into space for the sake of meteorological and radiological research. They get the prestige. The whole world applauds. But more than that. Suddenly they've got a satellite over Russian air space. They've set a new precedent – "freedom of space" – and the Russians can't complain. They're part of the same effort. And the next rocket that goes up might contain weapons. It might contain spy satellites. You see what I'm saying, James? Right now there's an opportunity for the Americans to take a giant step forward in the space race and the Russians are actually helping them on their way.'

Bond thought about the photographs he had seen in Sin's office. American rockets being studied by SMERSH – or perhaps by a small, specialised team within SMERSH. He remembered his meeting with M in London. Suddenly he saw the connection. 'You talk about prestige,' he said. 'The Russians were at Nürburgring because they were worried about their chap coming second. It was all about Soviet technology. They wanted to prove that the Krassny was the fastest car on the road. Suppose you took the same principle and applied it to space travel?'

'Russian rockets beating American ones? The R-3 against the Atlas or whatever? I suppose it makes sense. And it would explain what Sin was doing here in Germany. A bit like that chap in Crab Key…'

'Blowing up rockets. Setting back the American space programme…'

Duggan thought for a moment, then shook his head. 'I'm sorry, James. You might be right but I just don't see it. First of all, I don't know how Sin could get access to American launch stations: Cape Canaveral, Cooke, Wallops Island, White Sands.'

'He has a recruitment business.'

'Cooks and cleaners, maybe. Not engineers. He'd have a hell of a job getting anywhere near and suppose he did manage to blow up a couple of rockets. Would it really make that much of a difference? The truth is, the Americans are managing perfectly well without him. Last January they fired off a Thor rocket. It managed all of nine inches before it broke in two and blew up. They say you could hear the explosion thirty miles away. So they tried again in April. Same thing: thirty seconds and then bang! It turned out that it was some safety officer who'd got it in his head – quite wrongly – that the damn thing was going to fall on Orlando, so he put his thumb on the self-destruct button and blew it up. The last I heard, by the way, he'd been given a new job on a small island in the South Atlantic.' Duggan laughed. 'But that didn't stop them. One month later they were at it again. The third rocket sat on the launch pad quite cheerfully for a few minutes and then blew itself to smithereens. You see what I mean? Every failure just makes them redouble their efforts and the American public don't give two hoots about all their tax dollars going up quite literally in smoke. Half the time, they don't know. These launch stations are all remote, deliberately. And anyway, they think the prize is worth funding. Ownership of space. It would take a lot to make them change their mind.'

They had been walking through medieval streets largely untouched by the war. Station G loomed up in front of them; a red-brick building that could have been a guest house or perhaps the home of a minor government department. Nobody stopped them as they walked in. An elderly doorman, head buried in a newspaper, barely glanced up. But Bond wasn't fooled by the seeming lack of security. The doorman would almost certainly be armed. Their entrance would have been filmed by cameras concealed somewhere in the cornices. A fluoroscope would have been triggered as they passed and if they were known to be unidentified and carrying concealed weapons, the entire building would have gone into immediate lockdown. Duggan's office was on the second floor. He puffed and wheezed his way up the faded marble staircase, supporting himself on the handrail, and he was in a bad mood as he entered the room with its solid desk, comfortable chairs and antique, cast-iron stove.

'Greta!' he called out. 'I want two coffees. Strong – black. And have we had anything from London?'

A moment later, a smart-looking girl appeared, dressed in a severe, grey suit and with her hair in a Paris cut, framing her face. She was carrying a file and after a cool appraisal of Bond, she left it with Duggan and went out. Duggan opened the pages and read them. Bond lit a cigarette and waited for him to finish. The girl came back with the coffees. Once again they were alone.

'Well,' Duggan said at last. 'We're not really any the wiser. First, nothing's come up on Jeopardy Lane, not from the CIA or the FBI. But she certainly isn't a journalist – no articles under that name and she's not known at *Motor Sport* or any of the other magazines. Secondly, we've got a bit more information about your friend Sin Jai-Seong, but nothing to get too excited about. The Blue Diamond Recruitment Agency is an absolutely solid business with no associations, criminal or otherwise. It has a virtual monopoly when it comes to Koreans, obviously, but it also handles Puerto Ricans, Jews, Greeks ... you name it. There are millions of them, all cheap labour, but you can see that he's creaming twenty cents off every dollar they earn and he's making a fortune.'

'What areas are they working in?' Bond asked.

'Well, he has to be careful, particularly in New York. The

Cosa Nostra control rubbish collection and construction and he doesn't want to rub up against the unions. But he's got his finger in pretty much everything from meat processing to the rag trade. Labourers, hod carriers, elevator operators. A lot of the work is seasonal and, as I say, all of it's low-paid. He has a lot of people in transport – the subway system and buses. But no rocket scientists, James. The closest you're going to get is someone sweeping the floor.'

Bond took this information in. 'What else?'

'You asked about launches and this time you may have struck lucky. I don't know. The next one is five days from now.' Bond raised an eyebrow. 'Yes, I thought that might interest you. They're doing a satellite test, blasting off a Vanguard rocket from Wallops Island and they're determined this one's going to get off the ground. I've managed to dig up an image for you. Does it ring any bells?'

Duggan passed a photograph across the desk. Bond examined it: a strip of coastline, white buildings, the pencil shape of the rocket, the empty horizon. He recognised it at once.

'It's identical,' he said. 'Or as near as dammit. This was the picture I saw on Sin's desk.'

'Then you'd better be on your way, old boy. You've already got the go-ahead from M. I'll arrange the flight.'

That same evening, Bond left for New York.

PART TWO:

...MUST COME DOWN

13

The Man in Charge

'I'm sorry, Mr Bond. I think you've wasted your time… and, for that matter, mine too.'

Bond, still exhausted by the flight from Berlin, the long drive down from New York, a brief and unsatisfying sleep in the wrong time zone and the wrong motel, was not surprised. Somehow he had known from the moment he had been shown into this blank, comfortless office with its comfortless office furniture and single, rectangular window looking out onto a strip of uninteresting shoreline, that this wasn't going to go well. Behind the desk, Captain Eugene T. Lawrence USN sat with the easygoing obstinacy of a man too used to being obeyed. The Navy Liaison and Project Officer at Wallops Island was a man in his mid-forties, immaculately dressed in his summer uniform, khaki with gold buttons and three rows of ribbons nudging into his lapel, dark tie and shoulder boards. Buttoned up in every sense. He had the solid build and huge neck of a football player. The head, with its sandy-coloured hair, small eyes and smooth cheeks, was curiously baby-like. Bond guessed he went to church every Sunday. He would have a wife who would boast about him to her friends but who would wince at the sound of his coming home, and a son – Eugene Jnr – who would call him 'sir'. He was the man in charge here and it didn't matter if you had better judgement, more experience or new information. You did as he said.

Bond had been met at the gate by a younger man in a short-sleeved white shirt and flannel trousers who had introduced himself as Johnny Calhoun, Base Manager. Bond had quickly got the picture. This was what Duggan had already told him at Station G. Lawrence represented the military side of Wallops Island, Calhoun the scientific and civilian. Bond had seen his file and knew that he was a West Point graduate, employed by the Glenn L. Martin aerospace manufacturing company who had provided the majority of engineers working for the Vanguard Operations Group (VOG). He turned out to be slim and boyish with a crew cut, an easy smile and Ray-Ban Wayfarer sunglasses.

'Good to meet you, Commander Bond. Welcome to Wallops. This your first time?' Bond nodded. 'I've only been here a year. I got transferred here from Baltimore and it's been quite a ride. Please, come this way, sir. Captain Lawrence is waiting for you in his office.'

A single, wide track led from the car park, running parallel with the sea. There was a huge blockhouse on the left and, about fifty yards away, on the other side of the track and right next to the water, a great square of white concrete that was the launch pad. Bond stopped and gazed at the tower, ninety-five feet high, and the silver-white rocket standing there, its fury contained as it waited for the moment when it would finally be unleashed and blasted into space. Once again, he felt an irresistible thrill, something inside him that was both awed and inspired by the sheer power of the thing, the shimmering steel rising sleekly from the first stage rocket motor to the questing tip of the nose cone. From a distance, it looked almost lightweight, perfectly balanced on its platform about ten feet above the ground and surrounded by engineers and technicians – acolytes worshipping at the altar of modern science.

'Yes, it's quite a sight,' Calhoun muttered, following his eyes. He had a pleasant drawl and seemed genuinely friendly, the sort of man you couldn't help but like. 'Every time I look at it I find myself knocked out by how far we've come – and wondering just how far we still have to go. Will you be here for the launch?'

'I can't really say,' Bond replied.

'You should try to stay if you can. You won't have seen anything like it. It's a wonderful sight.' Calhoun faltered, then half smiled. 'At least, it is when they get off the ground.'

Bond had been present at the launch of one rocket – indeed, he'd had a unique, ringside view – but decided not to mention it. The two of them walked together, heading for a low white building surrounded by shrubs. The air was very warm, the sun beating down from a cloudless sky. There wasn't a breath of wind. Perfect launch conditions, Bond thought.

'You know... maybe I should mention a couple of things about Captain Lawrence,' Calhoun said. He already sounded apologetic. 'There's a great deal of pressure on him at the moment, just three days before launch. We all feel the same way. So when we got the communication from your London office via the CIA, well, it couldn't have been worse timed. I'm not blaming you, of course. I'm just trying to explain why you may find the captain a little... tired.'

'Does he get "tired" very often?'

'Yes, sir. You could say that.' Calhoun shook his head. 'He's not such a bad guy when you get to know him. He joined the navy the day after Pearl Harbor. Trained at the US Naval Academy and flew missions in Korea. You know he got the Bronze Star? He came here the year before me and actually he's run the place pretty well. Security. Discipline. Morale. He's kept open the channels of communication and that's quite something in itself, let me tell you. You have no idea how it is in this place. We've got so many different people involved, even ordering a light bulb or new toilet paper can take half a dozen forms and a committee meeting! If he's a bit short with you, just don't take it personally.'

Captain Lawrence *had* been short, from the moment Bond had walked into his office, not bothering to get up and examining him with the sort of disdain that he might reserve for a seasick Seaman Apprentice. Calhoun sat to one side, listening with a blank face as Bond told his story: the photographs found in Sin's office, the link with SMERSH, the attempt to sabotage the race at Nürburgring and the possibility that something similar might happen here. Bond read the disinterest in the captain's eyes and had to bite back his anger. He hadn't travelled halfway round the world to be casually dismissed by some brass hat behind a desk. He'd been up against SMERSH before. He could sense the danger in the air. He knew things that this man didn't.

And now, in his own considered way, Lawrence summed it all up. 'What it really comes down to is some photographs you said you saw in a castle in Germany. There could be all sorts of reasons for their being there, by the way, but putting that aside, what makes you think that this man Sin could have any reason to do us harm?'

'I told you, sir. The day before I had seen him with—'

'This Colonel Gaspanov. Has it not occurred to you, Commander Bond, that there could be a perfectly simple explanation for that, too? The Soviets were racing. Plenty of their top brass are into that sort of thing and you think some intelligence bigwig is going to pass on an excuse to get out of Moscow? Why, I bet you couldn't wait to get out there either. Sure beats paperwork.'

Bond ignored the insult. 'There was still an attempt to kill the British driver.'

'So you maintain. But again, in a court of law I'd say it was your word against theirs. And from what you tell me, the only act of violence on the racing circuit was committed by you.'

'Ivan Dimitrov was employed by SMERSH, Captain. We have the intelligence—'

'Which I haven't seen.' Lawrence glanced at Calhoun as if about to ask him his opinion, thought better of it, and turned back to Bond. 'What exactly are you asking me to do?'

'I came here to give you the facts, sir. Not to ask you to do anything. But if you're asking my opinion, I think you should consider postponing the launch.'

'That's out of the question.'

This time Calhoun agreed. 'That's true, Commander. And anyway, that decision would have to be taken at a much higher level.'

'But if you recommended—'

'We wouldn't recommend any such damn thing,' Lawrence cut in. There was a red flush on the sides of his neck. For a moment, he sat there. Then he tapped two fingers on the surface of his desk. 'All right. Let's see where this takes us. What exactly do you think these people – the reds, SMERSH, whoever – have in mind?'

Bond knew he was being played with but he had no choice. 'I think I've already explained myself, Captain. They may be planning to sabotage the rocket.'

'And how exactly are they going to manage that? Let's not forget that all three stages – engine, power plant and solid-propellant rocket – were all given thorough acceptance tests. Those were followed by systems tests. And then there were static tests for the propulsion systems, the stabilisation systems and all the controls. Are you telling me we overlooked something? There were alignment checks, system functional tests and a microscopic examination of all the instrumentation calibrations.'

'I'm sure you've been very thorough,' Bond said, patiently.

'Well, that's very kind of you, Commander Bond. But let's imagine that we've made a mistake. We're only dumb Americans, after all, and you're telling us that we can't look after our own security. So let us imagine that the commies pull it off. What exactly do they hope to achieve?'

'I was hoping you'd tell me that.'

Lawrence nodded at Calhoun who took over. He spoke with a tone of regret. 'This is a test flight,' he said. 'The rocket won't be carrying anything that's particularly valuable. In fact, we're loading on a grapefruit satellite. We call it that because that's about the size of it: 6.4 inches in diameter and it weighs four pounds.'

'All our rockets have to carry scientific equipment,' Lawrence added. 'That's the deal we have with the NRL.'

'We're testing the new spin stabilisation system,' Calhoun said. 'These days, thanks to miniaturisation, even the smallest satellite can do useful work. But it's true, Commander. There's nothing to be gained by shooting down the Vanguard or blowing it up or whatever. It would be annoying, of course. And expensive. But the navy is committed to this programme and it's going to continue.'

'Suppose it was redirected,' Bond said. 'Suppose it fell on a city.'

'That can't happen. Our safety officer will be following the launch from our central control office. He'll be watching every inch of the journey and if the rocket shows any faults, if it swerves away from its appointed trajectory, if there is even the slightest danger of a land-based impact... well, that's when he'll hit Trigger Mortis.'

'And what's that?'

'It's our name for the panic button, Commander. One of the technicians dreamt it up and it kind of stuck. Every single vehicle launched from this base carries a self-destruct mechanism. If we have any reason to believe that something has gone wrong, we pull the trigger and blow it apart... and the pieces simply fall into the ocean.'

Lawrence glanced at his watch. 'I hope that answers your questions, Commander Bond. Now, if you'll excuse me—'

But Bond hadn't come this far to be dismissed so abruptly. 'You talk about checks,' he insisted, 'but there must be a hundred people working on this base. Any one of them could have been bribed, blackmailed, threatened. Even your safety officer could be working for the opposition—'

'I happen to know Paul Glennan and his family and let me tell you I find that remark personally offensive. I have the recruitment files of every man jack on this island and I've gone through every one of them myself. That's part of my remit. There isn't one person I wouldn't vouch for.'

'And nothing has happened in the last few weeks or months? Nothing out of the ordinary?'

'Absolutely not.'

But as he spoke, Bond saw Calhoun flinch. He turned to him questioningly and the younger man blushed. 'Well, sir,' he muttered, 'there was that business with Keller.'

'Goddammit, Johnny!' Lawrence's fist crashed down on the desk. 'What happened with Keller had nothing to do with this base. You know it. The police confirmed it. And I can't believe you're contradicting me in my own office.' He came to a decision and when he turned back to Bond, there was a new coldness in his eyes. 'Let's get back to these photographs that you say you saw,' he snarled. 'That's where this all started. But where exactly are they?'

'I don't have them with me.'

'What happened to them?'

'They were stolen.' Something told Bond that Captain Lawrence already knew.

Lawrence hesitated, enjoying the moment. And then, sure enough, he reached down and pulled open a drawer. With a flourish, he produced a handful of photographs and scattered them across the top of the desk. 'Would these by any chance be the photographs you're talking about?' he demanded.

Bond glanced at them and knew at once that they were. Not just copies but exactly the same photographs that he had taken from the Schloss Bronsart and which Jeopardy Lane had subsequently taken from him. He could tell from the water damage. They had been in his jacket pocket when he hit the lake. 'I don't suppose the name Jeopardy Lane means anything to you?' he asked.

'Never heard of it.'

'Then where did you get these?'

'I think that's my business, Commander Bond.' Lawrence was smiling now. 'But you might like to know that I've had them for quite a few days and I've had a chance to examine them. As far as I can tell, they're fake.'

'Fake?'

'The ones of the base are real. Any tourist with a decent camera can take pictures. But this one ...' He picked out the photograph taken inside the hangar, the one showing three Korean scientists and the upper section of the Vanguard. 'I don't know what you think this is, but it's got nothing to do with us.'

'How can you be sure?'

'Because there are no Japs on Wallops Island. None at all.'

'These men are Koreans.'

'No Japs, no Koreans and no Chinese, except, maybe, in the laundry. This is not our hangar. I can tell you that at a glance.'

'But it's a Vanguard rocket.'

'No, sir. I don't believe it is. It may look like one – it's hard to say from this photograph – but America is the only country in the world that has the Vanguard and to the best of my knowledge we haven't had one stolen recently or, indeed, ever. I guess even we might notice if one of our rockets went missing, Commander. So, it's like I told you quite a while ago now, you're wasting your time.'

He stood up, signalling the end of the interview. Bond took one last look at the images strewn across the desk. Was it possible that Jeopardy Lane had been working for the NRL or even for the base itself? But if so, why hadn't Lawrence told him as much? He would surely have wanted to boast about recovering the photographs. The navy liaison man was standing ramrod straight. There was to be no parting handshake.

'I want you to know that I take particular exception to British Intelligence trying to undermine my authority,' he said. 'It's bad enough that you guys kicked us out of Barbados. It hasn't taken you very long to forget what we did for you in the war. But coming here like this, with your damn impertinent questions? Mr Calhoun will show you back to your car and make sure you leave the base.'

That was it. Johnny Calhoun walked over to the door and opened it and Bond followed him out of the office. Neither of them spoke until they were back in the open air and the sunshine. Then Calhoun broke the silence. 'I'm sorry about that, Commander.'

'Well, I can't say you didn't warn me. He was certainly tired. What was that jibe about Barbados?'

'It's actually true, sir. The NRL wanted to build a launch site in Barbados. When you launch a rocket, you always head for the east. You have to take advantage of the earth's rotation and the closer to the Equator you are, well, it would have been useful to have the equatorial kick but the British government refused. Environmental reasons, I guess, but it ruffled a few feathers.'

'How about that man – Keller?' Calhoun looked uneasy and Bond knew that he didn't wish to appear any more disloyal than he already had been. 'I can go to the local police if you don't want to talk about it. But it would help to get the facts from you and I can be discreet.'

'Sure thing.' Calhoun glanced back in case Lawrence had somehow followed them. There was nobody in the road. 'Thomas Keller was one of our supervisors.' Bond noticed the

'Thomas'. Not Tom or Tommy. There was no familiarity here. 'I hardly knew him and he didn't mix in very well,' Calhoun went on, confirming what Bond had already guessed. 'He was German, and the truth is, if the navy had its way there wouldn't be any Germans in the Vanguard Operations Group. They've got long memories. Anyway, a couple of weeks ago we were all very shocked because he was killed.'

'How?'

'According to the police, it was a domestic incident. His wife stabbed him and set fire to the house. She used to be a cocktail waitress – well, that's what the newspapers said – and she simply got fed up with him. She took the car and crossed the state line. The whole thing sounds like a cheap thriller, but the fact is that Captain Lawrence is right. It didn't have anything to do with us.'

'What was Keller's job here?'

'General Supervisor.'

'With access to the Vanguard?'

'Well, yes. Of course. But it's like I said. He was stabbed with a kitchen knife, the house was set on fire, and the wife disappeared, taking the car with her. As far as I know, they haven't found her yet.'

'Do you have his address? I still might take a look at his house.'

'Rainbow Lane, Salisbury. I don't recall the number but you can't miss it. How long are you planning to hang around?'

'I haven't really decided.' As far as Bond could see, there was no point kicking his heels in eastern Virginia but at the same time he had nowhere else to go. He would have to appeal to Captain Lawrence's superiors. At the very least, they might be able to tell him something about Jeopardy and her part in all this.

They had reached the car.

'Well, if you do decide to come for the launch, let me know and I'll fix you up with a pass.' They shook hands. 'Good to meet you, Commander Bond.'

Half a mile away, a man stood leaning against a four-door sedan. As James Bond drove through the gates at Wallops Island, the man took out a pair of Bausch + Lomb Zephyr 9x35 binoculars and raised them to his eyes. He focused until he had a clear view of the driver. Yes. That was the face he had been shown. Just as his employer had suspected, the British secret agent had followed the photographs here.

The man had been doing a crossword. The newspaper was still lying, half folded, on the bonnet of his car. He quickly threw it onto the back seat, then climbed in. A few moments later, Bond drove past. The man started his own car, turned round and followed.

14

Dead of Night

After his meeting with Calhoun, Bond went back to the motel where he was staying and made a phone call to the local police station. He was interested in Thomas Keller and wanted to know more. He arranged to meet an officer later that evening and went out to have an early supper of steak and fries in a nearby diner – a chilly little place called Lucie's. The waitress poured him coffee, which he hadn't asked for and didn't drink. American coffee, the standby of every diner, was barely more than brown water as far as Bond was concerned. But the food was good and after a cigarette – a Chesterfield, which made him think briefly of Pussy Galore – he paid and left. The car he had rented was parked outside. He checked the map, then drove up to Salisbury.

The burned-out remains of Keller's house were particularly shocking, an insult to the whole neighbourhood. It was as if a truck had come in the middle of the night and unloaded a great pile of charred wood and twisted metal. It had no right to be here. Bond drove slowly past the surrounding houses, all bright colours and perfect lawns. He could imagine children playing in each other's backyards, watched over by grand-parents sitting out on the porch, the whirr of a lawnmower on a warm summer's evening. And if there were fights, if there was violence, it would be done quietly, behind drawn curtains. 1261 Rainbow Lane gave the lie to all that. It was a black, ugly advertisement for hatred, violence and desperation; all those things that had no place in the American dream.

There was nobody in sight as Bond climbed out of his rented car and stood there, taking in the charred, sooty smell that lingers long after a fire. The grass had already begun to grow wild, the weeds gleefully grabbing the opportunity to break out. Someone had put up a sign: **KEEP OUT**. But there was no point in going any further. Bond could see at a glance that all the furniture and anything of any value had been removed. Eventually the bulldozers would come and remove the rest and soon Thomas Keller and his wife, along with all their secrets, would be forgotten.

A car pulled in behind him. Bond turned and saw that it was a Chevrolet Cruiser with the words 'Salisbury Police Department' printed on the door. A stolid, round-faced officer got out, wearing a shirt and tie with his badge pinned to his breast. He seemed to exude reliability and experience. He was exactly the sort of man that law-abiding citizens would want to have around.

'Mr Bond?' he asked.

'That's right. Thank you for coming out.'

'That's all right, sir. How can I help you?'

'Did you investigate what happened here?'

'Yes, sir. The Kellers . . . Thomas and Gloria. They'd been here quite a while. Kept themselves to themselves, but even so, plenty of people knew them. Met them in church or down at the mall. They seemed happy enough together. No financial worries, nothing like that. Nobody had anything bad to say about them.' The officer was utterly matter-of-fact, showing no emotion at all and Bond imagined he would be the same whether he was dealing with a murder or a parking offence. 'Mrs Keller came from Texas originally, but I believe they met in Mexico. He was German. No kids.'

'And you're sure she killed him?'

'It sure looks that way, sir. Mr Keller was stabbed in the kitchen and although it's hard to be sure, there doesn't seem to have been any struggle. He came home from work and she was here, waiting for him. And if it wasn't her who put the knife in, you have to ask why else would she take off like that?'

'Well, it seems strange to leave everything behind.'

'One of the neighbours actually saw her head off in a blue station wagon. That was just minutes after the house caught fire. Of course, we looked into her financial details. Turns out she'd remortgaged the property, taken a certified cheque made out to her. The two of them had a joint savings account and she'd walked into the bank and withdrawn the whole lot, in cash. This was the same morning it all happened.'

'Sounds pretty cold-blooded.'

'I agree. It looks like she had the whole thing worked out. You have to wonder – why now?'

And that was indeed the question, Bond reflected as he drove back to the motel. Why now? Or more precisely, why just a couple of weeks before the launch of the Vanguard? There was absolutely no evidence to tie Thomas Keller in with Jason Sin – for that matter, an attack on the rocket launch was still only a matter of conjecture. But everything in Bond's experience told him to look out for the unusual, for the little bump in the rhythm of life that demanded investigation. It could be that Gloria Keller had decided to get rid of her husband on the spur of the moment. Years of resentment could have finally led to a moment of violence that had been as sudden as it was unplanned. But wasn't it more likely that something in their lives had changed and that whatever it was had directly led to the murder? That's how it seemed to him.

Where next? Bond felt strangely disconnected, alone in the flat emptiness of the landscape, the fields stretching all the way to Chesapeake Bay and the sun already below the horizon. He was tempted to head north, back to New York. He could connect with the FBI and find out if they had managed to track down the absent Mrs Keller. It would also be interesting to know if Jason Sin had returned to America. But he could do all that by telephone and his every instinct told him to stay here, close to the launch. If the enemy was going to make a move, this was where it would happen. Above all, he wanted to know how the photographs, stolen from him in Germany, had turned up here. Lawrence wouldn't tell him but he seemed to have an ally in the base manager, Johnny Calhoun. It was too late to go back now. He would try his luck the next day.

The Starlite Motel was on Route 13, set back from the main road in front of woodland – mainly cedars and pines. Not surprisingly, the whole place was rocket-themed. The name was spelled out in white neon with a flickering red rocket blasting off from the lozenge-shaped sign. The rooms were arranged in three pastel-coloured blocks, each with two storeys and overhanging roofs – Redstone, Jupiter and Thor. Even the circular swimming pool was tiled to make it look like the planet Saturn. It wasn't the sort of accommodation that Bond would normally have chosen, but it was close to Wallops Island, surprisingly quiet and, with its AAA endorsement, as clean as he would have expected.

Bond had asked for a room on the second floor of Redstone, which was set slightly apart, on the edge of the compound. Eight dollars had bought him Redstone 205: a suite with a kitchenette and bathroom, TV and air conditioning and, what mattered most for him, an uninterrupted view of the gateway and main road.

Bond drove in, parked and walked over to the manager's office to pick up his key. There was a new man behind the counter, sleepy-eyed and well past retirement age, sitting in a rocking chair with his hands on his paunch. Seeing Bond, he got up with difficulty and searched out a scrap of paper from among many others. 'You gotta call,' he said. 'Man called Calloon or some such... you know? He call from outta that rocket place.'

'You mean Calhoun?'

'That's the one, boss. Yeah. He say he got summin' you might 'preshiate if you wanna hang 'round. He say iss important.'

'Did he leave a number?'

'I ain't got no number and you don' need none neither. He comin' here tomorrow at eight o'clock. That's wha' he say.'

'All right. Can I have my key?'

'Shoh ting.' The manager unhooked Bond's key from a wooden board that showed all the rooms in Redstone. He handed it over. 'Good night, sah. Yo getta good night's sleep.'

The four-door sedan eased into the compound at exactly two o'clock, the tyres crunching softly on the gravel. Twelve o'clock had come and gone but this was the true midnight, the time when the darkness was at its most absolute and people most deeply asleep. Wearing night camouflage and army boots, the man who called himself Harry Johnson stepped out and went

173

round to the trunk. He lifted something out. It was heavy and covered in tarpaulin. Behind him, a car and a van had arrived, parking in the street. Six more men unloaded themselves, similarly dressed in dark clothes with balaclavas covering their faces. They were all armed, with holsters hanging in plain sight beside their chests. At this time of the night, there were no witnesses and so no need for concealment. They closed the car doors quietly behind them and slipped into the shadows, taking up positions that had been agreed earlier on.

Two minutes past two. Johnson was lying on the ground with his legs spread out behind him. He was cradling an M60, the brand new, gas-operated, belt-fed machine gun currently being rolled out for the US army. With the plastic butt stock resting against his shoulder, he reached out and adjusted the rear sight. Room 205 in the Redstone building was directly in front of him, the window gazing blankly into the night. The machine gun had a quick-change spare barrel system, but it wasn't going to be needed. Johnson had meticulously cleaned and oiled every moving part and when he squeezed the trigger it would fire six hundred rounds a minute with a muzzle velocity of 2,800 feet. The target was barely five hundred feet away. The room and everything in it would be torn to shreds. Talk about nuts and sledgehammers. The people who were giving the orders were taking no chances. The British agent had to be killed – and if two thousand armour-piercing bullets didn't do the trick, there were half a dozen men waiting to deliver the *coup de grâce*. The entire operation would be over in less than ninety seconds. It would take the police at least seven minutes to arrive. A series of hoax telephone calls had already been made, diverting manpower to different parts of the state. Inside the van, a seventh man was monitoring police radio signals. He would give the alert long before the first patrol car came anywhere near.

For a few seconds Johnson listened to that intense silence that truly defined the deadness of the night. He could hear a few cicadas, scraping away in the trees. The hoot of an owl. The moment had come. Gently, he curled his finger around the trigger and squeezed.

Amplified by the stillness, the noise of the M60 was unbelievably shocking, white flashes erupting around the muzzle. On the other side of the compound, Room 205 simply ceased to exist, the wooden fascia, the door and the windows disintegrating as they were caught in the blast. In his mind's eye, Johnson could see inside the room and imagined the lights shattering, the pictures being blown off the walls, fragments of glass flying, the very air sliced open by a non-stop stream of white hot bullets. And the man in the bed? He might have woken up for just a few seconds, his body buckling and jerking as the bullets slammed into him, his blood boiling over, saturating the sheets. His death could not have been faster or more violent. It was the sort of ending that a British spy deserved.

He stopped. The silence now was almost physical as the night fought to regain its command. Nothing remained of Room 205. Lights were coming on in other rooms. There was a woman screaming. A baby had begun to cry. Some of the guests would already be scrambling for the phone, calling the police. But there was no hurry. There was plenty of time. Harry Johnson watched the dark figures chasing up the staircase to the second floor, moving in to check that the job had been done.

James Bond also saw them go past.

A secret agent working in the field develops an antenna. Having it or not having it is the difference between life and death. The moment Bond had got back to the Starlite Motel, he had been sure that something was wrong; not enough to leave but certainly enough to take precautions. Maybe it had begun with a glint of nervousness in the night manager's eyes, his message delivered lazily but still, somehow, evasively. It was always possible that Calhoun had been able to find out where Bond was staying although Bond hadn't actually told him the name of the motel. But if he had rung, why would he have mentioned that he worked at the rocket base? It wasn't the sort of information he would give out so carelessly, particularly with all the security surrounding the launch. And why would he come to the motel? Surely it would make more sense to meet in his office. Adding it all up, Bond was eighty per cent certain that somebody wanted to make sure that he stayed where he was. Which meant they planned to come for him that night.

And so he had taken his key and gone to his room as if there was nothing to worry about. Only once he was there had he acted. He had noticed from the keys on the board in the manager's office that the block, Redwing, was almost empty. It had been a simple matter to pack his single bag and slip downstairs to Room 105, directly beneath. All the rooms had doors at the front and sliding windows at the back. Bond went in round the back, effortlessly manipulating the latch with a knife he had taken from the kitchenette. The room was identical to the one above, even down to the abstract painting above the bed. He had lain down in the darkness fully dressed, waiting to see what would come. If it was the manager or perhaps a couple of late arrivals, he would be on his way before they had even opened the door. If it was trouble, he would be ready to face it.

Bond slept lightly; so lightly, he was barely asleep. Even before the car had drawn up at the entrance he had somehow sensed it and his eyes had flickered open, instantly alert. He knew at once that the rhythm of the night had been broken. The cicadas, sawing away, had paused briefly. Somewhere, a dog had barked three or four times and then stopped. He heard the metal legs of the M122 infantry tripod as it was placed on the gravel but did not know what it was. By not leaving, he knew that he had in part invited an attack – but what choice did he have? Whoever came for him, they would steer him to the person who had sent them. With no useful leads, Bond had to take any opportunity that was offered to him.

He knew that he was in trouble, that he had underestimated the enemy, when he looked out through a gap in the curtain and saw the six men spreading across the forecourt. That made it seven against one. They certainly weren't taking any chances! Surely they weren't going to start a war in the middle of a busy motel? Bond had only just asked himself the question when the machine gun opened up and demolished the room that should have been his. The noise was deafening, the blazing assault of the bullets as they hammered endlessly into wood and brickwork almost tangible. Crouching ten feet below, with just a few inches of ceiling and floor between him and the mayhem, Bond was shocked by the violence and by the knowledge that if he had stayed in the bed that had been assigned to him, he would most certainly be dead. Dust and wood splinters showered down. The smell of cordite enveloped him. For a few seconds he thought everything was silent, then realised that he had been quite literally deafened. As his hearing returned, he heard a woman screaming, then the cry of a baby. They were in the block next door. Looking out, he saw lights going on near the manager's office. He had no doubt that the night manager himself would already be far away.

Bond drew out the Remington M1911 semi-automatic pistol which had been supplied to him by the FBI, with their compliments, when he had arrived in New York. It was a little heavier than he would have liked but it had lain beside him as he slept and he was more than grateful to have it now. His mind was spinning. The machine gun should have finished him. The six men must have been brought along as backup, to make sure the job was done. Yes. Two of them were standing in the courtyard. He heard footsteps on the external staircase. Three of them were making their way up, covering each other – as if there was any chance that the occupant of Room 205 could have possibly survived to fire back! He had about fifteen seconds before they gave the alarm. Then what would happen? Bond weighed up the situation. His rented car was outside. They would know he was here. Once they realised their mistake, they would begin a room-by-room search.

He was already on his feet, making for the sliding window. Three men upstairs. Two at the front. That only left one at the back. Bond saw him almost at once, just a few paces away, staring up at what remained of Room 205. That was good. He was looking the wrong way and the balaclava he was wearing would reduce his field of vision. Bond came in low, covering the ground between himself and the man with lightning speed. He lashed out with the gun, driving it into the man's throat, feeling the full force of the steel muzzle as it crushed the thyroid cartilage and snapped the little hyoid bone just above. The man fell and would have screamed – or gurgled – in agony but Bond could not allow any sound to give him away. He struck again, this time using the grip, hammering it into the back of the neck. The man fell into Bond's arms. Bond lowered him to the floor.

It had taken ten seconds, maybe less. But there was no time to waste. Bond dragged off the balaclava – not even pausing to look at the face it revealed – and drew it onto his own head. He was wearing dark clothes. If he kept moving and stayed clear of the lit windows, he might get away with it. The machine gun was still silent but the dreadful memory of it hung in the air. The woman had stopped screaming. The baby was still crying. Then Bond heard someone shout out from above. Three words. 'He's not here!'

They knew he had tricked them. They were already looking for him. Bond's first instinct would have been to escape into the woodland behind the motel but the enclosure was fenced in and there was no way out. He ran round the side of the building, hoping that he could find a way to the main road. Five men, all armed – he could deal with that. The machine gun was the real problem. It would spit its fury at him before he could get anywhere near and with the light pouring out of half a dozen windows, he was an easy target. Would they recognise him in the balaclava? Had they arranged a method of visually referencing each other in case one of them went down?

Two men appeared, running towards him, and Bond knew instantly that his clothes, his height or simply the fact that he was heading in the wrong direction had given him away. He saw them stumble to a halt, bringing their weapons up.

Bond fired first, killing them both, then ran towards his car, knowing that the barrel of the machine gun would be following him, that the finger would already be tightening on the trigger. The car was a Plymouth, a typical piece of American automation, dull and predictable for all its attempts at style. Right now, that was all it needed to be. It was a metal wall, a barrier between Bond and his death. Even as he hit the ground, the machine gun started up its hideous racket and the car shuddered, the windows exploding, the metal panels buckling, the side mirrors spinning away. The key to the car was in Bond's pocket but as he lay there, cradling the Remington, he knew that he wasn't going to be driving anywhere. The car was rocking like a wounded animal. Then two of the wheels burst and it lurched sideways. The machine gun stopped.

Bond was trapped. He had the motel behind him. The gate – the only way out – was about three hundred feet away and whoever was positioned there would be out of range for his semi-automatic. He had taken out three of the men who had come for him but that still left four more and they would be closing in on him, making use of the shadows. They knew where he was. If he tried to break out, he would be cut down at once. Bond was furious with himself. He had known they were coming but he had decided to sit it out. He should have been on the other side of the fence, in the wood, or out by the road – anywhere but here. How many minutes had passed since the assault had begun? The police would have to be on their way by now. If he could just survive a little longer...

Bond ripped off the balaclava. He didn't need it any more and in the warm night air it was making him sweat. As an experiment, he threw it out from behind the Plymouth and instantly there was a single shot, this one fired from a pistol. So the foot soldiers had zeroed in on him too. What would he do if he were them? Keep him pinned down with the machine gun while the three moved into a position that would give them a clean shot. Bond gritted his teeth, waiting for it to come.

And then a car swung off the road, its headlights blazing. Bond glanced round the side of the Plymouth and saw it plunge into the motel compound, knocking the machine gun off its stand and hurling the whole thing aside. The man who had been firing it threw himself out of the way. Otherwise, he would have been killed. The car screeched to a halt in front of the Plymouth and the back door, already unfastened, swung open, carried by its own momentum. 'Get in!' a voice commanded. Bond didn't hesitate. He came out shooting and had the satisfaction of seeing one of the balaclavas fall backwards. He had to cover five paces before he could reach the car. He fired as he ran, then threw himself head first onto the back seat. The car was away instantly, Bond's feet and ankles still protruding from the door. The driver spun the wheel, hitting the accelerator and propelling them into a 180° spin. Bond dragged himself up and looked out of the front windscreen, for the moment ignoring the driver, not even caring who had saved him. The man at the gate had recovered. He had picked up the machine gun – Bond saw now that it was the new M60, said to be a game-changer for the US army. The man was bringing it round, aiming it at them. He had discarded the tripod and was going to fire from the hip. The car was hurtling towards him, the driver unflinching. It was just a game of chicken now, a case of who could move the fastest. Bond braced himself. He saw the man's face rushing towards him, short grey hair, a square face, narrow eyes. The M60 was in position. But before he could fire it, the car hit him full on. Bond felt the jolt and saw the man and the gun, the two of them separating as they were flung out of the way. And then they were past him, on the road, screaming away into the night. Bond looked out of the back window. The last two balaclavas had made it to the entrance but they weren't even trying to fire. The man lay between them, his legs and arms sprawled out and still.

The back door was still open. Bond pulled it shut, then leant forward so he could examine the driver. He had emptied the Remington but he knew he didn't need it any more.

'Thank you,' he said.

'You're welcome,' Jeopardy Lane replied.

15

Follow the Money

'All right, Jeopardy. No more mucking around.' Bond stabbed his egg and watched it bleed onto the plate. 'Who are you and how do you fit into all this?'

It was four o'clock in the morning and Bond was eating a breakfast that he didn't want in a place he didn't know. He wasn't hungry but nor was there any possibility of sleep. His nerves were still swamping his system with adrenalin, the organic chemical that had guided mankind from the moment it had stepped out of the cave. Epinephrine was created in response to danger and offered a simple choice: fight or flight. Maybe it was working overtime, Bond reflected, because in the end he had opted for both.

Jeopardy wasn't eating. She had a black coffee and a cigarette that she smoked lazily, as if she had barely noticed it was there. There was a bruised quality to her eyes. It was quite possible that she had killed a man a short while ago and although she was trying to pretend it didn't matter, it clearly wasn't something she was used to and she wasn't quite able to conceal the shock. 'I'm tired,' she said. 'We can talk in the morning.'

'It is the morning. And I don't want to wake up in another hotel room on my own.'

'I'm sorry I did that to you, James. OK? Is that what you want to hear? But try and see it my way. I didn't know who you were or what you were doing in Germany. I was just doing my job.'

'Who do you work for?' Bond tried a guess. 'Are you CIA?'

The two of them were alone in a long, desolate diner: Edward Hopper without the colours. Bond wondered why it stayed open all night. The waitress was half asleep behind the bar, the cook bleary-eyed and in need of a shave. The counter was a long slab of mahogany with a row of empty chairs.

'All right. I don't see why you shouldn't know. I'm with the US Secret Service, attached to the Department of the Treasury. I'm a kind of field agent. I investigate financial crime.'

'What sort of financial crime?'

'Well, all sorts. Mainly counterfeiting.'

Bond's head swam. Maybe it was too late – or too early – for this conversation. What could counterfeit money possibly have to do with the launch of the Vanguard and Sin's involvement with SMERSH? 'Go on,' he said.

'Are you sure you want to do this now?'

'Put it this way. I'm not letting you out of my sight until you've told me the truth.'

'All right.' She opened her purse and took out a brand new one-hundred-dollar bill which she laid on the table, as if she wanted to pay for the meal. 'Take a look,' she said. 'Maybe you can tell me. Is it real or fake?'

Bond picked it up. He knew that this was an impossible challenge. He was familiar enough with American currency but not down to the finer details and certainly not at four o'clock in the morning. Even so, he made a show of examining it, feeling the paper stock and holding it up to the light so that he could see the tiny red and blue fibres that had been woven in. Benjamin Franklin gazed at him impassively on the front. There was a building named as Independence Hall on the back but it occurred to Bond that he had no idea where it was situated. Washington, presumably. The note was brand new. He laid it down. 'It looks real enough to me,' he said. 'But I imagine you're going to tell me that it isn't.'

'The note is near perfect,' Jeopardy replied. 'One quarter linen, three-quarters cotton. It's been manufactured using an intaglio printer, with the ink applied at high pressure. The images couldn't be crisper. And this is just one of a hundred and eighty-five identical one-hundred-dollar bills received by my department about a week ago. We were suspicious straight away. First off, they were all brand new notes. Look at this one. You can see that it's never been in circulation. But what makes that really strange is that it's at least seven years old.'

'How do you know?'

'Back in 1950 they made a few changes to the design, particularly to the two seals. They added spikes to the Federal Reserve seal and the Treasury seal got smaller. This note predates that – and from the time it was produced, until now, it has never seen the light of day. There's got to be a reason for that. Of course, it could be real. It could have been stolen and hidden away for all that time. But look closer. The eyes are a little dull. And some of the details of the hair coming down over the collar are crude, unfinished. This is as good as I've ever seen – but it's counterfeit. There's no doubt.'

As she was talking, Bond noticed a different side to her. There was a passion that he hadn't seen before, a little spark of excitement in her eyes and a hint of colour in her pale, gamine cheeks. He knew plenty of women who enjoyed spending money but Jeopardy was the first one he had met who had such a passion for money itself.

'The stash of money, eighteen thousand five hundred dollars, was found by the Nevada State Police. There was a woman staying in a hotel in Las Vegas. The High Roller suite! She'd arrived a couple of nights before and she'd gone crazy, drinking and gambling – and losing like there was no tomorrow. They reckon that she managed to get through five thousand dollars in just one session, playing roulette. It was the casino owners who tipped off the cops. Those cold-hearted bastards don't mind taking money off anyone who comes through their doors but at the same time they're sensitive to trouble and they knew something was wrong. It's hard to be sure what happened, but a couple of patrol guys came knocking at the door and it seems the woman took fright. She went out of the window onto the balcony and when they broke down the door, she jumped. Shame she was on the twenty-first floor.'

'Her name was Gloria Keller.'

'Yeah. That's right. Captain Lawrence told you about her?'

'He didn't tell me anything.' Bond picked up the story. 'She saw the police. She assumed they were there because of her husband—'

'And she was so liquored-up she didn't stop to think. That's about it. They searched the room and found the cash in a suitcase and some bright spark in the LVPD decided to send it to us. We quickly saw that the whole lot was fake and I was put in charge of the case.'

'So how did you find your way to Nürburg?'

'Slow down. I'm coming to that.' She had finished her cigarette. She lit another. Bond pushed his plate away. He had only eaten half of the food. 'First of all, you have to understand that the cash was a big deal for us. How do you think I got onto this so quickly? These aren't the sort of crap you usually find in the streets; they're the best forgeries we've ever seen. In fact, they're so good, we believe they may have come from Operation Bernhard.'

'Sachsenhausen? The Nazi concentration camp?' Bond frowned, recalling the conspiracy that dated back to the Second World War. 'I always thought the Germans only produced sterling there.'

'The plan was to undermine the British economy by flooding it with fake cash. Using a team of prisoners stuck in a concentration camp, Major Bernhard Krüger counterfeited over a hundred and thirty million pounds and the bills were said to be the best ever made. Then, at the end of the war, he turned his attention to American dollars – with the same results.'

'He was shut down before he could complete them.'

'That's the official story. But there was always a rumour that a few batches of one-hundred-dollar bills were completed and – along with the printers – fell into Russian hands. As it happens, we already had proof of their existence. I'll come to that in a moment.' This was a very different girl from the one Bond had met in Germany. She spoke slowly, completely absorbed by her work. 'The point is, we had good reason to believe that the money we found in Las Vegas came from Operation Bernhard, and the moment we realised that Gloria Keller was married to Thomas Keller, who was a general supervisor at Wallops Island, we got very worried indeed.'

Bond's mind was already racing ahead. He had been right about the connection. So ... Keller is bribed by the Russians to commit some act of sabotage. He comes home with a suitcase full of cash but, with a typical piece of Soviet petty-mindedness, they've paid him off with counterfeit bills. His wife seizes the opportunity to break loose, kills him and runs off to Las Vegas with the cash. When the police knock on her door, she assumes they've tracked her down for his murder and kills herself. All very neat. Except… 'Do you know what they wanted him to do?' he asked.

'No.'

'But it must connect with the launch of the Vanguard.'

'The NRL doesn't think so. Look. They can't see any reason why the Soviets would want to blow up an American rocket. They don't understand what could be gained.' Bond understood. He'd already heard the same from Captain Lawrence. It was typical military thinking: if they couldn't see the danger, then it couldn't possibly exist. 'Anyway, if someone did want to hurt the American space programme, there are plenty of better targets.'

'So what were you doing in Nürburg?'

'That was the one lucky break. It's all down to those earlier counterfeit dollars I mentioned. Last year, one of our other investigators was called in to look into a payment of one thousand dollars that had been made using exactly the same fake currency. Operation Bernhard. Even the serial numbers were in sequence. The money had been put down as a deposit for a smart car and for some reason the dealer got suspicious. Anyway, the buyer was a multimillionaire New York businessman and when we went knocking on his door, he played the complete innocent. Why would a man in his position risk everything by using dirty money? Somehow it must have been passed to him by somebody else. No. He couldn't remember who; he often dealt in large sums of cash. He was shocked that such a thing could happen and that the Treasury Department was involved. Of course we had to believe him. The man was a major employer. A Korean. Highly respected in his community.'

'Sin.'

'Sin Jai-Seong. We looked into him, but as far as we could see he was clean. He'd come to the States from South Korea eight years ago. He'd started in Hawaii where he'd been taken in by distant relatives and he'd built up his business from scratch. There were some questions about where he found his initial funding – he got very rich very fast. In fact, for such a major operator, he's a completely blank page – and that's enough to set the alarm bells ringing. Anyway, in our business, we always follow the money. That's the first rule. Sin has homes in New York, Hawaii – all over the world – but I heard he was in Nürburg so I flew out to take a closer look. That was when I met you.'

'And the photographs?' Bond couldn't keep the accusation out of his voice.

Jeopardy shrugged. 'As soon as I saw those photographs, I had the connection back to Thomas Keller and of course I had to get them back to my people. I'm not going to apologise for running out on you, James. I was just doing what I thought was best. Anyway, you never told me who you were or what you were doing. I still don't know. You said you were an investigator but that could mean anything.'

Bond had already come to the conclusion that he was going to have to tell her everything. Jeopardy had just saved his life and now she was taking over the whole operation and being utterly businesslike and unapologetic with it. She was impressive in every way and even though it was half past four in the morning, he had a sudden impulse to grab her by the neck and to kiss those serious lips of hers so hard they bled. Instead, he told her what she wanted to know, taking her from the briefing with M to the point where she had come to his rescue.

'So we're in the same business,' she said. 'I should have guessed. The British Secret Service!'

'That's right.'

'Why didn't you tell me to begin with?'

'You weren't telling me anything either.' There was a moment's silence. Bond examined the round, boyish face, the cropped hair, the watchful eyes. 'It was lucky you showed up,' he said. 'I wasn't expecting quite such a reception at the Starlite Motel.'

'It wasn't exactly luck,' she replied. 'I sent the photographs to the NRL but they weren't having any of it. How much more stupid could these people be? So I came down to Wallops Island to see if I could find out more about Keller and his work on the space programme. I was actually there when you came out of the office and walked to your car and I decided to follow you. I wasn't the only one. As you drove off, a second car pulled out and drove behind you. I saw it right ahead of me. You led them to your motel and I decided to stick around and see what happened.' She shrugged. 'Maybe that was luck. I don't know. All I can say is, they were pretty serious about wanting you dead.'

'Well, it looks like we're in this together now,' Bond said. 'We're both involved in the same operation. We've just come at it from opposite ends.' He met her eyes. 'Do you agree? Or am I going to wake up and find you gone again?'

'Of course I agree. I just need to talk to my office. But don't worry. I'm not going anywhere.' She stubbed out her cigarette and put some dollars – real ones – down on the table. 'I'm in a hotel on the other side of Salisbury.'

'Are you offering me another night on a sofa?'

Jeopardy ignored the insinuation. 'There's no need for that,' she said. 'They've got plenty of rooms. Let's get some sleep and tomorrow we can decide what to do.'

She called over the waiter and paid the bill. Outside, the sun was already beginning to rise, the first tendrils of dawn feeling their way over the horizon. It was the last full day before the launch.

16

The Lion's Den

Bond awoke reluctantly. The flight from Europe, the events of the day before and the long night that had followed, all pressed down on him, forcing him to fight his way through the tunnel back to consciousness. He was in a room that was perfectly square and perfectly uninteresting and, a depressing thought to start a new day, he was in it alone. He threw back the covers and got out of bed. The curtains were drawn but the sunlight was blasting its way in at the sides. He opened them and looked out onto a patio, a swimming pool, a figure knifing through the water, reaching the end, then turning and beginning another length.

He knew at once that it was Jeopardy. Her shoulders were bare, her arms well-developed, powering her forward in a slow, steady rhythm. The strands of fair hair, darkened by the water, kissed her neck. She was wearing a flesh-coloured costume that, for a moment, gave the illusion of complete nudity. Bond looked at the water separating on either side of her behind, which was small and round, like a child's. She reached the end of the pool and, without stopping for a breath, corkscrewed back, her whole body contorting. Bond had seen enough. He went and had a shower, then made phone calls to London and New York.

Later, at breakfast, her hair still damp, Jeopardy came over and joined him.

'Jason Sin is back in America,' Bond told her. 'I've spoken to the CIA. He landed at Idlewild two nights ago and disappeared from sight, but yesterday he was seen being driven into a compound just outside Paterson, New Jersey.'

'Blue Diamond?'

'Yes. Some sort of depot.'

Jeopardy nodded. 'I've seen pictures. He does a lot of work in construction and he has his own heavy plant: excavators, dump trucks, lowboys ... that sort of stuff. It's quite a place. Totally fenced in. There are security guards, the whole works.' She thought for a moment. 'But why? What do you think he's doing there? What's he's hiding?'

'Whatever he's doing, I think we should go there.' Bond had instantly made up his mind. There was nothing to be gained by hanging around in Maryland. Both the British and the US Secret Service had given the Naval Research Laboratory every warning they could possibly need but they were determined to press ahead. Which left the two of them with no choice but to take the fight to the enemy. 'If Sin is there the day before the launch, there must be a reason. If I can find a way in, at the very least I can take a look around.'

'I'm coming with you,' Jeopardy said.

Bond smiled. 'I wouldn't dream of doing this alone. Seriously, Jeopardy, what you did last night was amazing. I think the American Secret Service are very lucky to have you.'

'Forget it. I've settled the tab. Let's get the hell out of here.'

There was a seven-hour drive between them and New Jersey. Jeopardy drove a two-door Chevrolet Bel Air and they left together, stopping after half an hour at a low wooden cabin that advertised itself as Harry's Gun Shop (*Everything for the Outdoorsman*). Bond had left his ammunition back at the motel but he had his gun and his wallet which, he decided, was all you really needed to get by in America. He bought what he needed from an old, gap-toothed sales manager who handed the goods across as if they were loose change and they set off again. For a while they drove in silence. Bond lit a cigarette and offered one to Jeopardy but she shook her head. 'Not while I'm driving.'

'So are you going to tell me about yourself?' he asked. 'How did you get to be a spy?'

'I'm not a spy,' she replied. 'I told you. I'm a field agent. I don't have a gun and I don't creep around sending people messages in code or things like that. I'm not like you.'

'Then how did you get to be a field agent with the American Secret Service?'

'Why are you asking?' She was suddenly defensive.

'Because I'm interested.' Bond rolled down the window, releasing the smoke. 'You don't have to worry, Jeopardy. This is just between the two of us and if we're going to get into trouble together, it would be nice to know who I'm with.'

She softened. Not taking her eyes off the road, she answered him. 'There's not much to tell. I was brought up in a pretty rough neighbourhood, if you want the truth. You could say I was born on the wrong side of the tracks – and I mean that literally. Our house backed onto a big railway depot at Coney Island. There was a fence at the end and all the kids used to break in to play on the tracks and sneak around the workshops. Of course it was dangerous – and the transit people put up a big sign on a chain. It had a single word on it, written in red ink. JEOPARDY. That was how I got my name. My mom looked out and saw it the day she was having me and somehow she just thought it was right.'

She slipped the car into a higher gear, using the three-speed Synchro-Mesh transmission, and pulled out, overtaking a Pontiac in front of her. Bond liked women who drove confidently. He wasn't surprised that Jeopardy was in total command of the road.

'My dad drank himself to death when I was six years old,' she went on. She said it in such a matter-of-fact way that she could have been discussing the weather. 'My mom tried to look after me but she couldn't even look after herself. I spent my childhood out on the streets, playing Stoopball with the other kids, hanging out at Nathan's hot-dog stand. That sort of stuff. When I was about thirteen, I got sucked into the carnie. A lot of kids did. It was easy money and nobody asked any questions. I spent three months working in a sideshow. I was "Olga the headless girl". Did you ever see it? I had to sit there with my head hidden behind mirrors and with all these tubes running out of my neck and the showman would step out: "You've all heard of artificial hearts and artificial lungs. Now here's the girl with the artificial head." I used to quite enjoy it, sitting there, taking off my gloves and crossing and uncrossing my legs. I could hear all the people gasping in horror. And they paid me ten cents an hour.

'After that, I did a stint on the Wall of Death, tearing around this giant barrel on an old Indian Scout Motorbike. You had to go about forty miles an hour to stay on and they made a big deal because I was a girl. "Little Miss Daredevil" they called me, but I don't think anyone was very impressed because I looked like a boy and a pretty mean one at that.

'Maybe I'd still be there now, although even then the whole

place – the boardwalk, the amusement park – was beginning to shut down. But then my mom died – it was liver cancer – and an uncle I'd never heard of turned up, took one look at me, and dragged me off to Washington DC. That was when my whole life changed. Actually, it was more than that. It was like it had never happened. Ralph and Gracie were good people. They had no kids of their own and they were horrified by what they saw. They were determined to turn me round. They put me into school and then college and forced me to catch up on six years' lost education. They changed the way I looked. They changed everything about me. It was church every Sunday, meals round the table, no drink – and definitely no swearing. Ralph worked at the Treasury Department and he got me a job as a secretary in research. Now I'm an investigator. I still live in DC. I have a nice apartment. I live on my own. That's how I like it.' She changed gear and pulled into the outside lane. 'And now let's talk about something else. Or you can turn on the radio. We've still got another three hours to go.'

The sun had begun its downward curve but the afternoon heat was still close and intense when they arrived at the construction depot that belonged to Blue Diamond and where Jason Sin was now based.

It was five o'clock – exactly thirty hours until the Vanguard launch. But what possible link could there be between this place and an event happening more than four hundred and fifty miles away? What interest could SMERSH, with all its power and ambition, have in a grimy industrial wasteland where industrial diggers sat next to beaten-up forklifts and garbage trucks with spools of wire, cement blocks and all the other detritus of the construction industry? Even as Bond watched, crouching beside the car on the edge of a slight hill, a low-loader – Jeopardy had called it a lowboy – arrived at the main gate and began the painful manoeuvre that would allow it to enter. There was certainly plenty of security. A single-storey office, brick with a large observation window, guarded the entrance and there were at least half a dozen men in attendance, some of them Korean, checking the driver's papers, the vehicle, the driver himself. The compound, shaped like a rectangle and at least two hundred yards in length, was dotted with metal poles supporting night vision cameras and arc lights, the whole thing surrounded by a chain-link fence topped with rolled barbed wire. CAUTION – HEAVY PLANT ENTERING. NO TRESPASSING read the sign in large letters that meant it. There had to be something here that was worth protecting but, crouching on the outside, Bond couldn't imagine what it might be.

The left-hand side of the compound was dominated by a huge warehouse, corrugated iron with a soaring zinc chimney that reminded Bond of Enterprises Auric in Switzerland. It was triple-height, with massive sliding doors that were already opening to let in the lowboy. Inside, Bond heard machinery – hammering, and the scream of an electric saw – and got a glimpse of gantries and a dull yellow light, but he could see nothing more. Opposite, there were temporary offices and living quarters built like Nissen huts, a car park with around a hundred cars, and some sort of administration block. And Sin himself? He had to live in the house that overlooked the central courtyard, a building that seemed strangely familiar to Bond. It was white, elegant, two-storeys high, built some time in the nineteenth century and definitely not American. Of course! It was crazy, but he knew exactly what he was looking at. Like many schoolboys before him, Bond had been dragged round the house where the poet John Keats had lived in Hampstead, north London. This building was an exact copy.

How were they going to get in? Bond was aware of the ticking clock. At Wallops Island, final checks – ensuring that all vehicle systems were in order – would be well under way. They couldn't cut through the wire. Even assuming they could purchase the necessary equipment, Bond was certain that there would be some sort of alarm device built in. Making any sort of move in full daylight was out of the question. There were people everywhere, men and women criss-crossing each other's paths, taking no notice of each other, some in hard hats, some carrying pieces of equipment. Like it or not, they would have to wait for darkness. And then? The main gate was the only way.

They had a meal together and Bond outlined his plan. At first, Jeopardy was reluctant. If he was going in, she wanted to be with him, but he managed to persuade her to see things his way.

'I can't do this without you, Jeopardy, and whatever I find, you'll be the first to know.'

The sun had set by the time they returned and the long shadows colluded in their approach. The evening had a close, clammy feel, indigo clouds passing sluggishly overhead. The compound was quieter now, at least on the outside. Bond could hear the work continuing inside the warehouse, the grinding of machinery, the sound of a man shouting. The smell of dust and machine oil lingered in the air. Jeopardy was beside him. The two of them had a good view of the main gate and they could see that there were still many vehicles coming in and out. That was good. That was what they needed.

A truck was approaching. Bond could tell it was going to turn into the compound; it was already slowing down. He nudged Jeopardy and together they scrambled down the side of the hill until they reached the fence, then followed it along to the main gate. They were both wearing dark clothes. Provided they kept away from the side of the road, it was unlikely they would be seen. They stopped about ten yards from the security office. The truck turned and its headlights swept briefly across them.

'Now,' Bond said.

Jeopardy left him, straightening up and walking towards the entrance as if she had every right to be there. Four men had come out, once again checking the driver and the inside of the front cabin, but suddenly they had something else to contend with, a young woman who had appeared from nowhere.

'Can you help me?' Bond heard her say. 'My car broke down. It's just up the road.'

'I'm sorry, lady. You can't come in here.'

But she was already inside the complex. She had walked in front of the truck, through the open gate. She was moving forward, making for the door of the office.

'Lady! Do you mind?'

'I just need to make a call.'

Three of the men were closing on her. The fourth had stayed with the driver. Nobody noticed Bond on the other side of the truck as he slipped through the open gate then followed the fence as it stretched into the darkness. He had done it! The warehouse was in front of him. He had already decided that it was there that he would begin. Sin might be inside the white house. There might be files and photographs inside the administration block. But it was whatever work had to continue beyond nine o'clock at night that interested him. Jeopardy would make a nuisance of herself for the next ten minutes, refusing to leave until she had made a call to a non-existent garage. Hopefully, that would leave the way clear for him.

He kept close to the fence, being careful not to touch it. There were no cameras anywhere near, at least, not that he could see. The sliding doors had closed again, apart from a narrow crack. No way in there. He reached a wall of corrugated iron and began to follow it round, hoping for a secondary entrance. And he found one, round the side, not used often. He could tell from the clumps of wild grass that had been allowed to grow in front of it. There was a single lock – a Yale cylinder. Provided it hadn't been allowed to rust, it would present no problem to Bond who had come equipped. He knelt down and slid open the heel of his left shoe. There was a miniature pick and a tension wrench embedded inside. Bond set to work. Less than two minutes later there was a click and, using all his strength, he was able to wrench open the door. He was in.

The door led to a metal staircase surrounded by a rough, concrete wall. Bond took out his pistol – now fully loaded – and made his way up, listening out for any sounds above the dull throbbing and the clatter of metal against metal that had met his ears the moment he entered. The stairs continued. There were no doors, no corridors on the first two floors. At last he saw an opening ahead of him and, through it, the yellow glow of the warehouse interior. He still had no idea what he was about to find. Could there be a perfectly simple explanation for all this activity? No, dammit. Blue Diamond was meant to be an agency for low-grade contract work and employment and this place advertised itself as storage for heavy plant. Sin was hiding something. There could be no doubt.

Bond emerged onto a narrow gantry high up in the ware-house, with the sloping ceiling just above his head. He looked down in disbelief. He had thought this would be the moment when everything made sense but instead he was more baffled than ever.

The lowboy he had seen earlier had been parked in the middle of the warehouse and now it had been loaded up. A Vanguard rocket was lying there on its side, strapped down by a series of chains in a manner that was somehow reminiscent of Gulliver taken prisoner on the beach. It was an exact duplicate of the rocket he had seen at Wallops Island – even down to the colours and the markings. But there was one significant difference: this rocket clearly wasn't intended to fly. Only the second and third stages had been constructed – from the nose cone down to the oxidiser tank and rocket motor. The first stage, the one that would actually propel it into the air, was missing. Worse than that, it seemed to have been cut off. The metal skin was torn and truncated as if some giant (Gulliver again) had snapped it in half. Workers – about half of them Korean – were securing it. Others were unfolding a huge tarpaulin. It was about to be transported somewhere and no one was to see what it was.

Looking around him, Bond realised that he had seen the warehouse before. This was where the photograph had been taken – the one he had found in Sin's office in Germany. There was a second load on the far side of the enclosure, this one, unfortunately, already covered. It wasn't rocket shaped. It was a large box, big enough to contain a car. The men were preparing to lift it, using a heavy block and tackle. Presumably it was a companion to the rocket. A launch pad? But how could that be when there was only half a rocket to launch?

At any event, Bond now knew that Sin wasn't sabotaging the Vanguard. He was copying it. Except that couldn't be right. Why would he bother? And where on earth could he be taking it? Only one thing was certain. Bond had to get out of here and tell Jeopardy what he had found. The two of them had to pass on the information to their respective secret services.

But he couldn't leave, not yet, not with the puzzle still unsolved. He was in the lion's den and who could say what other secrets it might conceal? He had seen enough in the warehouse and hurried back down the stairs to the door. Crossing the courtyard would be too dangerous with all the cameras and the guards but that still left the house. And that, surely, was where he would find Sin.

He emerged into the warm night air and continued around the back of the warehouse. The replica of John Keats's house was ahead of him and there were just fifty yards of open ground to cover. Bond had taken the first three steps when, with a silent explosion, night became day and the entire compound burned itself into the back of his eyes. Every single arc lamp had been turned on, the combined wattage almost blinding after the soft acquiescence of the night. Bond froze where he was, one arm thrown protectively across his face, the Remington M1911 clutched above his head. At the same time, a voice burst out of speakers positioned all around.

'Attention, Mr Bond! Step forward and show yourself. Throw down your weapon. We have Miss Lane and if you do not comply in ten seconds, she will be dealt with.' There could be no mistaking what the speaker meant. 'You will see her at the main gate. The countdown begins now. Ten… nine…'

Bond squinted through the light. Yes. There she was, standing between two men. She had been hurt. They were having to hold her up.

'…eight… seven…'

A third man was holding a gun, pointing it at her head. Behind them, the entrance was shut with several more men on guard. More workmen were closing in from all sides. If Bond was going to run, if he seriously thought he could fight his way out, he had to do it now.

'…six… five… four…'

The countdown continued, a grisly reminder of the one that would be taking place on Wallops Island in just over twenty-four hours. What had happened? How had they got the upper hand?

'…three…'

Bond had to get the information out. He had to stop the launch. He had to let M know that he had stumbled onto something as bizarre as anything he had ever encountered. But the man with the gun was solid, implacable. Jeopardy was helpless. He couldn't leave Jeopardy to die.

'…two… one…'

Holding his Remington so that everyone could see it, Bond walked out into the open. He threw the gun down and stood there waiting as Sin's men closed in.

17

No Gun Ri

There were forty-seven white tiles stretching from left to right along the back wall. Thirty-five tiles reached from the floor to the ceiling. The window was barred and had no view beyond a patch of sky but Bond could tell that the building was being patrolled. He heard footsteps pass outside every twenty minutes, without fail. He could actually time them by his watch. There were other sounds too. The rumble of lorries, a distant telephone, somebody shouting. Bond had been left alone for nearly twenty-four hours. And then, finally, the door had been unlocked and there was Jeopardy, standing in the corridor between two guards, a gun pointing at her neck. There was an ugly bruise on the side of her face.

'I'm sorry, James.' It was the first time they had seen each other since they were taken and the words came pouring out. 'They knew who I was. At the gate. They made me tell them—'

'Enough! No talk now!' One of the guards was Korean. He spoke bad English and it suited him. Bond could not imagine a single sentence that was intelligent or civilised coming out of that blank face with its spiky black moustache and swollen lips. 'You come!'

'Yes. I come straight away,' Bond replied, laconically. 'I don't suppose there'd be time for a shower before dinner?' It was five o'clock by his watch. Six hours until the launch.

'No shower. You come now.'

They were allowed a brief lavatory stop. After that, they were taken out of the building and into the courtyard, Bond following Jeopardy with two more guards bringing up the rear. These men knew what they were doing. Two in front, two behind, all of them exactly the right distance away, all of them of course armed. The little group walked towards the white house. Bond glanced at the construction that he had infiltrated the night before. It was empty. The lowboy, presumably carrying the upper sections of the Vanguard rocket, had gone.

They entered the building and at once Bond saw that the interior was very different from the one he had visited as a child. He had vague memories of a home that was sparsely but pleasantly decorated with carpets and embroidered curtains, oil paintings, busts, antique furniture ... everything you would expect of a nineteenth-century poet at the height of his powers. The replica, like the castle in Germany, had been stripped of any comfort or animation. As they continued forward past blank, undecorated walls, their feet resounded against bare wooden floorboards. Here and there the wallpaper hung down in shreds. The windows were naked, the place lit by lamp bulbs without shades. At first appearance it might have seemed abandoned but everything was well-lit and there were air-conditioning units, working against the warmth of the night. So what did these strangely barren living conditions tell him about the man who owned the place, a man who seemed to have little or no connection with the human race? Already, Bond feared the worst.

They reached a door and for a moment Bond and Jeopardy were side by side.

'Leave any move to me,' he said, quietly. 'If there's an opportunity, I'll take it.'

Jeopardy glanced at him scornfully. 'If I can bust out of here, I'm busting out of here,' she muttered. 'You try and stop me!'

One of the men knocked on the door and opened it. Bond and Jeopardy were ushered into a square dining room with two symmetrical windows, a fireplace, a chandelier. A Regency table stood in the middle, flame mahogany with splayed feet. It was a beautiful piece of furniture, spoiled by the chairs, modern and ill-matched, that had been set against it. With so little effort, the room could have been warm and welcoming. Instead it had the same dead quality as the rest of the house. Jason Sin was already sitting on one side of the table, facing them. He was dressed entirely in black: jacket, barathea trousers, roll-neck jersey. With his black hair and olive skin, he appeared almost as a silhouette of himself. His hands were crossed in front of him, unmoving, on the table. Curiously, there was a deck of cards beside them.

'Do, please, come in, Mr Bond, Miss Lane,' he said. There was nothing in his voice; no welcome, no enthusiasm. He sounded bored. The table was laid for three. Bond and Jeopardy moved to the far ends, opposite each other, with Sin in the middle. Bond had expected the four guards to leave but they stayed in the room, two at the door, two on either side of him, so close that they could reach out and touch him. Their eyes were fixed on him. Bond looked down and saw that he had been supplied with a full set of cutlery with which to eat whatever meal was about to be served and it occurred to him that, given a few seconds, he could have snatched up the knife and used it on Sin. But not with the men there. Not so close.

'Let me tell you where you are and how you came to fall into my hands, Mr Bond,' Sin began. 'This is one of many quite similar depots that I have in America. This one belonged once to a silk manufacturer who had emigrated from London. He had this house built to remind himself of his origins. As to your arrest, I will admit that you were unlucky. There is a camera inside the office beside the front gate and there is a relay to my office on the first floor. I was working at my desk and happened to see Miss Lane on my monitor. I recognised her at once from the Schloss Bronsart. It is my habit never to forget a face and it seemed a very strange coincidence that a so-called journalist at a race track should suddenly turn up, pretending to have had some sort of mechanical breakdown, here. I gave orders for her to be apprehended at once and, after inflicting a certain amount of pain on her, she informed me that you were also inside the compound. The rest you know.'

'I don't need to listen to this,' Jeopardy muttered. 'Why don't you just take me back to my cell?'

Sin turned to her slowly. 'You will do what I tell you to, Miss Lane,' he said in his matter-of-fact way. 'You are here for no reason other than that it pleases me. But if you interrupt me again, I will indeed have you taken back to your cell. And when you are there, I will instruct my guards to do anything they wish with you. So I would advise you to keep your infantile remarks to yourself.' Jeopardy opened her mouth to speak, thought again and said nothing. Sin turned his attention back to Bond. 'Shall we get the basics out of the way?' he continued. 'I have a feeling you will have been in this position before. We only have a certain amount of time together so I shall explain the house rules, as it were, and then we will eat.'

'You have less time than you think,' Bond cut in. 'Our people will be looking for us, both the British and the Americans. They know we're here. If they don't hear from us very soon they will most certainly come knocking at your door.'

'That may well be true – and I thank you for drawing it to my attention. My door will always be open to them, but I rather doubt that they will find you on the other side.'

There was a second door leading into the room and as if on cue it opened to admit a Korean man, dressed as a waiter, carrying a silver tray with two cocktail glasses.

'I am told that your favourite alcoholic drink is a martini cocktail,' Sin explained. 'Three measures of Gordon's, a little vermouth, a twist of lemon, the whole thing to be shaken not stirred. It sounds to me a ridiculous amount of effort for what is, after all, no more than an inebriant, but as you are my guest I have endeavoured to satisfy you. Miss Lane will drink the same, I am sure.'

Bond took the drink and sipped it. It was ice cold but unpleasant to taste, completely overpowered by too large a measure of vermouth. He said nothing but stored away the information that Sin lacked the expertise even to make a decent martini cocktail.

'You will see that I know everything about you, Mr Bond, 007 of the British Secret Service. You have a licence to kill. Does that mean you came here to kill me, I wonder? Or is it SMERSH that is your true target? They were very pleased that you and I had crossed paths. They have a very high opinion of you, you might like to know. Colonel Gaspanov asks me to send you his very warmest good wishes.'

'Tell the colonel I look forward to catching up with him.'

'That is unlikely to happen. Your cigarettes are made by Morlands of Grosvenor Street. I was unable to procure any given the short space of time but you are welcome to smoke if you wish.' Sin nodded and one of the guards placed a packet of Viceroys and a book of matches on the table. Bond took one and lit it. He noticed he had been supplied with just two matches: one for now, one perhaps for later. 'We have made an elaborate ritual out of eating, which is what animals simply do with their head in a trough,' Sin went on. 'But these extraneous habits, drinking and smoking, I find completely incomprehensible. Still, I would not wish to deprive you of your last pleasures. At the same time, we must get down to business.

'I am going to tell you the story of my life, Mr Bond. It is a unique story, quite remarkable in its own way. I am sure it will be of interest to you and I will admit it gives me some satisfaction relating it. I also know that I can confide in you for the simple reason that, as I have already indicated, in a short while you will be dead. This was inevitable from the moment we met and you would have done better to have stayed away. Knowing you to be a man of considerable resource, I am sure that even now you are considering what action, what countermeasures to take. I should therefore warn you that the four guards in this room will be watching your every movement, every second that you are here. Their attention is focused on you one hundred per cent. If you so much as twitch a little finger in a manner that causes them concern, they will react. Do I make myself understood?'

'Perfectly,' Bond replied. His face revealed nothing but at

the same time he folded away a tiny note of hope. Once again, Sin had said more than he had perhaps intended, revealing a weakness that might just possibly be used against him.

'Good. Your drink is satisfactory? Then let me begin.

'I imagine you do not know very much of the country that gave birth to me, Mr Bond. To the world, Korea is a faraway place of great strategic significance but of little interest in itself. When I was born, in 1927, it was occupied by the Japanese, a brutal race who treated us as little more than animals, stealing our food, crushing our traditions and trampling our heritage underfoot. We were finally liberated from them on the fifteenth of August 1945, a day I will never forget. The entire country celebrated. It was the first time in my life that I had seen our own flags waved in the street and at last we thought our identity would be returned to us. This optimism was short-lived. First of all, the country had been quite arbitrarily divided into two with a line crossing the thirty-eighth parallel and this would soon have disastrous consequences. After rigged elections, and with the support of the Americans, a new president – Syngman Rhee – was voted into office and quickly proved himself to be ruthless and dictatorial. Strikes and demonstrations, assassinations and acts of terror quickly followed. Even large cities became prone to attacks by communist guerrillas. The police and government were incompetent and corrupt. We had nowhere to turn.

'I should explain that I was fortunate in that I was exempted from much of the suffering of my country. My parents were wealthy. My father was what was called a *yangban*, which is to say that he was well-connected, part of an elite family. He was a Confucian scholar and a senior official in local government. His mother, my grandmother, had attended upon the Empress

Myeongseong – Queen Min as she was known – and had lived for a time at Changdeokgung Palace during the dying days of the Chosŏn dynasty. This fact is central to my narrative. As for myself, I had been sent to a first-class liberal arts college and then to Seoul National University where I studied business and law. I was also fluent in the English language before I was twenty.

'My life changed for ever on Sunday the twenty-fifth of June 1950. I recall that I was walking to my home in Seoul without a care in the world when I heard a siren break through the air. I hurried into the house to find my mother and two sisters listening to an announcement on the wireless. The North Korean communist army, comprising 135,000 men, supported by Russian-made T-34 tanks and artillery units, had crossed the thirty-eighth parallel at four o'clock that morning. They were on their way south and there was nothing we could do to stop them.'

Sin broke off as the waiter returned with the dinner, a simple plate of steak, rice and salad. Bond felt the guards' eyes boring into him as he picked up his knife. He was determined to eat. Apart from a sandwich and a glass of water brought to his cell at lunchtime, he'd had nothing in the past twenty-four hours and he would need his strength for whatever lay ahead. Sin had been served the same. 'I hope you don't mind if we talk and eat at the same time, Mr Bond.'

'You're the one doing the talking.'

'Indeed so.' He turned to Jeopardy. 'Do you have everything you need, Miss Lane?'

'Yes, thank you.' She didn't look up.

The waiter poured two glasses of wine for Bond and Jeopardy, placed the bottle on the table – another weapon? No, the guards were still too damned attentive – and left. Sin returned to his narrative.

'My father decided we should leave at once. He knew that the North Koreans would enter the city in less than a week – in fact it took them just three days – and as a government official he might well be taken out and shot. He was a very dignified, very quiet man and none of us would have dreamed of arguing with him. In Confucian teaching, the bond between the father and his children is a sacred one. He instructed us to take very little with us. He placed his valuables, including some artworks and my mother's jewellery, in a secret compartment beneath the *ondol* floor in the dining room. There was a system of flues there that carried the heat from the kitchen and I had never seen it opened before. Nor, for that matter, would I ever see it again. My mother, my two sisters and I carried one small package each. We locked the front door and, without saying a word, set off into the night.

'Our destination was the village of Chu Gok Ri where my grandparents had lived. My grandmother was now alone, my grandfather having died two years before. We took a bus as far as the River Han, then crossed the main bridge on foot. We were lucky to do so. One day later, our own army would blow it up without any warning, killing hundreds of our own people at the same time. And I should mention that there were many other stories of dreadful, hideous errors. American planes – we called them "shriekers" – had attacked our own forces, mistaking them for the enemy. Already it was apparent that this was not war in any modern sense. It was a mess. The American military in Korea were untrained, ill-disciplined and ignorant. Many of the soldiers had not even received basic training. It might interest you to know, and it has a great bearing on my tale, that they were unable to distinguish between the communists of North Korea whom they were supposed to be fighting and the terrified refugees of South Korea whom they were there to protect. The Korean word for "Korean" is *Hanguk-saram* and so they called us *gooks*. It did not matter where we came from. We were all gooks to them.'

Sin lifted his glass and took a sip of water. Unlike Bond, he had not been served wine. His own food lay, getting cold, in front of him.

'By the time we reached Chu Gok Ri, the flow out of Seoul had become a flood and the main highway was a seething mass of humanity with vehicles and possessions abandoned everywhere. We saw a few planes pass overhead and also some trains, carrying Republic of Korea soldiers north to the fighting, but we felt safe out of the city. My grandmother had a beautiful house with a traditional tiled roof, surrounded by persimmon trees. I remember her as a wonderfully poised and smiling woman, impossibly old, although she must have been only in her mid-seventies. She had enough space for all of us although my sisters – Li-Na and Su-Min – had to share a room and I had a mattress on a sort of platform, tucked into the eaves. We stayed with her for almost a month.

'Inevitably, the troubles followed us. More and more refugees poured into the village and, having nowhere to stay, they slept in the streets even though it was pouring with rain. The ground soon turned to mud and the night brought clouds of mosquitoes. Every day we saw new families arrive, the men bent double under their *chige* – wooden A-frames loaded down with all the possessions they had been able to carry. Some of the women had brought their cooking pots even though it broke their backs to do so. There were children carrying their little brothers and sisters. And at the same time the war was getting closer, too. We could hear explosions on the other side of the valley and at night there were flashes in the sky and the whole air smelled of petrol. Then American soldiers arrived. They came in trucks and jeeps and set up a camp just outside the village. They lounged around, playing cards, and some of the children went up to them to try and get chocolate or chewing gum. But my father was afraid. He had heard rumours of civilian deaths. Apparently an order had gone out that if anyone was found to be in groups of ten or more, they could be taken for enemy infiltrators and shot. The American commanders were afraid of communists disguising themselves as civilians. Most people, both from the north and the south, wore the same, traditional white clothes. That would be enough to identify you as the enemy. And there were other rumours regarding the American soldiers, many of whom were young and had never been with a woman before. My mother cut off my sisters' hair to make them less attractive and forced them to stay close to the house. I still remember the fear in her eyes. To her, the soldiers were as dangerous as snakes.'

Bond was listening in silence. He already had an idea where this story was going and it struck him how strangely emotionless Sin was in the telling. His voice was soft and monotonous. He was not looking for sympathy or understanding. It was as if all this had happened to someone else.

'And then the day came when the Americans told us that we had to leave. They had suffered many defeats in the north and the communists were advancing. We were in the middle of what would soon be a battle zone. I remember a jeep that came driving into the village with a fat American in military dress, a driver and a Korean interpreter. Between them they explained that we had two hours to leave our homes, taking only what we could carry. There was a sort of controlled panic throughout the village. My father, who seemed to have lost all his authority during the previous few weeks, told us that we had no choice. We must do as we were told. He went to the back of the house to collect his mother. She had not been well and had taken to her bed but it was unthinkable that she should stay behind. At least, that was what we thought. He was gone for a long time and when he finally came back, his face was grave.

'"She is not coming," he said, simply. My mother began to argue but he cut her off. "She has made up her mind." He turned to me. "She wants to see you. Be quick. We have to leave now."

'Mystified, I made my way to her room. She was sitting in bed, looking for all the world like the dragon queen that I had often seen in temples. There was something in her face that disturbed me. Her eyes were hard and I remembered what my father had said.

'She called me over to her bed and told me to sit down. "I am not coming with you," she said. From the way she spoke, I knew I was here to listen, not to interrupt. "I am not afraid of the northern soldiers. Why should they want to hurt me? The Americans are worse. They are stupid and violent – but they will soon be gone. Anyway, it doesn't matter. I am too old for all this and I don't really care if I live or die.

'"I want to give you something. It is important that some-body in the family should have it and because you are my oldest grandchild, I have chosen you." She drew her hand out from beneath the bed cover and I saw that she was holding a small silk envelope. "Do not tell your father," she went on. "He will think I have no faith in him and perhaps he is right. He will be angry. But I see in you the same steel that I had when I was a young girl and I know that you will use this wisely, to help your sisters and your family. Do not open it now. Wait until you are somewhere on your own, far from this house." She pressed the envelope into my hand then fell back, the very life force ebbing out of her. It was as if she had handed me her soul. "Now leave me," she said. "Go quickly. And trust no one. Everyone who has ever come to this little country of ours has always betrayed it. Nothing changes. Go now!"

'I left her and a short while later I left Chu Gok Ri, stripped of my identity, just part of the straggling line of villagers that included my sisters and my parents, making our way through a narrow valley with rice paddies on one side and pine groves on the other, escorted by American GIs. The weather was already very hot, very close and that evening the clouds broke and we were instantly drenched. In the distance we could hear guns firing and we felt the earth tremble. By the time night came, we were exhausted and hungry but we had no choice but to carry on. And so it was that we came to the bridge at No Gun Ri.'

It was what Bond had been expecting. He had seen an intelligence report on No Gun Ri. There were many Americans – politicians and generals – who were trying to pretend that the place didn't exist.

'The name comes from old words meaning "forest" and "deer",' Sin explained. 'The bridge had been built by the Japanese. It was a very solid – I would say brutal – construction, comprising two concrete arches supporting a railway which ran overhead. A rough track led from the bridge to a cluster of mud huts, used by local farmers. There were more rice paddies nearby. By now we were too tired to carry on and this is where we stopped and rested, with fireballs crossing the night sky, the dull thud of explosions punctuated by gunfire, and then silence filled with the excited whispers of the cicadas.

'When the sun rose, there were about six hundred of us huddled together below the railway track at the foot of White Horse Mountain with American soldiers, clearly visible in their green uniforms, dug in on the slopes, some of them watching us through binoculars. My mother had brought food and we ate a hurried breakfast, wondering what would happen next. It seemed incredible to me that an ordinary family who, a short while ago, had been living comfortably in a modern city, should have been reduced to little more than peasants. But I knew not to complain. My sisters had said almost nothing since we had left the village. We had followed my father here and we trusted him to get us out. It was his belief that the Americans would send some sort of transport for us and, indeed, just after midday, with the heat growing ever more intense, we heard the sound of planes approaching. I remember thinking how strange that was. There was nowhere for them to land.

'The planes were American. They drew closer until the scream of their engines filled the air. They were very low. Nobody moved. Nobody even thought of running away, not until they opened fire and began to kill us.

'I cannot describe the horror of what followed, Mr Bond. I have no idea how long the attack continued. All I can tell you is that the day turned to night, the world exploded and all around me people were torn apart as they were hit by bombs, by rockets and by machine-gun fire. When I say that the noise was deafening, I mean it quite literally. It was as if a gigantic fist had punched me in the head and all sound – the screams and the explosions – no longer seemed to belong to what I was seeing. And what was that? Fire and blood, stomachs ripped open, limbs torn off. My father died in front of me. One minute he was an elderly man, a man I had loved and respected all my life, standing there with a mixture of outrage and indignation, the next his head had gone and his body was toppling to one side and my mother was screaming hysterically, covered in his blood. The bridge was directly in front of us and I saw that the concrete arches would provide the only cover. Other people had had the same idea – the ones who were still living. It is impossible to say how many mangled bodies were already strewn over the ground. Something incredibly hot seared across my neck and I realised that a bullet had missed me by a fraction of an inch. Where had it come from? That was when I saw that the Americans on the side of the mountain were also firing at us, picking us off not one by one but ten by ten. There were bodies falling everywhere.

'I scooped up Li-Na, the younger of my two sisters. She was twelve. My mother and my other sister, Su-Min, were close by. We began to run towards the bridge. I tried not to look at the people around me. It was too horrible, too unbeliev- able. All my energy was focused on trying to find a place to hide. Something hit my face. I thought for a minute that it was a bullet – but no. It was a piece of human bone. Li-Na shuddered in my arms and I shouted at her to keep still, not to trip me up. She said nothing. The bridge was ahead of me. It filled my vision. In front of me, terrified villagers seemed almost to be flailing their way through the air. In a field to one side I saw a cow crash to the ground as its legs were scythed away beneath it. And then, incredibly, the concrete archway reached out and embraced me. I was sobbing. My neck was on fire and my sister was a dead weight in my arms. I threw myself against the wall, gasping for breath. The machine guns were still firing. The air was thick with smoke.

'I tried to set Li-Na down but she would not stand on her own two feet. I spoke to her and at the same time I felt something warm and wet gushing down onto my trousers. I let Li-Na go and recoiled in total shock and dismay. There was a huge hole in her back, made perhaps by a bullet intended for me for, inadvertently, she had become a human shield and for much of the time I had been carrying her, she must have been dead. This was a little girl I had played with. I had made up stories for her when she was going to bed. And now her eyes were empty and her blood was all over me. I looked for my mother and for Su-Min. I knew at once that they had not made it. There were people everywhere, screaming and sobbing. Many of them had horrible wounds. But my family was not among them. I was alone.

'In the next twelve hours, as day once again became night, I found myself in an unimaginable hell, surrounded by a sort of madhouse of the dead and the dying. I saw wounds too horrible to describe: little children with their flesh torn open. The heat was intense and fat black flies descended in their droves. And still the Americans were not finished with us. Their warplanes continued to attack us. If we tried to leave, they shot at us. If we tried to get water, we would die. I was torn apart by thirst. As night fell, I licked the concrete wall in the hope of finding moisture. I thought of my father and my one sister whom I knew to be dead and wished that I could join them, and in the end I could bear it no more. Half delirious, and with the last of my strength, I walked out of the tunnel, expecting to be cut down in a hail of gunfire. But at that moment the moon dipped behind a cloud and somehow I was not seen. I had emerged on the side away from the main road and managed to escape into the darkness. The one hundred survivors that I left behind me would remain inside the tunnel for three more days.

'I made my way back to Chu Gok Ri, thinking of returning to my grandmother. But the house was no longer there. The Americans had adopted a scorched earth policy and a pall of smoke hung over the place where the village had once been. All the houses had been burned down, often with the inhabitants still inside. There were a few people picking through the ruins and I was able to beg a little food and water from them before I left, walking the fifteen miles to a town called Yakmok. From my childhood, I remembered that there was a station there and sure enough, as I arrived, a train packed with ROK troops was about to leave. I threw myself on the mercy of the soldiers. I told them what had happened. They took me with them.

'The train took me to the port of Pusan on the south-eastern tip of Korea, a city jam-packed with soldiers and civilians, the streets swarming with refugees who were struggling to survive. Some of them had managed to get work, helping to unload the ships which had arrived from America. The quays and jetties were piled up with military supplies. I had no money, nothing. I knew nobody. There was a sort of burning emptiness in my head as if my brain was being devoured from inside. And then I remembered the little packet my grandmother had given me. Hiding in the shadows of a temple, close to the sea, I opened it. A dozen little stones fell into my hand. I knew at once what they were even though I had never seen such things before. They were blue diamonds, Mr Bond, quite rare and worth more money than I could begin to imagine. Where had my grandmother got them from? I have mentioned that she was close to Queen Min. Maybe she had been given them for her service. Maybe she had stolen them as the Chosŏn dynasty disintegrated around her. But these questions were immaterial. She had given them to me and they were to be my salvation.

'I sold one of the diamonds to a jeweller who had a shop in the business district of Gwangbok-dong. He cheated me, of course. He gave me a fraction of its true value. But it provided me with enough cash to bribe an American marine who helped me stow away on a boat leaving for Hawaii. Many thousands of Koreans had emigrated to Hawaii at the start of the century, mainly to work on the sugar plantations, including members of my own family, and I had no doubt that I would find help and support once I arrived, certainly with eleven blue diamonds in my hands. And so it proved to be. I will not tire you with the journey nor with the problems that I faced when I arrived. Suffice to say that I lived among the Korean community in Hawaii for some months before moving to the United States where I established a recruitment and construction business which I named Blue Diamond, and that brings us very much to where we are now.

'But this is what you must understand. This is the point of my story. We have a belief in Korea that if you die away from home, you will be condemned to wander for eternity, that you will never come to rest. That is what has happened to me. I died at No Gun Ri. It was not my life that was taken from me, but my soul, my very humanity. Even as I sit here now, I still see the dead bodies. I can see my father's head as it separates from his body. I see my dead sister. I smell the blood. Those ugly, black flies are still crawling behind my eyes.

'I have become very wealthy. My business empire is worth many hundreds of times more than those diamonds with which I began. And yet I myself am dead. I feel nothing. I have forgotten the meaning of pleasure. For me, food has no taste, the air has no scent, the sun no warmth. I do not hate the Americans although I will never forgive them for the atrocity that led to the death of my family and so many others. I feel nothing for them, and the same is true of all humanity, including you and Miss Lane. In a way, I have become like death itself. I throw parties because it is expected of me. I wave to cameras and I smile when my rich American friends call me Jason Sin, carelessly trampling on my culture and my origins, and secretly I want to kill them all. In fact, I have been responsible for the deaths of many, many people. Some of them have worked for me. Some were business rivals. Many of them have been complete strangers. I exist now only to destroy everything around me and I understand that this is what makes me so useful to SMERSH. Well, they are useful to me too. I have no interest in their ideology. I would be just as content to work for the American Secret Service or for anyone else. They simply give me the excuse to do what I do.

'There is only a little more to add. I am aware that I have been speaking for some time and I thank you for indulging me but I only get the opportunity to say these things very occasionally. It may further interest you to know what it is that I am doing here, what exactly it is that I have arranged. It will please me to tell you. Am I acting out of vanity, I wonder? Am I, perhaps, a little too pleased with myself? I do not know – but I suppose I must be as there can be no other reason to explain everything to you. Even so, I must be brief…'

Sin reached for the deck of cards and drew them towards him.

18

'...any Card.'

Bond laid down his knife, once again contemplating the sharp steel blade and the almost indecently heavy Bakelite handle. It had certainly made easy work of the steak, which he had finished while Sin talked. Eating the meal had been very much as Sin had described, nothing more than a biochemical act. Bond needed the nutrients, the proteins and the carbohydrates that even now his body would be processing, turning into energy for whatever lay ahead. He had tasted none of it and had even been slightly repulsed by the pretence of sociability while all he wanted to do was hurl himself at a host who, at the same time, was preparing to murder him. How tempting the knife was, just inches from his hand! But the four guards hadn't moved. Not for one second had their attention strayed. At the other end of the table, Jeopardy had barely touched her food. She was sitting very still, her face giving absolutely nothing away. As for Sin, although he had been served the same food as them, he had not eaten at all.

'Your story is a very interesting one,' Bond said, using the second of his two matches to light a cigarette. 'Although I wonder if you've considered telling it to a qualified psych-iatrist? We have some very good ones in England. I could put you in touch with the Tavistock Clinic who have plenty of experience dealing with former Japanese prisoners-of-war and the like, although I grant you that probably none of them was as disturbed as you.' He blew out smoke. 'As I understand it, the very fact of having survived brings with it a sense of shame and dishonour which in turn leads to serious mental issues. In your case, these would seem to be raging paranoia and self-loathing, and left to yourself you'll probably go on to commit suicide. It's a shame. But anyway, you were about to tell us what particular little madness you've got planned. Do go ahead. The steak was very good, by the way.'

Sin's lips tightened and what could almost have been a thin mist passed across the glass discs that enclosed and magnified his eyes. Bond was reminded of the portraits he had seen in the castle in Germany. The extraordinary thing was that Sin briefly resembled them. He had been vandalised by his experiences in Korea. Look behind the eyes and you would find... nothing.

'I think you are trying to make me angry, Mr Bond. If I am angry, you hope I will make mistakes. But I will simply ignore your facetious remarks and continue with my narrative. Unless, that is, you wish to proceed directly to the last section of the evening's entertainment, the one that concerns your own particular fate.'

'We know what you're planning.' It was Jeopardy who had spoken. Her voice was level, controlled. Bond knew that she had stepped in to take the heat off him. 'You bribed a rocket scientist called Thomas Keller with money supplied to you by the Soviets. Did they tell you the money was counterfeit? Or maybe they didn't trust you enough. I'd be worrying about that, if I were you. The NRL is launching a Vanguard rocket tonight and you've arranged for it to fail. That's not such a big deal. We've got plenty more where that one came from.'

Sin said, 'You are half right, Miss Lane. But the question you should be asking is – *why* will it fail and what will be the result?' He turned back to Bond. 'My friends in Moscow have taken a considerable interest in American and, indeed, European technology. It is important to them, for their own prestige and for economic advantage, that they should be seen to be leading the field in whatever industry you care to mention – and to this end, SMERSH quite recently put together a specialist team with that particular aim in mind. It was headed by Colonel Gaspanov.

'One of their earlier operations involved the Krassny motor racing car which brought them into an arena with which I am already familiar. The Russians were keen to win at Nürburgring and arranged for the English driver to be assassinated by one of their agents. The race was, in my view, a trifling matter and one that could well endanger my own, much more significant operation. Even so, the colonel ordered me to meet him at Nürburgring. This is the trouble with working with the Soviets. They trust nobody, and they had concerns following the quite unexpected death of Thomas Keller, murdered by his wife, as it turned out.

'At any event, they insisted on a meeting although I thought it foolish and told the colonel so, in no uncertain words. It is a shame he did not listen to me. You only became involved in our affairs because of it and since then you have caused us a great deal of annoyance. But for your bad luck last night you could have caused us serious harm.

'Yes. The Vanguard will fail. Mr Keller was able to gain access to the turbo pump in the first stage rocket engine following the acceptance tests, the systems tests and even the static tests when the liquid propellant was ignited without the rocket actually being fired. At the very end of the process he made certain adjustments that will ensure that the pump is not able to deliver enough pressure to take the Vanguard into orbit and, as a result, the central control room will have no choice but to activate a device which they refer to as Trigger Mortis. The rocket will self-destruct and the various pieces fall harmlessly into the Atlantic Ocean.

'But let us imagine for a moment that due to some catastrophic piece of negligence, the rocket – or part of it – fell onto a major city in America; New York, for example. Can you imagine the devastation that would be caused by twenty thousand pounds of metal, filled with kerosene and liquid oxygen, falling at 220 miles per hour onto a populated area? It would be the equivalent of a million tons of TNT, something not far short of a nuclear explosion. That is what I am going to cause to happen—' He held up a hand before Bond could interrupt. 'At least, that is what I am going to *simulate*.

'Last night, when you broke into this compound, you saw a perfect replica of the Vanguard rocket that is going to be launched at Wallops Island tonight. As we have been speaking, it has been carried to the rapid transit yard at Coney Island. A very large number of people working in the New York transit system have been recruited by Blue Diamond and I have my own workshops there. The replica rocket will be loaded onto a train which will also be carrying a very large bomb which you may also have seen here last night. It might interest you to know that I will be using C4, a plastic explosive originally developed by the British and one of the most destructive materials on the planet. Just a couple of pounds of it would be enough to destroy a small building, but my train will be carrying one hundred and fifty pounds connected to a series of quite basic detonator caps.

'Half an hour before the launch, the train will leave Coney Island, travelling non-stop to 34th Street and Sixth Avenue. I have ensured the line will be clear and your knowledge of Manhattan will tell you that the train will have arrived at the very heart of the city, less than two blocks away from the Empire State Building. That is a considerable distance – some 1480 feet – but we are helped by the presence of an underground stream, which appears on old maps as the Sunfish Pond. It will provide a channel through the metamorphic rock. Technicians working for SMERSH have predicted that the explosion will be enough to bring the Empire State Building down. This will not be a result of the initial shockwave itself but because of a process known as soil liquefaction in which the effective stress of the soil is reduced to zero by the force of the blast. You might imagine an old man with a stick having that stick kicked away from beneath him. I do not know how many hundreds of people will die or how many millions of dollars' damage will be done. These are not my concern, although there will be a useful corollary in that Blue Diamond will greatly profit from the reconstruction work. Nor is this an act of war. No. The aim is simply to ensure that the Russians win what has become known as the space race and that, ultimately, control of outer space – weapons, communications, the exploration of other planets – is theirs.

'This is what will happen, Mr Bond. Some time after eleven o'clock, the real Vanguard space rocket will fail. It will be destroyed. Five minutes after that, a gigantic explosion will take place in the heart of New York. I have representatives gathered around the city who will swear that they saw an object falling out of the night sky. At the same time, I will ensure that news leaks out of the failure at Wallops Island. This will be supported by photographic evidence of an explosion a mile or so above the Atlantic. The American media and the general public will quite naturally put two and two together. What goes up, must come down. Of course the government and the Naval Research Laboratory will deny any culpability – but who will believe them? It was their missile that destroyed a vast tract of New York that happened to include the Empire State Building, in itself a symbol of American pride. And when the crater is examined, parts of a Vanguard rocket will be found, the final evidence. The fact that a subway train has also been destroyed at the same time will be nothing more than a coincidence. It will be seen as irrelevant.

'The result will be a public outcry. There are already enough people in America who believe that the exploration of outer space is a colossal waste of money but as a result of this catastrophe, all projects will be frozen and future funding cut off. And the beauty of it is, although the NRL will be furious, although they will know that the public have been deceived, they will be completely powerless. The louder they shout, the more people will turn against them and even retrieving the debris of the real rocket from the ocean – if such a thing is possible – will make no difference. It is my belief that the events tonight will end the American space programme for ever. At the very least, it will set them back a decade or more, by which time the Soviets will be in total command and unstoppable. You could say that the very future of the world will be in their hands.'

Silence took its place at the table as Bond reflected on

what he had just been told. Would it work? In the long run, the American authorities would surely be able to persuade the public of the truth. But Sin was right. That might take years, during which their entire space programme would be in stasis. And what proof did they have that the Russians were involved? Only the counterfeit money (which could have come from anywhere) and Bond's word – that he had witnessed the meeting between Jason Sin and Colonel Gaspanov.

He had to stop the launch taking place. There was very little time left but somehow they had to break out of here. Bond considered all the possibilities. What was it that Sin had said? The four guards were watching his every move. He could feel their eyes on him even now. Yes. In that lay his only hope.

'You have nothing to add?' Sin demanded.

'Only that you're wasting your time,' Bond replied. 'Miss Lane and I have both made separate reports. I have photographs of you with Gaspanov. We have the pictures that we took from your office and they show quite clearly that you've built a replica of the Vanguard. We already knew about Thomas Keller and we have the counterfeit money. The scenario you're trying to set up won't be believed.'

'You still fail to understand me, Mr Bond. It is not *my* scenario. I am merely serving – and being handsomely paid by – the Russians. To be honest with you, I don't care if it works or not. Causing multiple deaths whilst destroying a large part of Manhattan will give me satisfaction in itself.' Suddenly, his hand closed on the stack of cards. He cut it several times, then reassembled the deck. 'But, speaking of death, it is now time to discuss yours…'

Briefly, Sin described the Hanafuda playing cards and how he had adapted them to his own ends. Out of the corner of his eye, Bond saw Jeopardy grow pale. It was strange that this one death should seem more horrible than all the others that Sin had described and he hoped she wouldn't try anything that would cause her harm. Sin talked for another minute. Then he spread the cards out across the table for Bond. 'I have cast myself in the role of death,' he explained. 'The mechanism is in some respects a slightly clumsy one but I could think of no other way to marry the unpredictability of death with its inescapable certainty. Well, here we have both. It is your choice. Any card. The manner of your death will be revealed on the other side.'

Bond looked down on the colourful arc with its gaudy images of leaves and flowers. With a sick feeling in his stomach, he wondered how many other people had been given this choice, forced to select their own deaths. 'You can ———— yourself, Sin,' Bond replied. 'I'm not playing your squalid little games.'

'There are three blank cards that could save your life.'

'I don't believe you.'

'Why would I lie?'

'I want to see them.'

Sin hesitated, with downturned lips. He had never heard this before and Bond was pleased that he had spoiled the game, removing some of his control. Almost sulkily, he said, 'Very well. You can look.'

Bond reached out and turned the cards over. Sure enough, they were all printed with capital letters, in English. He saw POISON, STARVATION, STRANGULATION but did his best not to look at any more. At her end of the table, Jeopardy was sitting dead still. Sin hadn't said anything about her. Bond wondered if she would be next. He found the three blank cards. They had been evenly distributed through the deck. He pushed them forward, sliding them across the tablecloth.

'Are you satisfied? Sin asked.

Bond said nothing. He gathered up the cards, including the blank ones, gave them a thorough shuffle and spread them again. For a long minute, he sat staring at them.

'Choose,' Sin said.

'Don't, James!' Jeopardy was fighting to keep herself under control but Bond knew that all of this was far outside her experience and she was terrified.

He didn't reply. He stabbed forward with a single finger and pushed a card out from the centre of the deck. 'Are you happy now, you maniac?' he asked, pleasantly. 'Why don't you turn it over?'

Sin leant forward and turned the card.

It was blank.

'Well, that would seem to be that,' Bond said. 'I assume you're going to obey your own rules, so if you'd get one of your men to show me to the door, I'll say goodnight.'

'No!' Sin's voice was high-pitched, somewhere between a whimper and a scream.

'I hope you're not going back on your word—'

'No. You saw the cards! You cheated!' Sin was like a petulant schoolboy and, alone in the room, Bond knew that he was right.

There had been no greater card manipulator in the world than the American magician John Scarne, and Bond had spent long hours with his book, *Scarne on Cards*. When he had assembled the deck, it had been a simple matter to in-jog one of the blank cards, control it to the bottom and then, using the rather more difficult single-handed Annulment, to bring it to an exact position in the centre of the spread. In doing so, he had nicked one corner with his fingernail, making it instantly identifiable, and had simply drawn it out. He knew that it would do no good. There was no way that Sin was going to let him walk out of here. But it was always worth unsettling the enemy and at the very least it would have spoiled his squalid fun.

Sure enough, Sin came to a decision. 'I'm choosing for you!' he snapped, and turned over the card next to the one that Bond had taken.

BURIED ALIVE

The two words screamed at Bond from the table.

Sin was satisfied. He leaned back in his chair. 'A slow death and a very unpleasant one. You deserve nothing less.' He glanced briefly at Jeopardy. 'I will keep you alive a little longer, Miss Lane. You are not a threat to me and you can provide useful services to some of my men. Many Koreans are fascinated by Western women but, of course, unless they are prepared to pay for prostitutes, it is forbidden fruit. I will give you to them as a reward. As for you, Mr Bond, you will be taken from this room, nailed into a box and buried underground. If you try to resist, my men will shoot you in the knee so that you will end this life not only in darkness and in terror but in pain.' He repeated his words in Korean for the benefit of the guards who, without moving, seemed to have closed in on Bond. Sin stood up. 'I myself must now leave for New York. I will wish you good night. They are the appropriate words.'

Bond also stood and at once two of the guards seized hold of him. The other two were opposite, their guns aiming at his stomach. And that was when Jeopardy broke. With a sob, she threw herself forward, rushing into Bond, one arm around his neck, the other around his waist. 'No! Please!' she cried out. 'Don't leave me, James. I can't bear it.' She tried to pull him free but the guards were unmovable. She turned to Sin. 'Please!' There were tears rolling down her cheeks. 'I'll do anything you want. Just don't hurt him.'

'Enough!' Sin called out in Korean and two more guards entered the room. He nodded and they made straight for Jeopardy, pulling her away. Bond stood with his arms pinned behind him, two guns trained on him. 'Make the preparations. Take him away.'

'You turned the cards today, Sin,' Bond muttered. 'But one day, very soon, they will turn for you. Trust me. They're being shuffled even now.'

The guard who was holding him muttered something in Korean and he was dragged out of the room.

19

Six Feet Under

It was a box, not a coffin, but about the same shape and size, made of thick plywood with the lid resting against it. Sin's men had carried it to a patch of land behind the Keats house (a man building a replica rocket in a replica house ... even now, the irony wasn't lost on Bond). A mechanical digger, marked with the Blue Diamond marque, had been used to scoop out a trench that was six or seven feet deep. It was being driven by a sandy-haired, very ordinary-looking worker, an American – who had gone about his task with blank-faced efficiency. He couldn't have been more than twenty years old. Bond wondered what must be going on in his mind. Was he a willing part of all this? As an added piece of obscenity, Bond had been made to stand in the sullen evening air, watching the entire process. His own grave being dug. He was still surrounded by guards who were clearly determined to make no mistakes. The digger finished its work and backed away. So the moment had come. Despite himself, Bond felt a hollowing in his throat and stomach, the primal fear of death – and a particularly horrific sort of death – which no amount of training could quite subdue.

Sin had arrived to see the final act of the drama he had instigated. He had dressed himself, bizarrely, as a New York motorman, with baggy coveralls, black leather boots and an engineer's cap. He waited until the digger had retreated, then gestured at the box. 'Step in, Mr Bond. You might like to know that it will take you approximately sixty minutes to die, although it is quite likely you will go mad before the end. Do you have anything to say? Any last witticisms?'

Bond swore, simply and meaningfully.

'Do it,' Sin said.

Bond weighed up his options. He could fight it out. There were four men with guns, but if he moved fast enough he might be able to get his hands around Sin's throat and use him as a human shield. Even if he was killed in the gunfire, would that not be preferable to the other option he was being offered? At least it would be quick. But he soon dismissed the thought. There was something he knew that Sin didn't. There was still hope.

He took a deep breath of the night air and briefly considered the sickness that motivated Jason Sin. Was he actually sick? Did he have some sort of cancer of the brain, triggered by the horrors of the massacre at No Gun Ri? Bond could almost imagine the abnormal cells, black and virulent, eating their way through the neural tissue inside the man's skull. Or was that simply to excuse him? Like all truly evil men, Sin knew what he was doing. Bond wondered how many other victims he had tortured with his Hanafuda cards. He had boasted of killing rivals and employees. They would never have known danger in the way that he had, and faced with whatever unspeakable death they had been forced to choose, they would have been terrified. Standing on the edge of his own grave, Bond promised himself that he would bring Sin to account. But he said nothing. He took a few steps forward and climbed into the wooden box, then lowered himself so that he lay flat. Two of Sin's men picked up the lid. Bond caught one last glimpse of the night sky, the roof of the house, Sin himself looming over him at the edge of his vision. Then the box was sealed.

Darkness punched him in the face. It was an extreme sort of darkness – shocking, immediate, total. Already Bond felt his pulse racing, his heart furiously beating and he had to stop himself struggling for breath. Instinctively, he raised his hands, his palms pressing against the solid wood just inches above his face. A moment later, he heard the sound of hammering, loud and incredibly close. They were driving nails into the sides of the lid. How many of them? It might be important. Bang, bang, bang, pause. Bang, bang, bang, pause. It wasn't just the sound that was hideous, it was the methodical, almost robotic way in which the nails were being applied. A tiny amount of light was filtering in through the crack between the box and the lid. Bond could vaguely see the shape of his hands if he held them in front of his face. He focused on them, trying not to panic, knowing that all too soon they would disappear. Bang, bang, bang pause. Four nails on either side. One at the top, one at the bottom. Ten in all. How long were they? That was important too. Bond wished he had caught sight of them before the work began.

Silence. Then a lurch as the coffin was lifted off the ground. He could feel himself swaying from side to side as he was carried towards the grave and could imagine it opening up in front of him. Then came a sickening sensation, real or imagined, as he was lowered into the ground. The feeble light was extinguished. Now he was completely blind. The descent seemed to last for ever but then there was a thud as he hit the

ANTHONY HOROWITZ

bottom and he felt the wood that he was lying on jolt into his shoulders and the back of his head. He pressed against the lid with the palms of his hands and pushed. Nothing. It didn't give at all. There was another long pause. Utter silence. Was the digger coming back or were they going to fill the hole in by hand? It might make a difference. Why? Bond tried to focus but his nerves were screaming and it was impossible to think.

He couldn't see. He could hear nothing but the sound of his own heart beating, his blood being pumped through his arteries. How could it be this loud? It was beating too fast. Slow down, he thought. Slow down. Once again he was breathing too much, snatching at the air. It was almost impossible not to. He was aware of the tiny space in which he was trapped, the wooden panels pressing down left, right, above, below, so close. Every fibre of his being wanted to stand up, to break out even as his brain replied that it was impossible. Somewhere, deep inside him, Bond recognised that panic was now his worst enemy. Come on. Think about this. You're not going to die. Not tonight. Not in this place. Close your eyes. That's better. Now you've got a reason for the darkness. Breathe normally. You're not underground. You're lying on your bunk, back on the *Trespasser*. Bond had spent six weeks in the T-class submarine during his time at the RNVR. It had taken him a while to get used to the claustrophobia, to the sense of being trapped, but in the end he had done it. What was that bloody captain's name? Bond remembered him. He had taken a shot at a dead whale, mistaking it for the enemy. A torpedo and a whale. The whole crew had laughed and, trapped in his coffin, Bond half smiled at the memory. After a few moments, his heart responded by slowing down. It had taken a huge mental effort, but he was under control.

And then the earth came tumbling down. It thudded against the lid. They were using spades – he could tell from the rhythm – as if to taunt him, to make this more like a real funeral. Two, maybe three men. And they were working quickly. Already the sound was getting softer as the wooden surface was covered and earth fell on earth. Finally he could hear nothing and knew that the hole had been filled in. The silence had an extraordinary heaviness, the whole world pressing down on him. It was already getting warmer inside the box. The sweat trickled off his stomach and round the back of his neck. So now you are buried alive, he thought. The grave has been covered. They are walking away, leaving you here. He could feel the pressure in his ears and despite his efforts, the madness of panic and despair were close by, the other side of a mental barrier that could collapse at any minute.

So dark in this tiny space. Blind. No room to move. The weight of the earth pressing down. No air.

No – that wasn't true. The box was about the size of a coffin. Let's say eighty by thirty by twenty-four inches. Do the maths. That's about thirty-two cubic feet of air, but you've got to lose about half of it for your own body displacement. You're breathing about twelve times a minute. (Breathe gently. There's no need to gulp. Keep your eyes closed. You're lying on your bunk. That's all.) Allow how much for each human breath? Let's say a sixth of a cubic foot per minute giving you ninety minutes. But then there's the CO_2. Every breath exhaled is 16 per cent oxygen and 4.5 per cent CO_2. That was something he'd learned on the *Trespasser*. It was what would kill him. Hypercapnia – or CO_2 poisoning. First there would be dizziness and confusion. His heartbeat and blood pressure would go off the map. He would go into convulsions. And he would die.

But he still had time. Certainly more than an hour. Maybe as much as an hour and a half. So Sin had been wrong. He was always wrong, always too clever by half.

Like at the table, for example. *'Their attention is focused on you one hundred per cent.'* That was what Sin had said about his guards and Bond had instantly realised that if that were true, then they wouldn't be watching Jeopardy. And she had known it too. Bond had been unable to steal his own knife but she had taken hers and, at the end of the meal, when she had run, sobbing, into his arms, she had slipped it into the waistband of his trousers. It was there now. Awkwardly, Bond felt behind him and pulled it free.

It was the knife, the knowledge that it was there, that had kept him sane. Even if it turned out that he was trapped, that there was no way out, he could use it on himself. If he pierced a carotid artery, it would all be over in seconds. But that had never been Bond's intention. Using a finger to guide himself, he inserted the blade into the gap beneath the lid. And pushed. The knife slid easily. Plywood is a form of composite wood that has been engineered. It's cheap but it's not particularly strong and the piece that made up the lid was straining under the weight of all the soil. It was already buckling in the middle. And Sin had ordered the lid to be nailed down, perhaps for effect. Screws would have been much more of a problem. Bond twisted the knife. He had to be careful. He didn't want to break the blade. He felt the side of the lid rise up, drawing the nail out. He was lucky, too, that the digger hadn't been used. (That was why it had been important.) The earth, falling in smaller quantities, was more loosely packed. There was room for the lid to move.

He felt with his hand and inserted the knife a second time, about halfway down his body. It was a difficult manoeuvre. He could barely move. He couldn't find the space to give his arm freedom to do its work. But moving slowly, he was able to release three of the ten nails that he had counted, then passed the knife across his chest and, using his left hand, did the same on the other side. At one point his breath caught in his throat and he had to stop as all the fears that he had been keeping at bay came rushing up on him. There was no more air left! The deadly CO_2 was attacking his system. He closed his eyes tight and forced himself to relax. The bunk on HMS *Trespasser*. That bloody whale. OK. Now get to it again.

The lid had been partly freed on both sides. It was bowed in the centre and Bond knew that actually it was keeping him alive. Without it, he would suffocate, buried in the dirt which would come plunging down. He slid the knife into his waistband and undid his shirt. It had to come off – but that too wasn't easy in the confined space. Bond contorted himself, using his elbows to lever himself up and dragging it over his head. Every time he touched the lid, he was reminded of his predicament. You're underground. You're buried alive. Your air is running out. Relax. Don't scream. The shirt had come free. His vest was sodden with sweat, sticking to his skin. Utterly blind, he felt for the top button of his shirt and did it up so that the collar formed a seal around his neck. Then he untucked the fabric and drew it over his chest and above his head, clumsily tying the bottom end to create a sort of balloon. It would prevent the earth rushing into his mouth and nostrils and allow him to breathe as he fought his way to the surface.

But could he even reach it? Bond was six feet tall and estimated that ground level – fresh air – was about eight inches above that. Well, there was no other way. With the fabric pressing against his face, he stretched out, then kicked upwards with his feet. Nothing happened. He rested his left foot and kicked out with his right, once, then several times. He felt the other nails come free and the lid slipped slightly to one side. A flurry of soil, soft and cold, trickled down onto his right foot and ankle. He felt with his hands. The lid was tilting. Most of the nails had come out. He kicked again and there was a sharp crack as the lid split along the edge and the earth cascaded in, burying him again, pressing down on him, threatening to pin him down with its weight.

This was the moment that mattered most. Bond had to get himself vertical. Then he would be able to use his outstretched hands to burrow his way up. He twisted sideways, at the same time forcing himself to his feet, exiting the coffin through the half-splintered lid. Bond made no sound but he was screaming. The soil was like some alien creature, swallowing him whole. It was pressing into his face and but for the shirt it would already have killed him. He could feel it, damp against his skin. He could smell it. Using all his strength, he uncoiled his legs, pushing himself up. Now his feet were flat, on the bottom of the coffin, and as he stood up he propelled himself towards the surface. He had been holding his breath but he needed more oxygen and breathed in. Somehow he found the necessary air, filtered by the fabric. He punched out with his fists, then hooked his hands, trying to find the leverage to pull himself up. He had hoped his outstretched hands would break through but he was too deep. He wasn't moving. Christ! To have managed so much and to die now. It wasn't going to happen. Bond was standing up, fully extended. He slid his feet apart, found the edges of the box and stood on it. Part of the lid was still in place and he used it as a platform, giving himself an extra twenty inches' height. Once again he pushed and felt his hands break through the surface. Had Sin left any guards up above? If so, this would all be for nothing. He still had the knife though. He could feel the blade pressing against his skin. It was a moonless night. He might have a chance.

Bond was still buried. Only his hands were free. Like two spiders, they explored the surface, searching for the edge of the grave where the soil would be more compact. He brought his palms down and pressed. Yes. He could drag himself out. Did he dare take another breath? He was suffocating. The shirt wasn't working any more. In fact it was gagging him, wrapped tight around his mouth and nostrils, held there by the pressure of the earth. Time to go. Do it now. Using all his strength, Bond pulled – and felt the earth sliding past him. His deltoid muscles were burning but he ignored the pain. He was dragging himself upwards, almost as if he was being reborn. His head broke the surface. He felt the weightlessness of the night air and, gasping, tore the shirt off his face. He had done it! He was free, lying crookedly with the earth still reaching up to his neck. He stretched out and pressed one hand into the ground, then pushed again. As the rest of his body emerged, he reached down and drew out the knife. But there was nobody there. Sin had left. (The rocket. The bomb. The Empire State Building. New York. It was only now that Bond remembered them but decided that even M would have forgiven this brief dereliction of duty). The Keats house was empty, the lights switched off. The entire compound seemed to be deserted.

For a full minute, Bond lay there breathing in the sweet night air. Then he went to find Jeopardy.

20

Naked Aggression

He needed her. Jeopardy had told him that she had been brought up close to the train yard on Coney Island, and that was where Sin had taken his rocket. She would know her way around. She might know a way in. And anyway, Bond wasn't going to leave her behind after all they had been through, even if finding her might eat up time he didn't have. How many hours could there be until the launch of the Vanguard? It was only now that Bond realised he had lost his watch – a Rolex Submariner that was barely three years old. It had somehow been dragged off his wrist as he fought his way through the earth – just one more thing that Sin would have to pay for. There was a glint of something savage in his eyes as he stalked through the darkness, his shoulders low, keeping close to the perimeter fence, away from the security cameras. He was making for the accommodation block where he had been held for twenty-four hours, assuming she would have been taken back there.

Bond was filthy. The dirt from the grave was all over him, in his hair. It had penetrated his clothes and covered every inch of his skin. It was under his nails. He could smell it in his nostrils and it reminded him of the suffocating death that had almost been his. His clothes were damp and uncomfortable, clinging to his frame. He wiped sweat off his forehead and looked down, disgustedly, at the back of his hand. The brown streaks made him wonder what the rest of him must look like – something out of a horror film.

There was more security than he had first thought. Sin might have departed but he had left a full night staff behind him: the exit gate was still guarded, the barrier down, and there were uniformed men prowling around the central workspace as if anyone might be interested in stealing the builder's junk it contained. Bond had parked a quarter of a mile away, further up the road. He and Jeopardy would have to steal another car to get out of here. There was a floodlit parking area with about a dozen vehicles to one side, but it was unlikely that anyone would have left their ignition keys behind the sunshades. As Bond reached the accommodation building, he saw a car pull out, drive over to the gate and stop while the driver showed his ID. It told him what he had already guessed. Getting out of this place was going to be as difficult as getting in.

He entered the building, following a long corridor – bare walls and parquet flooring – back towards the room where he had been held. The lights were on but there didn't seem to be anyone around. As he crept forward, he passed an open door. He looked into an office with a desk and a telephone. Quickly, he slipped inside and lifted the receiver. Surely he could reach someone at the FBI in New York? One word from him and they could shut down the entire New York subway system, stopping Sin before he had even left the transit yard. But the telephone was dead. Sin must have taken the most elementary of precautions, cutting off the exchange to make sure that nobody could call out. Bond swore quietly and put down the receiver. He would just have to do this on his own.

He continued down the corridor, stopping as a door opened and a man appeared, carrying a sports bag which he swung back and forward as he walked away. Bond waited until he had disappeared around the corner, then opened the door and found himself looking into a staff changing facility with lockers, sinks and toilets, a pile of fresh towels and a row of showers. It was exactly what he needed but could he spare the time? A clock on the wall showed that it was half past nine. Just one and a half hours to go. Bond made an instant decision. He could shower and steal new clothes. It might cost him five minutes but the physical and, for that matter, the psychological gain, would be more than worth it.

He stripped off the filthy clothes and kicked them away, glad to be rid of them. Then he stepped into the nearest shower and turned the taps on full. He was rewarded by a burst of hot water that blasted the dirt away even before he picked up the soap. American plumbing at its typical best. He looked at the brown water swirling around his feet and just for a moment, as if a shutter had fallen across his eyes, he was back in the coffin, nailed in, underground. Furiously, he rubbed his shoulders and his face, washing away not just the dirt but the memory.

And then the door opened again and someone came into the room. Bond had pulled the shower curtain across. He couldn't be seen. But with the rushing water it would be obvious he was there.

'Jack? Is that you?' a voice asked. Bond didn't reply. 'Jack?' the voice insisted. Bond grunted non-committally, hoping that whoever it was would go away. But the man was puzzled.

Bond saw his shape on the other side of the plastic curtain as he drew nearer. 'Who's in there?'

Bond knew what he had to do. He turned off the water, threw the curtain back and stepped out, already tensing himself for the action that would result in the certain death of another man. He would simply pile-drive into whoever was there, sweeping them forward and kicking their feet away from beneath him. Then, even as they fell, a hand-edge blow delivered hard into the larynx would finish them. The man wouldn't even have time to cry out. It was straight out of the textbook, even if the authors had never factored in the possibility that the attacker might be stark naked. He had already grabbed hold of the man and unbalanced him but before he could deliver the *coup de grâce*, some instinct screamed at him to pause and he stopped with his hand rigidly locked, the muscles in his arm already strained.

The man who had come into the changing room and who had been less than a second from a violent death was very young, perhaps eighteen or nineteen. He had sandy hair and eyes that were wide with shock and innocence. He had been about to wash before bed. He was wearing a white, sleeveless T-shirt and he'd had a washbag and a towel in his hand, although they'd slipped onto the floor. There was a tattoo of an eagle and a girl's name on his shoulder. Everything about him was crying up at Bond not to hurt him.

Bond knew him. An hour ago he had been driving the mechanical digger that had dug his grave. This man – this boy – had been part of the team that had set out to bury him alive.

'Don't hurt me, mister!' the boy rasped. He had the good sense to keep his voice low, not to cry out. 'Please!' He raised both his hands, palms out, in the universal symbol of surrender.

Bond released him, then reached down and took the towel, wrapping it around himself. 'I know you,' he said. 'You were out there tonight.' There was a cold fury in the midnight eyes. 'Give me one good reason why I don't kill you now.'

'Mister, I swear to God I wasn't part of it. I just do what I'm told.' The boy fumbled in his pocket and produced a security pass with his photograph as if it were some sort of talisman, as if it would protect him from Bond. 'My name's Danny. I'm from Queens. Don't hurt me. I've got a wife and a kid…'

'You buried me alive.'

'No, sir. No, I didn't. I swear to God. They just told me to dig a hole.'

'Don't lie to me.' Bond's voice was ice. His hand was still poised to strike and the boy cowered. 'You saw what they were doing.'

'Look… I know. They do crazy things here. I've seen things, horrible things, but what can I do? I came here because I needed a job. I'd been in trouble. I gotta rap sheet and nobody'll touch me. Then I came here. They offered me good money and I gotta pay for my family. But I don't do any of that shit, I swear ta you. I keep my head down. I'd leave if I could. I'd leave now. But I can't. Nobody walks out of this place. They'd kill me before they let me go. I know that.' He was on the edge of tears. 'Honest to God, I hated what they did to you. It made me sick to my stomach. But what could I do?'

Bond lowered his hand but his expression didn't change. 'You live here?'

'During the week. I have a room.'

'Where's the girl?'

'What girl?'

'Her name is Jeopardy. She was taken prisoner with me.'

Danny was going to lie. He was going to deny that he knew anything. Bond saw it in his eyes. He knew he shouldn't give out any information and was as afraid of Sin as he was of the man he had tried to kill. But then he relented. He changed his mind. 'Down the corridor,' he said. 'Through the doors. Then it's the last room on the right. We're not allowed to go near it.'

'Is it guarded?'

The boy shook his head. 'I don't think so. And there are no keys. Just bolts. You can open them.'

'I need clothes.'

'You can have mine. There are spare clothes in my locker. You can have my keys. You can have my pass. You can have anything. Just don't hurt me.' The boy fumbled a set of keys out of his pocket and held them in front of him. 'I won't tell anyone,' he went on. 'I'll say you stole my stuff while I was in the shower. I've got a kid. His name is Frankie and he's six months old. I've got a mom – she's sick. I'm not a bad person, mister. What they wanted to do to you … that was nothing to do with me.'

'What's your locker number?'

'Sixty-four. There's a shirt in there, pants … I've got money too. You can take it all.'

Bond knew that he had to kill him. That was the only safe option. There was no time to tie him up and gag him (how much time had he wasted already?). And yet, looking at him, pale and trembling, he had to ask himself – wasn't this what it had always come down to? The thin man who had prepared him for torture at the hands of Le Chiffre, the disciples of Mr

250

Big, the simpering women – Sister Lily and Sister Rose – who had welcomed him into the world of Dr No, all the workers at Goldfinger's plant in Switzerland … he had never asked where they had come from, why they had agreed to do the devil's own work. Were they just trying to scratch a living? Did they have sick mothers and six-month-old babies? Bond had killed many of them, snuffing out their lives without even thinking of them as human beings at all. And here was Danny, working his three-dollar-an-hour shifts. Danny Slater, his security pass read. He was crying. There were real tears seeping out of the corners of those blue eyes, tricking down his cheeks. Did he deserve to die?

But this was the same Danny Slater who had dug a hole seven feet deep and who had known that a living man, nailed into a box, was going to be buried in it. With the fingers rigid, Bond's hand flashed out, aiming for his throat. The boy didn't even have time to cry out.

Bond examined his work, then snatched the keys up off the floor and went over to the locker. There were spare clothes inside. The boy hadn't lied about that. He dressed himself quickly, put his own shoes back on, then dragged Danny into one of the shower cubicles. If someone came in, they could think he'd slipped on the soap. He took the keys and the security pass, turned off the lights and hurried out into the corridor.

Down to the end and through a set of double doors … Bond found himself back where he had started a few hours before. His own cell was open and empty. Jeopardy had to be in the room opposite. He drew back the bolts, opened the door and stepped inside, ducking down as a wooden chair missed his head by inches, smashing into the wall behind him. Jeopardy was holding the other end. Her face was filled with pent-up fury which rapidly turned to alarm as she saw who it was.

'James!' she rushed into his arms. 'Oh my God! I could have—'

'Are you all right?' he asked her. Someone had hit her. There was a second bruise high up on her cheek.

She nodded. 'I cut up rough after they took you away and started throwing myself around. I smashed a few plates and threw a whole lot of stuff on the ground and in the end they did this to me.' She pointed. 'But I didn't mind. I didn't want them counting the knives and forks. And I guess it worked.'

'You were brilliant, helping me the way you did.'

'Jesus Christ, I was worried about you. Did they actually bury you? Don't tell me. I don't want to know, and anyway we've got to bust out of here. We don't have much time.'

Bond showed her the keys and the security pass. 'These might help. How far do you think we are from the Coney Island depot?'

'We can do it in less than an hour.'

'Can you contact your people?' Bond had already worked it out. The best way to stop Sin was to throw the switch in one of the power stations and close down the entire subway system. If he couldn't move the rocket, he would be finished. But had he left it too late? By the time they found a phone, called the FBI or Secret Service, established their identity, explained the situation and tracked down someone with the authority to do what was needed, the whole thing might be over. For all Bond knew, Sin was already sitting underneath New York with his bomb and his phoney rocket.

Jeopardy was ahead of him. 'They're in Washington,' she

said. 'And it's the middle of the night. I can call the duty officer but I'm not sure...'

'Then we're going to have to do this on our own.'

Ten minutes later the guards at the gate heard the sound of an engine starting up but it was immediately obvious that it wasn't a car. Puzzled, they edged forward then shouted as, in the far distance, a mechanical digger rumbled towards the fence. A couple of them managed to bring their guns round and fire but the vehicle was too far away, moving too quickly through the darkness. Behind the controls Bond squeezed on the throttle and crouched down as a bullet clanged into the metal close to his head and ricocheted into the night. Jeopardy was next to him, the two of them squeezed together on the narrow seat. Ahead of them, the fence loomed up. Bond hoped it wasn't electrified but it was too late to worry about that now. The vehicle's blades were raised up and elongated, stretching out in front of them. Bond saw them tear into the wire, ripping it apart as if it were cotton thread. More bullets spat past but they were already out of the compound and the nearest trees were only a few feet away. Once they were in the scrubland, they could quickly work their way up to Jeopardy's car. She had left her keys in the exhaust pipe.

Meanwhile, in the changing room, Danny Slater opened his eyes and drew in a deep breath. It hurt. He was lying, crumpled, in the shower cubicle. Slowly, he dragged himself to his feet, staggered out and looked in the mirror. His throat was swollen and there was a livid discolouration in the flesh. His head felt as if it had been beaten with a baseball bat. He could barely swallow. But he was alive.

As Bond abandoned the digger and set off with Jeopardy on foot through the woods, he recalled the final second when he had changed both the direction and the velocity of his strike and had knocked the boy unconscious instead of killing him. What had made him change his mind? Bond was one of three agents who had been given the double zero assignation – a licence to kill. But that didn't mean he *had* to kill or that he would ever enjoy killing. Somewhere inside him he felt a measure of satisfaction. A great evil had been done to him but it had not made him evil. Sin might claim that what had happened at No Gun Ri had turned him into the monster that he undoubtedly was but Bond had escaped from the hell of a living grave and he had left nothing of his inner self, not an inch of his humanity, behind. That was the difference between them. It was why he would win.

21

The Million-Dollar Train

The fence, topped with barbed wire, stretched in both directions, a point of no return for the city which had crept almost to the very edge and then fallen back, knowing it was beaten. On the other side, there was a wilderness of gravel, discarded oil drums, concrete blocks, telegraph poles with drooping wires and seemingly abandoned pieces of industrial equipment. And railway lines, miles and miles of them, a labyrinth of intertwining metal that seemed to have been laid out almost randomly, a vast playset that had run out of control as more and more pieces had been added. The empty space was somehow all the more shocking on the edge of Brooklyn. It was as if the fence divided two quite separate worlds. Bond could imagine the distant apartment blocks, filled with families, all of them crammed into small, dark rooms, one on top of the other. They would look out onto the Coney Island depot, forbidden to them, except as a view through a grimy window pane, offering more space than they would ever enjoy in their lives. It was almost like the difference between life and death – with a cold, white moon bathing both in its spectral glow.

The break in the fence was exactly where Jeopardy remembered it. It had been repaired, then broken again, repaired, broken, then finally abandoned in a tangle of redundant wire. The two of them squeezed through the gap and examined the landscape around them. The nearest buildings were about two hundred yards away: a line of workshops made of brick and corrugated iron, tall and rectangular, with the tracks disappearing inside. There didn't seem to be anyone in sight but as they watched, crouching in the shadows, there was the sound of an engine and a lone motorcyclist appeared, rattling to a halt. Bond recognised the oversized nacelle and the chrome, 'mouth organ' tank badge of the 650cc Triumph Thunderbird. He couldn't help smiling. This was the bike that had fuelled the hopes and ambitions of a generation of GIs after the war. It wasn't enough that it was faster and lighter than the old Speed Twin, it had to be gaudier too; shouting to the world with its bright colours and chrome. He watched as the driver dismounted and strolled nonchalantly through a sliding door and into the workshop. Was he just a railwayman or did he work for Sin? Bond hoped it was the former. Let him have his innocence and his simple pleasures and at the end of the day let him get back on his bike and go home to his wife or his girlfriend. Enough people would die tonight without him.

'These sheds are all private contractors,' Jeopardy whispered. She was crouching beside him, gazing through the darkness. 'Anyone working here at this time of the night ... it's got to be Sin.'

'I'm going in,' Bond said. 'You get out of here, try and find a phone.'

'I'm not leaving you.'

'We don't have time to argue, Jeopardy. I wouldn't have got here without you. But now it's my turn. I'm going to stop Sin's train from leaving.'

'How? You don't even have a gun.'

'I'll find a way. And if I fail, you have to talk to the Secret Service and get the entire railway network shut down. What are the substations? Fifty-ninth Street? Long Island?'

'James – I've told you. It's too late.' Jeopardy looked at her watch. 'Fifty minutes to launch.'

'Find a phone. Call your people.'

He was off before she could say any more, running beside the tracks towards the workshop that the motorcyclist had entered. The tracks ran all the way to the sliding doors and then, presumably, continued on the other side. At least there didn't seem to be too much security – but why should there have been? This was nothing more than a railway depot, grimy and uninteresting except perhaps to the local kids who might sneak in for a dare, just as Jeopardy had done all those years ago. Nobody saw him as he reached the brick wall with its evenly spaced windows, the glass panes frosted to allow no view in or out. Bond didn't want to risk the sliding door – not until he knew what was on the other side. A spiral staircase led to a platform with a smaller, wooden door tucked away to one side. He edged his way along the wall and climbed up.

The door was locked. But the bolt was old and rusty and Bond decided to risk breaking it open with his shoulder. Hopefully, there would be enough activity inside the workshop to cover the noise. He took one look back. There was no sign of Jeopardy and he hoped she'd had the sense to get out while she could. There was no time for delicacy. Bond slammed into the door and felt the lock give way. It swung open. At once he heard music – a radio playing – the clang of metal, men shouting, the whine of an electric motor. If anyone had been looking up they might have seen him enter but there was no chance of his being heard. He eased himself inside. The first person he saw was Jason Sin.

He was surrounded by his men, a whole squadron of them, this time predominantly Korean. Well, it was an unusual American who would willingly participate in the destruction of New York's most famous landmark and the hundreds, even thousands, of deaths that it would bring. They were all dressed as railwaymen, gathered together as if for one final briefing in a vast hangar of a place with railway lines stretching from one end to the other. Each of the men cast five shadows, spilling out from beneath their feet. All of them were armed. Bond couldn't hear what Sin was saying. There was at least a hundred yards between them and he was concealed behind a latticework of criss-crossing steel girders. In fact, nobody could have seen the door as it crashed open. Even as Bond watched, Sin came to the end of his peroration. As one, the group moved towards the waiting train.

Bond recognised it at once. The R-11 cars, built at the end of the forties, were among the most beautiful that had ever been rolled out on the New York City Subway. With their shot-welded stainless steel body and distinctive porthole windows, fluorescent lighting and steel strap-hangers, they had caught the spirit and the dynamism of the age and as each car had cost $10,000, they had inevitably come to be known, together, as the Million-Dollar Train. Of course, this one had been bastardised by Sin who had reshaped the whole thing, engine and carriages, for the operation that was about to take place. No train like this had ever entered the subway system. Nothing like this would ever run again.

First there was the engine. The driver, a Korean, was already climbing up, letting himself into the front cabin with Sin right next to him. He was evidently going to ride with him, perhaps fulfilling some childhood fantasy – didn't everyone want to drive a train? Next came some sort of maintenance vehicle, a flat car that resembled the lowboy that Bond had seen earlier that evening but on rails, not on the tarmac. It had no roof. A series of short, steel pillars surrounded a load which had been covered in tarpaulin to conceal it as it made its final journey. It was the fake Vanguard. There could be no doubt about it. Bond noticed that it had been secured with dozens of thin, lightweight chains. Presumably they would melt in the explosion, leaving no evidence behind. It was attached to another R-11 car which contained the bomb. Bond could see the bulk of it behind the windows. Two men were climbing in to accompany it on the journey, one small and wiry, the other corpulent, both dressed as railwaymen, both Korean.

There was another car right behind it and this was where the rest of Sin's men would ride. Bond counted seven of them as they climbed in, making eleven in all, including Sin and the driver, against just one of him. Not great odds. Finally, at the back, there was an empty car and a second engine. Bond was puzzled by that, but he quickly worked it out. Sin would ride into the tunnel. His men would arm the bomb and uncouple the car that contained it. Then they'd travel back the way they had come in the rear engine, leaving a scene of devastation and the wreckage of a train behind them. Nobody would know what had really happened.

And somehow he had to prevent it. Standing on the gantry, looking down on the train, Bond made a cold-blooded assessment of the situation as he saw it. There were only forty minutes until the launch of the real Vanguard at Wallops

Island. Sin was overseeing the operation himself. Bond was unarmed and alone. Jeopardy might be on her way to a telephone and there was still a chance she would be able to alert the authorities, but it was only a small one and anyway, he still couldn't assume they would have time to act. The R-11 would have to travel through Brooklyn before it reached the network of tunnels that would take it under the East River and up, into the heart of Manhattan. At what station would it go below ground? Fifteenth Street? Seventh Avenue? Or later? If Bond could reach the train and detonate the bomb while it was still on the surface, in Brooklyn, the damage would be minimal (though possibly not to himself). Once the train reached Manhattan, it would be game over. Bond had to move now.

He was already too late. Sin and his team were inside the train. He had left the rest of his men behind him in the workshop and they had pulled back the oversized doors to reveal the tracks that stretched across the depot on the other side. Suddenly, without warning, the train jerked forward. Bond cursed and at the same moment set off, back through the door and down the spiral stairs. There was nothing for it now. He had to reach it before it picked up much more speed.

And he might have made it. But as he got to the bottom of the stairs, an American appeared, bald with tattoos on his neck and shoulders, coming out of nowhere. Suddenly the two of them were face to face. Somehow, he must have seen Bond. Perhaps, after all, he had heard the door crash open. He was armed with a knife, and even as Bond fell instinctively into a defensive position, the blade slashed down. Bond was ready for it. He used a simple forearm block, then reached up under the man's knife arm and grabbed his wrist, jerking it down to break the bone. The tattooed man screamed. Bond followed through with a single, vicious blow to the chin. The lights went out in the man's eyes and he crumpled. Bond reached down and snatched up the knife, wishing it had been a gun. He tucked it into his waistband, the blade against his skin.

He had only been delayed for thirty seconds but it had been enough. Already the train had cleared the entrance to the work shed and it was picking up speed, the rear lights dwindling into darkness. Bond began to run. The nearest coach – in fact, the driver's cab which would be used for the return – was about a hundred yards away and the distance was growing with every second that passed. At least it was empty. There was nobody who might look out and see Bond as he pounded down the railway line, all his energy focused on the task of catching up. Part of him was dimly aware of the third rail, elevated and somewhere on the right of the line itself, which carried the electricity supply. If he accidentally stepped on it, it would kill him instantly. Bond was already sweating in the heat of the night. The clothes he had stolen fitted him badly and the synthetic cloth was cutting into him. The Coney Island depot seemed to stretch on for infinity and no matter how fast he ran, the R-11 wasn't getting any nearer. Bond's breath was rasping in his throat. His foot came down on a loose piece of debris and he was almost sent sprawling. He passed a maintenance vehicle with a crane looming over him. He couldn't run any faster but he forced himself on, his arms outstretched, willing himself onto the train. But the train was accelerating. Bond's nostrils were filled with the stench of dust and defeat.

The R-11 pulled away, measuring out the space between them, and Bond came to a stumbling halt. It was hopeless. Sin had got away. But for the American with the knife he might have had a chance, but those lost thirty seconds had made all the difference. And what now? He had failed! He accepted the inevitable with a sense of closing darkness. How could he have expected otherwise? He was only human. So many missions in the last ten years... Could he really have believed he would succeed in every one of them? As he stood there, hunched over and gasping for breath (all those cigarettes – he was feeling them now), watching the tail lights of the train as they slid away from him, there were black spots of anger in front of his eyes. He could already see himself sitting at his desk in London. 'Having made the decision not to alert the authorities, I attempted to head off Sin Jai-Seong at the Coney Island depot but, despite my best efforts, regrettably I arrived too late. The subsequent explosion, the major damage inflicted on Manhattan and the attendant loss of life all resulted from this failure on my part.' No matter how he couched it, he wouldn't come out of this well. Would he be typing a report or a letter of resignation?

The R-11 had gone, the lights swallowed up in the dark. About a dozen stations, without stopping, of course, and it would plunge into a tunnel. Bond straightened up even as the sound of the OHV vertical twin engine came roaring in from behind and he turned to see the Triumph Thunderbird race across the gravel, sliding to a halt beside the track. Jeopardy was in the driving seat.

'Get on!' she commanded.

Bond didn't argue. He slipped his arms around her, feeling the warmth of her body against his, and then they were off, not in the direction of the train but crossing the depot diagonally towards the fence. He could tell at once that Jeopardy was in complete control of the bike and he remembered what she had told him of her experience at the Wall of Death. Well, it was certainly coming into its own now. God! What a girl!

But where were they going? With no helmet or goggles and the wind and dust buffeting his eyes, Bond found it easier to bury his head behind Jeopardy's shoulders and trust to her good sense. They came to an open gate. There was a night watchman stationed here but he had been half asleep in his cabin and shouted at them uselessly as they stormed by. And then they were out, away from the rails, accelerating up a deserted, four-lane avenue with patches of scrubland and low-rise buildings, mainly industrial, on both sides. There was almost no traffic at this time of night and the sidewalks too were deserted. Jeopardy opened the throttle and the bike surged forward, the tarmac sweeping past beneath the wheels. Now the sky was cut off by a steel construction, a sort of tunnel resting on pillars and stretching in a dead straight line far into the distance. It was carrying train tracks and Bond looked up, wondering if he might catch sight of the R-11, but his geography told him that they were far to the east of the depot and he wondered if it was part of Jeopardy's plan to intercept it somewhere up ahead. If so, what would they do then? A motorbike would be no match for a speeding train. Could they derail it? First, they would need to get access to the track and that depended on how familiar she was with the area.

She certainly wasn't hesitating as she gunned the bike on. They left the steel tunnel behind them and swung right onto the Bay Parkway, a more residential street with solid-looking houses and decent cars neatly parked. So far the traffic lights had all been green but Bond doubted that Jeopardy would have stopped anyway. He was quickly proved right. At the next crossroads, a garbage truck pulled out across their path. She didn't even slow down. Leaning to the right, she swerved round the obstacle then ducked back, just in time to miss the oncoming traffic. Bond smiled to himself. Instinctively, he had tightened his hold around her waist. Although immediate danger was past, he didn't relax his grip.

The buildings were still low-rise. The sky was empty, washed through by a pale moon. They were speeding through some sort of village with a few more signs of life: an old man sitting on a bench, a deli still open late into the night, a couple walking a dog. Jeopardy pulled out to overtake a beat-up roadster and Bond caught a glimpse of the driver, hugely obese, jammed behind the steering wheel. They came to their first traffic jam at the lights at 60th Street and ignored it, overtaking the cars that were waiting and dodging between the cross-traffic with horns blaring. Suddenly there were gravestones all around them, hundreds of them stretching out to another elevated section of the railway, but no sign of any train. Make room for two more, Bond thought to himself, as Jeopardy overtook one truck and missed another by inches. And then they had hit Ocean Parkway, a much more serious road with six lanes of traffic.

There was another snarl-up ahead of them, a policeman waving the traffic around a roadwork and at last Jeopardy was forced to slow down. Bond took the opportunity to shout in her ear.

'Where are we going?'

She twisted round. 'Fourth Avenue. There's a subway station there. They're doing repairs. We can get there ahead of them.'

'And then?'

'You tell me!'

The traffic cop waved them on. They rocketed forward.

All the way up Ocean Freeway and onto the new Prospect Expressway, still under construction, now heading north on the last run up to Manhattan. However fast Sin was travelling in the R-11, the Thunderbird had to be going faster, but he had the more direct route with no obstacles in the way. Had they got ahead of him? They were rushing past the traffic on the expressway, smashing through the wind and the glare of the oncoming headlights. They came off at Prospect Parkway, skirting the park, then swung a hard left onto 10th Street, a narrow thoroughfare hemmed in by warehouses and dominated by a massive steel structure that loomed over the houses on the right-hand side. Looking up, Bond saw the railway. And there was the R-11! There could be no mistaking the sleek, aluminium shell streaking along. They had caught up with it and the two of them were level. But where was the station? If there was any traffic ahead of them, if a single junction was blocked, they would be too late. It was going to be a damned close thing.

They crossed Fifth Avenue. A car screamed at them, swerving to avoid their path. Bond peered to the right but now, impossibly, the railway had disappeared. Where was it? Where was the train? They passed an ugly block of apartments and there, suddenly, it was. A grey concrete wall with the railway above and a temporary road that had been built specially for the construction workers rebuilding the station. Bond saw the R-11 racing them neck and neck even as Jeopardy veered off the road, across the sidewalk and up the ramp that would take them into the station itself. There was a low gate ahead of them, closed and padlocked. Jeopardy twisted the throttle and, propelled by its own momentum, the Thunderbird left the ground and soared over the obstacle.

The wheels hit the ground. Somehow they stayed upright. And then, impossibly, they were inside the station, rushing along the platform with a brick wall on one side, a canopy overhead and the R-11 right next to them, a silver blur slicing through the night. Bond saw the lights in the windows. The howl of the engine echoed in his ears. There was a flash of electricity as the train rolled over a contact point, as if a storm was about to break. Jeopardy had slowed down. She had no choice. The platform was narrow, strewn with debris left by the builders. It was also about to come to an end. The R-11 was pulling ahead. Bond tensed himself, knowing what he had to do. One last desperate throw of the dice. It was all he had left. They had almost reached the end of the platform. The last carriage, the driver's cab, was slipping past.

Bond let go of Jeopardy and balanced himself carefully, transferring his weight to the balls of his feet. They were still travelling at forty miles an hour and she must have guessed what he was going to do. She had steered the bike to the edge of the platform so that the rushing wall of the train was only eighteen inches away. She continued straight and at that moment Bond threw himself sideways, using the muscles in his thighs to propel himself across the gap, reaching out for the silver railings that formed a safety barrier across the rear driver's door. For a single moment he hung in mid-air. If he missed, he would fall onto the tracks and break his neck or electrocute himself. But somehow his flailing hands caught hold of the railings. There was a terrible shock as his arms were almost pulled out of their sockets by the forward momentum of the train. But then he was being carried along, hanging onto the back. He had one last glimpse of Jeopardy, on the platform, bringing the Thunderbird to a scything halt. Then she was gone. The station walls flashed past. And finally darkness took over as he was swallowed up, instantly and irrevocably, by the mouth of the tunnel.

22

Tunnel Vision

The train, with Bond attached to the back of it, thundered through the tunnel. It seemed to have picked up speed, perhaps an illusion caused by the walls and ceiling pressing in on three sides – but certainly the R-11 was making a journey like no other. It was stopping at no stations. It was the only train making the journey on the Sixth Avenue line from Coney Island, the points changed and the signals turned green by a trainmaster in Sin's pay. It was almost a straight line from the northern edge of Brooklyn to the Empire State Building. The bullet had been fired. Nothing could stand in its way.

For the first minute he stayed where he was with his arms spread out, clinging onto the railings, a bit like a fly on a windscreen, it occurred to him. He needed to regain his strength, but at the same time he was already making his calculations, reminding himself of what he had seen. Five carriages. The one in front of him with the engine for the journey back. Then came the carriage with Sin's taskforce: seven men, probably armed. Bond only had the knife, still pressing against the small of his back, in the waistband of his trousers. Not good. If he could get past them, he would arrive at the carriage which contained the bomb. Two more men were travelling with it. Then the fake rocket. And finally there was Sin and the driver. Think, Bond. Think. You can reach Sin and kill him. Presumably his men will abort the operation. But suppose the C4 explosive is on a timer? Sin had talked about blasting caps but that could mean anything and the bomb might go off anyway. Forget Sin. Think about the bomb. You still have half an hour. Twenty minutes, certainly. Get into the carriage, deactivate the bomb, make New York safe, then worry about the rest of them. Ten against one. You've had worse odds than that.

The train erupted out of the tunnel and into a station. Bright lights sliced Bond's eyes. He saw white tiles, an empty platform, a sign – CARROLL STREET – benches, iron maiden turnstiles. He was rushing through the open space and then, just as suddenly, it was dark again. Cautiously, he looked round the side of the train and was rewarded with a blinding rush of warm air and soot. OK. Time to make a move. Clinging on with one hand, he swung round with the other and tried the handle of the door of what, on the return journey, would be the driver's cabin. It was locked.

So he was going to have to go over the top. Moneypenny had accused him of the same often enough. Slowly, Bond pulled himself upwards. He was protected while he was on the back of the train but he knew that he would be pulverised by the wind rush the moment he tried to crawl along the roof – and anyway, there wouldn't be enough room. Much of the subway system had been built using the cut-and-cover method, digging into the soft earth as close as possible to the street surface and then rebuilding over the trenches. The shallower, the cheaper – and the workmen had made sure money wasn't wasted. The trains were twelve feet and two inches high. The top of the tunnel was only a few inches higher and although it was hard to tell in the darkness, Bond was aware of steel beams, lethal weapons, rushing past. If he raised his head at the wrong moment, it would be knocked clean off his shoulders. Even lying flat, there was every chance that a loose cable or any other projection could scrape him off and send him to an instant, bloody death. With the wind beating at his head, Bond examined the roof of the carriage. Yes. Perhaps it could be done.

The roof curved. It was an integral part of the design, making the R-11 sleeker, more streamlined. If Bond made his way along the very edge, half his body actually touching the side of the train, just above the windows, he should be out of harm's way. But it would be incredibly difficult to hang on. The aluminium roof was ribbed and that would give him fingerholds. But he would be absolutely dependent on the strength of his right hand. If the train rocked, even slightly, he would be thrown off. If he relaxed for a second, he would simply slide into oblivion. And what if a train came the other way? The blast of compressed air might be enough to dislodge him. Bond could see himself falling between the two silver monsters. A blast of light. A scream of metal. And then minced up between the wheels.

But there was no other way and Bond had already wasted enough time hanging on here. The tunnel was shattered by light as they entered the next station – Bergen Street – and swept through. That was something else to consider. If there was anyone standing on any of the platforms, they would see him as he made his way across the carriages. Better to get started while he was in the dark. The train entered the next tunnel and Bond pulled himself onto the roof, making sure that he was on the edge of the curve, an inch or two below the highest point. He hooked onto the ridges with his right hand and pressed his left palm against the vertical side of the carriage. At least the friction would provide him with a modicum of support. Then he began to edge forward, his eyes closed, feeling the wind hammering at his shoulders and head, desperately trying to force him back. It was even harder than he had expected. If he could have stretched himself out along a flat surface, he would have been able to crawl forward at a steady pace. But he was tilted, on the edge of space. He had to use half his strength and all his concentration simply to stop himself from falling. Looking up, he could just make out the top of the tunnel, rushing past, reminding him how fast he was travelling. There was a sudden crackle and a searing burst of electricity. For a few seconds, Bond was blind, as if his eyes had been burned out. The train didn't care. It seemed determined to travel ever faster.

With half his body hanging off the edge, Bond pulled himself forward. His progress was painfully slow. He felt something swipe across the top of his head, shockingly hard. A loop of wire must have been hanging down. If he had accidentally raised his head at that moment and allowed it to catch around his neck he would have been garrotted. Another thought scratched away at his consciousness. How long did he have? How many stations would he pass before the train dipped under the river and entered Manhattan? As if to answer him, they burst into Jay Street. Bond saw the name, black letters on a white panel. They were going faster and faster. He wasn't imagining it. They were no sooner in the station than they were out again, another tunnel reaching to swallow them up.

He reached the end of the first carriage and manoeuvred

himself across the narrow gap that separated it from the second. Now he had to be more careful. Sin's men were directly underneath him and although the noise of the train would cover almost any sound, there was still the chance that one awkward move, his foot striking metal, might give him away. The effort of keeping himself on the sloping surface was taking its toll and Bond's right hand, supporting most of his weight, was aching. The pain was spreading to his shoulder. It was hard to breathe. It felt that as much soot as air was entering his throat and his eyes were smarting. He pulled. He shuffled forward. He pulled again and eventually reached the next gap in the carriages, on the other side of Sin's men.

The gap was barely eighteen inches wide. Bond had to contort himself to fit into it. There was only one porthole window in the centre of the door and he was careful to avoid it so that Sin's men would not catch sight of him as he wriggled down. He glanced at the rails, flashing along beneath the spinning wheels, then lowered his foot onto the coupling. It was a tight squeeze. He was trapped between two metal walls, both of them vibrating, shifting, as if about to crush him. He found the handle of the door and pressed down. This time, it moved. The door was unlocked. He glanced in through the window and saw the guards sitting about halfway down, facing each other with the dull faces of two commuters on their way to work. The bomb was at the far end of the carriage, beyond them. Bond checked that the knife was still in his waistband. Then he pressed the handle, threw open the door and tumbled in.

He was only vaguely aware of the inside of the compartment as he propelled himself forward: a bright red floor with empty seats, battleship grey, scattered around him, facing different directions. Three lines of neon lights. Advertisements. Slender silver rods reaching from the floor to the ceiling. The two guards hadn't heard him enter. How could they have with the roar of the train in the tunnel? But now they saw him and rose to their feet, scrabbling for their weapons.

Bond dealt with the smaller one first, guessing that he would be the faster of the two. His hand reached behind him for the knife and, as the man drew his gun out of a shoulder holster he'd been wearing outside his coveralls, Bond plunged the blade into his chest, aiming for the on/off button that was his heart. Blood fountained out and the guard fell back, carrying the knife with him. The second guard had also produced a gun, moving surprisingly quickly given his bulk. He brought it round and fired. Bond felt the bullet pass over his head as he plunged forward, slamming his shoulder into the man's stomach. The guard twisted round, trying to break free. The train rushed on and, propelled by its momentum, the two of them were sent in a macabre dance, spinning down towards the door through which Bond had come in.

They crashed into the metal surface. The guard was trying to bring the gun round to aim at Bond but the angle was wrong and Bond was gripping him too tightly. Instead, he pounded it against Bond's head and the back of his neck. Bond chose his moment and jerked upwards, one hand flying out to seize the guard's wrist, the other closing against his throat. The two of them were trapped in a recess with the door behind them. It seemed that Sin's men in the next carriage hadn't heard the shot but surely one of them would look up and see the fight taking place on the other side of the porthole windows. Bond tried to free the gun with one hand while the other burrowed through the folds of flesh that surrounded the guard's neck, searching for the larynx. He had it! Bond pushed with all his strength, cutting off the airflow. The guard panicked and grabbed hold of Bond's wrist. At once, Bond let go of the gun and, straightening up, used his extended fingers to jab the guard three times, viciously, in the throat. The man went down. Bond hit him again for good luck. He wouldn't get up again. That much was sure.

The door handle rattled and a furious Korean face appeared at the window. Sin's men had finally seen what was happening. They had opened the door of their own carriage and were attempting to enter this one, but they had reacted too slowly. The body of the guard – dead or unconscious – had slid to the floor and was lying inside the recess, blocking the second door. Well, that was useful. They could push all they liked. There was no way they were going to get it open. But it was only a brief respite. One of the men raised his gun to fire and Bond only just had time to step out of the way before a torrent of broken glass came rushing in with the wind. A hand reached through, searching for the handle. Bond snatched up the fat man's gun and fired three times. The hand fell away. That would show them! The door was stuck and the porthole was too constricting to allow them to aim and fire simultaneously. The moment they showed their faces, they would make themselves too obvious a target. Nor could they climb through. They would have to come at him another way.

Bond had no doubt that they would find it. He had perhaps minutes to deal with the bomb, with Sin, to stop this whole thing in its tracks. Being careful to keep out of the line of the window, he lurched through the carriage, jerking the knife out of the body of the man he had stabbed. As he moved forward, the advertising billboards mocked him with their inane, irrelevant messages. *BET YOU COULD DO BETTER IN A HAT. 84 OUT OF 100 WOMEN PREFER MEN WHO WEAR HATS. SUNNY BROOK WHISKEY. CHEERFUL AS ITS NAME. SUNKIST CALIFORNIAN LEMONS. INSTEAD OF HARSH LAXATIVES.*

Ahead of him, the bomb sat like a church altar. It was utterly alien, dominating the space around it, warning him not to come close.

Bond took out the knife, then spun round as the sound inside the carriage changed. Had the Koreans somehow managed to open the door? Had Sin himself heard what had happened and come to investigate? No. Bond turned his attention to the bomb. C4. Sin had volunteered the information, as always giving too much away. What did Bond know of it? It was a British invention. Cyclotrimethylene-trinitramine. Also known as RDX. He had handled one of its precursors during the war and still remembered the feel of the putty, the smell of almonds. It was stable and insensitive. He could set fire to it. Nothing would happen. He could empty the gun into it. The same.

He used the knife to cut the string holding the tarpaulin in place, then pulled it back to reveal the block itself. The substance was a dirty white colour and Bond saw that there were half a dozen detonators pushed into it, with wires leading to a single battery pack. These were the blast caps, first developed in Germany but now in use across the world. In essence, they were little more than oversized matchsticks. A spark from the battery would fire the ignition charge – silver acetylide or lead styphnate. The result would be a small explosion which would immediately cause a chain reaction, setting off the whole thing. Sin didn't need six blast caps. He was taking no chances. One would have done.

But for the first time in a while, luck was on Bond's side. Sin had expected to prime the bomb without any interruption. Nobody would know it was there. The tunnel would be empty and he would have plenty of time. So he hadn't needed a complicated detonation system with fake wires or a capacitor concealed inside the C4. In fact the whole thing was connected to a simple, cheap alarm clock sitting between the blasting caps and the battery. Sin would set the minute hand to give himself enough time to leave, and that would be it. It was about as crude a device as Bond had ever seen and it would be simple enough to defuse … provided he concentrated and kept a steady hand. The trouble with blast caps was that they were unreliable. During the war, Bond had seen trainee agents crimping the fuses with their teeth before inserting them into the ignition mix. It hadn't been that uncommon for them to blow their own heads off.

He glanced at the door. It was being rocked back and forth, thudding into the body of the man who lay across it. But he wasn't moving. A face appeared behind the shattered window and Bond fired off a fourth round, smiling to himself as the head jerked back with a bright red crater between the eyes.

Quickly, he disconnected the battery. Then, crouching in front of the altar, he gently removed the first blast cap and laid it on the floor. He wished now that the train wasn't moving so quickly. He could feel every jolt, every vibration and knew that even without an electrical charge, the detonators could all too easily go off. The train howled through York Street. Was the R-11 accelerating or were the stations getting closer together? Keeping half an eye on the door, Bond focused on what he was doing. One after another, he removed the other blast caps, laying them gently on the nearest seat. The last one came out. For good measure, Bond threw the alarm clock on the floor and smashed it.

He looked back. The Koreans had given up trying to open the door. The window was clear. Bond could imagine them trying to work out a plan. Would they pull the emergency handle? No. Stopping the train was the last thing they would want to do. Should he pull it himself? He dismissed the idea. If the train came to a halt, it would only make him an easier target. But even as he'd been working on the blast caps, he'd forced himself to realise the truth of the situation. It wasn't enough just to dismantle the bomb. For Manhattan and the Empire State Building to be completely safe he had to get rid of the plastic explosive altogether.

There was one way he could do that. At the same time he could separate himself from the Koreans before they found a way to reach him. And he could give Sin the shock of his life. Bond half smiled as he worked out his strategy. He wasn't just going to neutralise the C4. He was going to use it.

He used the knife to cut off two pieces, the blade easily slicing through the soft putty. Working as quickly as he could, he used his hands to mould the pieces into balls, each one about the size of a hand grenade. And that, of course, was exactly what they were about to become. He grabbed two of the detonators and pushed them into the putty. Would it work? Why not? All it would take was the pressure of 81,000 pounds of steel pressing down – that and a sniper's eye.

They were under the river. Bond knew it from the change of pressure in his ears. They had left Brooklyn and were on their way to Manhattan. He cut a makeshift sling out of the tarpaulin, carefully suspended the two missiles inside and slung the whole thing over his shoulder. It was still horribly dangerous but he had no other way to carry them. He made sure they were secure, then hurried to the far end of the carriage and the other door. There was a gunshot – he barely heard it above the sound of the train – and a bullet slammed into the back of the seat closest to where he was standing. Bond twisted round and returned fire but whoever had taken aim at him had already gone. He had just three bullets left. Should he search for the other gun? He decided against it. If this was going to work, it had to be done now.

Bond opened the door. This time there wasn't a conventional carriage in front of him. Instead, he found himself leaning into the full expanse of the tunnel with the wind tearing past, the wheels and undercarriage clattering, the tunnel walls a continuous, black streak. The maintenance vehicle carrying the rocket, chained into place, was in front of him. Ahead, there was the carriage with Sin and the driver. Well, very soon, if Bond had his way, they would be parting company with their precious load. It almost amused him to think of Sin turning up at the Empire State Building with nothing but the engine and the carriage in which he sat.

Bond had tucked the gun back into his trouser pocket, knowing he might need it. He started forward, inching his way as quickly as possible in the narrow space between the rocket – concealed beneath its tarpaulin – and the edge of the lowboy. He had just reached Sin's carriage when the train burst into East Broadway, the first station in Manhattan itself. There were just six more stops until 34th Street, where Sin had planned to stage the fake crash of the Vanguard. Bond grabbed hold of the rail that ran across the door. He was tempted to look in through the porthole, just to check that Sin was there. But he didn't need to put himself at risk. He had seen the train leave. He knew where everyone was. Bond was filthy again. The wind had blasted him with years of accumulated dirt and soot. He could taste it in his mouth. It had penetrated his skin. The very clothes he was wearing had turned black. But he didn't care. He grinned and his white teeth flared in the darkness. This was the moment of reckoning.

He reached the roof and almost split his head open on a low metal girder that came rushing past. He actually felt it swipe across his hair and cursed himself for the moment of over-confidence that had brought him within an inch of getting himself killed. It was so nearly over. Don't make mistakes now. He twisted round so that his feet were stretched out towards the front of the engine and his head and shoulders were protruding over the edge of the roof, above the replica Vanguard rocket. He reached round and took one of the makeshift hand grenades out of the sling. It shouldn't be too difficult. All he had to do was drop it onto the rail. The maintenance truck carrying the rocket would run over the C4 and the huge pressure would set it off. If he had got it right, there would be a small explosion which would shatter the coupling between the rocket and the carriage with Sin and the driver. By the time the train stopped, there would be half a mile between the engine and its payload. And Sin's remaining men would be out of the picture too.

It was so easy. The rail was right underneath him. But then, before he could do anything, there was a spark in the darkness and a bullet ricocheted off the stainless steel, inches from his hand. He looked up and saw one of the Koreans on the other side of the rocket, lying sprawled on the roof of the carriage that Bond had just left. There were two more men behind him. They had realised that the only way round the blocked door was to climb over the top. They were crawling towards him even now. The man aimed a second time.

Bond had to choose. Shoot back or use the grenade?

He took careful aim, then threw the first of his two missiles towards the rails.

23

Final Countdown

T minus four. Stage one and stage two auto sequence initiated.

It was a perfect night for a launch. To the spectators who had parked their cars and who were lining the shore in expectation of the world's most spectacular – and expensive – firework display, the sky was an inky black with a glittering panoply of stars reflected in the water below, which was still and sluggish as if in anticipation of the event to come. The scientists and technicians within the Wallops Island launch facility would have described it a little differently. There was an optimum weather outlook, the temperature 39 degrees, the wind speed a comfortable 18 knots with a wind-shear element of 4.5 knots factored in. A small amount of lightning activity had been reported but it was well outside the safety limit of ten nautical miles. There were no clouds.

The Vanguard stood on its launch pad, tiny and defiant against the night sky, pinned into place by powerful spotlights closing in on it from three sides. A tiny red beacon was glowing at the top. At T minus sixty-five the gantry cranes had been slowly retired and now only the so-called umbilical cords connected it – tenuously – to the ground. A mixture of liquid oxygen and kerosene was being fed into the oxidiser tanks and the base of the rocket was wreathed in the dense white smoke that made it appear sacred and deadly at the same time. In just a few minutes the engine would ignite, achieving 27,000 pounds of thrust – enough to send the rocket on its way with a vertical velocity of 3,903 feet per second. If it all went well. Everything had been checked and rechecked but there were still a thousand things that could go wrong.

T minus three. Telemetry and command receivers switched to internal power.

There were thirty men and women inside the central control room, many of them sitting behind desks that had been positioned in front of the long, narrow window that faced the launch site. They were surrounded by dozens of monitors, all of them displaying information from the brand new IBM 709 data synchroniser which in turn was hotwired into the AN/FPS-16 radar system.

Every single piece of data relating to orbit determination would be recorded instantly and at the same time transmitted to Washington. Ultimately, in the event of serious system failure, the launch could be aborted or, in a worst case scenario, the rocket destroyed. This was the responsibility of the Range Safety Officer... a man in a suit, in his early thirties, pale and silent, standing in the middle of all the activity and yet somehow removed from it. He had a desk with a bank of machinery and a red toggle switch in a grey box. It was strange that so many years of research, so many millions of dollars, could be wiped out by something as simple as this. For the switch and the box were the Vanguard's self-destruct mechanism, christened, with graveyard humour, 'Trigger Mortis' by some of the VOG technicians.

T minus one twenty...

The countdown had switched to seconds and the tension

in the control room was cranked up accordingly. It was dark inside. The heavy blockhouse doors had been drawn across and the overhead lights dimmed. Most of the illumination now came from the monitors and from the NO SMOKING signs which had flickered on as the final countdown had begun. Captain Eugene T. Lawrence was sitting – in full uniform – as close to the centre as he had been able to get, ignoring the fact that he was the one person in the room who had absolutely nothing to do. He was rolling an unlit cigarette between his fingers, slowly shredding it. The Base Manager, Johnny Calhoun, was standing close by, watching him carefully. Neither of the two men had spoken again about Bond's visit but they had both been affected by it. And they both knew it. A secret agent does not fly all the way from Europe to deliver a tissue of lies and, whatever Lawrence might have said at the time, a cloud of uncertainty hung over them, all the worse because there was nothing they could do. If something did go wrong, if the launch failed, it would be their fault. But it was too late to stop it. Far too late.

It hadn't worked.

The ball of C4 with its detonator had hit the rail but it had harmlessly bounced off before the wheels could crush it. As if realising what had happened, the Korean on the roof of the other carriage fired off a second shot. Bond scrabbled for his own gun and fired twice. The man screamed and rolled sideways, disappearing into the darkness. But behind him, his companion had raised himself up to get a better aim. His gun was pointing directly at Bond and Bond had nowhere to hide. Time seemed to have been cut into a series of snapshots. It was a sensation that he knew well from moments of extreme danger when the adrenalin was pumping through him. Somehow everything slowed down and he was able to separate it into distinct moments.

The Korean aimed.

Something hit Bond on the shoulder. Not the bullet. Whatever it was had come from behind.

The Korean smiled. He knew he couldn't miss.

Bond didn't move. He was going to be all right after all. He knew that the bullet wouldn't be fired.

A wire dangling from the roof of the tunnel caught the Korean around the throat and jerked him backwards, horribly, breaking his neck, sweeping him into oblivion. This was what Bond had felt just a second before. He had been lucky it hadn't done the same to him.

There were three more men on the roof behind him. But they wouldn't move forward. Not now. Not yet.

Bond took out the second grenade. Another station rushed past so abruptly that he didn't have time to see the name. Broadway? West 4th Street? The train was showing no sign of slowing down but they had to be getting close to the target area.

Lying flat on the edge of the roof with the stale subway air rushing over his shoulders, Bond held the ball of explosive as low as he could before releasing it, the top half of his body folded over the edge. He wondered how long he had before the other Koreans fired at him. He had to concentrate on what he was doing. He didn't dare look up. But he could imagine them crawling forward, climbing down onto the platform with the rocket. From there, they would have an easy shot. He had to be careful. He'd only manufactured two of the makeshift bombs. If he missed this time, that would be it.

He opened his hand, whipping back up as the missile fell, using the horizontal surface of the roof as a shield. Had it worked? Bond didn't see the train ride over the C4, crushing it completely. He didn't see the steel edge of the wheel biting down, triggering the blast cap. But he heard and felt the explosion. There was a burst of bright, crimson light and for a moment the tunnel glowed as if the train were travelling through a circle of fire. The shockwave travelled up, bouncing off the walls and ceiling of the tunnel and Bond had to flatten himself, clinging onto the metal ridges, to prevent himself being thrown off. He felt the entire carriage shudder and then there was a terrible screaming sound and he knew that his plan hadn't worked out quite as he had hoped – that, in fact, he had done more than he had intended. The explosion had cut the train in half. There was the maintenance truck disappearing into the distance (he just caught sight of it in the corner of his eye) and the rest of Sin's men were going with it. Well, good riddance to them. But the front section of the train was in trouble. Bond felt the roof jolt and then tilt to one side. A million sparks blazed all around him. There was a terrible shuddering, like an earthquake.

The train had derailed. He only understood when the entire thing buckled and split apart. Bond was wrenched free. His shoulder slammed into a steel bracket. Not part of the train. Part of the tunnel roof. He was flying through the darkness and the carriage was no longer beneath him. His whole body was limp. He heard the shattering of glass, metal being ripped in half, the engine howling, out of control. Something smashed into his head. He felt his neck breaking and there was a huge electric shock behind his eyes. He was unconscious before he hit the ground.

*

All across Wallops Island, the sirens were blasting out their final warnings, the sound starting low then climbing into the night sky. The crowds standing far outside the compound knew that the moment had come and this was the real reason for the alarm. Anyone who might be in any danger had long withdrawn.

T minus thirty. Ground disengage...

The umbilical cords fell away. Now the rocket really was on its own and the night sky seemed darker than ever, fearful of the assault that was about to take place. A sudden spark, brilliant, elemental. With just six seconds to lift-off, the pyrotechnic igniter had been activated. This was the moment of truth. Inside the central control room, nobody moved. The loudspeakers had fallen silent. Even the television screens seemed to have frozen.

Lift-off...

One second later, the spark reached the oxygen and kerosene fumes and exploded, swallowing up the darkness, expanding into a blinding ball of light as bright as the sun. Behind the rocket, the sea danced white. The gantry, the other buildings... the entire island was consumed and the Vanguard itself was barely visible as torrents of dust and smoke swirled around. At the same time there came the sound of the loudest explosion in the world, not sudden but sustained, pulsating through the air, through brickwork, deafening everyone for a mile around. The ground was shaking. The vibrations were tearing the fabric of the night apart.

The Vanguard rose, painfully slowly, hesitantly, hovering above the ground as if reluctant to begin its journey. Inside the control room, the Fire Control Technician stood at attention, his hand close to the water deluge lever that would release thousands of gallons if the rocket fell back to earth. For what seemed like an eternity it hung there, then began to move, a silver dagger cutting into the sky. The gantry was trembling, bending in and out of shape as it soared past.

All systems stable. Flight proceeding normally.

Captain Lawrence smiled, a thin crease spreading across the wide expanse of his face, the intense glare reflecting in his eyes. This was the moment when he was vindicated, when the English spy was proven wrong. The Vanguard was picking up speed, moving effortlessly now, leaving behind a billowing carpet of smoke and light. The howl of its engine was louder than ever. In fifty seconds it would be supersonic. At the same time it would ease itself into a pre-calculated arc, taking advantage of the earth's curve. The first stage would burn out and fall away, allowing the second stage to take over. The rocket had a journey of just seventy-six miles. After that it would have broken through the earth's atmosphere. It would be in space. Already it was tiny, little more than a blazing star, climbing through the sky, beautiful and silent.

System malfunction. Stand by. Repeat. System malfunction.

A gasp of disbelief. The Range Safety Officer looked round as if he had been slapped. In a chamber to one side the Electronics Telemetering crew were whispering urgently, examining the data as it appeared on the screen. Something had gone wrong. There was some sort of blockage in the nitrogen supply lines feeding the fuel tank and insufficient propellant was being pumped into the combustion chamber. The readings showed that the thrust had only reached twenty-one thousand pounds. Not enough to complete the journey. The rocket wasn't going to make it – and suddenly it was a threat.

Seventeen thousand pounds of hardware with thousands of gallons of kerosene and liquid oxygen. It was no longer a rocket. It was a bomb, one mile above the earth's surface. If it fell back. If the second stage ignited. If it lost control...

Abort mission.

They were the two words the Range Safety Officer most dreaded. But his training told him not to question them, not to hesitate. His hand hit the toggle switch of the self-destruct system that they knew as Trigger Mortis. He fumbled it. There was no feeling in his arm. But then his fingers closed round it and he pressed upwards, sending out the radio signal that meant instant death. There was a brief pause, a last half-second in which everything might be all right after all, and then a vast explosion as the Vanguard blew itself apart, the star stretching itself in every direction, doubling, tripling in size before disappearing altogether. Then darkness; total, absolute. Inside the control room the scientists were staring in shock and disbelief. A few of them were in tears. Calhoun caught Lawrence's eye but the Navy Liaison and Project Officer looked away. He was feeling sick.

Launch team, launch team. Be advised. Stay at your consoles...

Along the shorelines the spectators cried out, witnessing what had happened. Many of them had captured it on their cameras. All of them would be talking about it the next day and for the rest of their lives. In the darkness, none of them saw the broken pieces of the Vanguard as they fell back to earth, splashing harmlessly into the Atlantic.

They could, of course, have fallen anywhere. Among the crowd, Sin's agents piled into their cars and drove away, taking their cameras with them. The photographs would be developed overnight. Every newspaper in the country would have them following the catastrophe that had been supposed to take place in the next two minutes in a city three hundred and thirty miles to the north.

Bond was in pain. His whole body was in pain. He hadn't broken his neck but he had landed awkwardly, one leg bent underneath him, his ribs resting on one of the rails. His shirt had been torn off. He could taste blood in his mouth. And he smelled burning. Something was on fire. He felt a great blow, a heavy object slamming into his stomach, and as his brain switched back on it informed him that this was actually the third or fourth time it had happened, that whoever was hitting him was going to do it again, and that this was what had woken him up.

He opened his eyes and saw Jason Sin standing over him. His black hair was hanging down over his eyes and his spectacles had been knocked sideways so that they hung, ridiculously askew, on his nose. There were dark streaks on his face and a deep, weeping wound on his forehead. The railwayman's uniform he was wearing included heavy leather boots and he had been kicking Bond repeatedly and deliberately, his face utterly blank, just two little pinpricks of madness flickering in his eyes. He was holding a gun, a Browning .22 Compact, but he wasn't going to use it yet. It was hanging limply, slanting sideways and towards the ground. All his attention was focused on the half-naked body in front of him. Bond knew that the kicking would only stop when he died.

What was left of the train was about a hundred yards down the track, lying on its side at a point where the tunnel emerged into another station. The steel was crumpled, the engine on fire. Smoke was billowing out, filling the tunnel and Bond's eyes were already smarting. He twisted the other way. There was no sign of the carriage with the bomb or the rocket. Sin's men had probably been killed. The two of them were alone.

Sin had seen him open his eyes. He kicked out one last time and Bond felt one of his ribs crack as the leather toecap made contact with the bone. 'Why are you here?' Sin asked. His voice was thin, high-pitched. He might have been on the edge of tears. 'How are you here? You should be dead. Who helped you?'

'It's all over, Sin,' Bond said. It hurt him to talk. 'The American Secret Service will be here any minute. Your whole plan's gone off the rails. Like the train.'

'Who helped you?'

'You did. Your ego and your stupidity.' As he talked, Bond reached behind him, wondering what had happened to his own gun. It had been torn out of his grip when the train had crashed but was there any chance that it was somewhere near? His fingers passed over loose gravel, then brushed against a length of chain. He groaned and, at the same time, pulled it towards him, trying to think where it had come from. It could have been part of the train. There had been chains holding down the fake Vanguard rocket. It could have snapped off from one of them. He guessed there were three or four feet lying on the ground behind him. A weapon?

He winced as Sin kicked him again, but this time he had anticipated it, turning his body, taking the main force of the blow on his lower back. He pulled the chain closer towards him, at the same time manipulating his body so that he lay between the rails, not touching either of them. 'You should get away while you can,' Bond said. He didn't care if he was making any sense. He had to talk, simply to cover what he was doing. 'And you won't need to worry about the Americans if the Russians get to you first. It'll be interesting to see who actually kills you.'

'No!' Sin remembered the gun in his hand. 'I am not the one who is dying, Mr Bond. You are.' Slowly he lifted it. 'Even now, I can make your death protracted,' he went on. 'A bullet in the stomach or the groin. I will leave you here, like a rat, in the darkness—'

'You're the rat, Sin.' Bond swung his arm. He had almost no strength. The position he was lying in made it impossible to put any force into the blow. The chain caught Sin on the ankle and draped itself over his foot. But it hadn't hurt him. He looked down and, at last, something close to a smile appeared on his lips. 'Is that the best you can do, Mr Bond?' he asked.

'No,' Bond replied. 'This is.'

He threw the other end of the chain over the third rail.

He hadn't been certain that there would be any electricity in the subway system. It might have turned itself off automatically when the train derailed. But he knew at once that, when it most mattered, the gods were on his side. There was a sharp crackle, another shower of sparks and, at the same time, a terrible scream from Sin as seven hundred and fifty volts surged into him. His fingers splayed. The skin on his face rippled outwards. The glasses fell away and the eyes, finally revealed, turned white. His hair stood on end. He had surely been killed instantly but he stood there, jerking and shuddering until suddenly, as if a plug had been pulled, the electricity released him from its hideous grip. Smoke trickled out from between Sin's lips. The sweet smell of burning flesh reached Bond's nostrils and Sin fell sideways and lay still.

Bond got unsteadily to his feet. He was careful not to touch the metal rails. The train was still blazing but if he moved quickly he might be able to get around it and into the station. Sin's gun had fallen free. He took it ... just in case.

Choking, with the smoke burning his eyes, Bond made his way out.

24

Travelling Time

Rain swept into London like an angry bride. It rattled off the streets, swirled round the gutters and drove anyone who happened to find themselves outside back into the doorways. The traffic slowed down, then came to a halt. All the lights – headlights, rear lights, traffic lights and the neon lights on the hoardings, blurred into a single turmoil of colour. Thick clouds, reflected in the puddles, rolled over the rooftops. There was no escape. Any memory of the August sunshine had been wiped away. This was the day when the birds would fly south and the leaves would begin to die. Soon it would turn cold. Another year was disappearing down the drain.

Bond liked the sound of the rain, hammering on the roof of his Bentley. As the windscreen wipers drew back an endless series of curtains, he looked out on the sodden expanse of Regent's Park and felt very much at home. It had been twelve hours since the Pan American 'Super 7' Clipper had deposited him at Heathrow. Flying back in first class, courtesy of a grateful CIA, Bond had taken full advantage of the on-board cocktail lounge, flirting with a pretty, over-severe stewardess at thirty thousand feet before stretching out on the bed-length Sleeperette and falling into a comfortable sleep. He'd had plenty of time to remember his last night in New York.

Don't want to leave you
Sorry to grieve you
It's travelling time, and I must move on.

The Frank Sinatra song had been playing in the cabin before take-off. It couldn't have been better chosen.

Things had happened very quickly in New York once the Secret Service had become involved, although, back at the Coney Island depot, Jeopardy had been right. Finding the right person in the right office in Washington had taken half the night and if Bond hadn't gone after the R-11 on his own, it would have all ended very differently. As it was, they both knew it had been a near miss. The train had come to a halt just south of 23rd Street and, according to the experts who had examined it, it had been packed with enough explosive to do serious damage to the heart of Manhattan. There was a very real chance that it would have brought down the Empire State Building. It would certainly have devastated any number of the offices, apartments and hotels in the immediate neighbourhood, bringing chaos, multiple deaths and a billion-dollar reconstruction bill to the city. The loss of the Vanguard space rocket was regrettable but it was a small price to pay in comparison and Captain Eugene T. Lawrence had already been told that his services would no longer be required by the NRL. It was still unclear how Thomas Keller had managed to sabotage the feed to the turbo pump in such a way that it had passed unnoticed until the very end. But there are huge differences between static tests and an actual launch and Keller had certainly known what he was doing. The whole truth would emerge when the engine was finally recovered and since it was somewhere at the bottom of the Atlantic that might take some time.

Jason Sin was dead. The American authorities – the CIA, the FBI and the Secret Service – could not have been happier with that particular outcome. They were still tying up the loose ends of the Goldfinger business and it would have been difficult for the government – particularly a Republican one – to explain why so many multimillionaires were suddenly ganging up on the United States. Sin's people were already scattering. A raid on the Blue Diamond depot outside Paterson had found the place virtually empty. But there had been one grisly discovery. Two more coffins had been dug up in the loose earth where Bond had been buried alive. Each of them had contained the bodies of men who had died horribly, trying to claw their way out. These were clearly less fortunate victims of Sin's grim deck of cards.

Jeopardy was out of town for two days, going through her various de-briefings, and in that time Bond took it easy, recovering from the worst of his injuries. He had got away with serious bruising and one broken rib but he still felt as if he had been put through the wringer. He knew he was lucky. In those last few minutes in the tunnel, Sin had finally shed any semblance of reason or sanity. The kicking he had given Bond had been painful. But it was almost as if he had forgotten he was holding a gun.

Bond was glad to be left alone for a couple of days' quiet time. He had arranged to meet Jeopardy for dinner, just the two of them, when she got back to Manhattan. And he had made all the arrangements. He was staying at the Plaza Hotel in Fifth Avenue – not somewhere he would normally have chosen. It was a little too pleased with itself for his taste, a little too ostentatious. How much gold-plated china could one hotel seriously contain? And weren't 1,650 crystal chandeliers taking it a little bit too far? But once again, the US authorities were paying – 'It's all on us, Mr Bond. Just charge anything to your room.' He had a suite overlooking Central Park and he had already ordered a bottle of Clicquot Rosé champagne on ice and two glasses to be set beside the king-sized bed with its luxurious, 300-count Frette sheets (the same linen, the porter had proudly explained, had been used on the *Titanic*). He had booked dinner – the best table – in the Rendezvous Room. The stage was most definitely set.

Jeopardy arrived late, hurrying between the tables. She had dressed for the occasion and looked stunning in a black silk velvet evening dress – Christian Dior, Bond guessed – with square shoulders, long sleeves and the waist drawn in almost cruelly by a black leather belt. The bruises on her face had faded or she had covered them artfully with make-up. She was wearing a simple necklace with three sapphires clustered together. A nod towards Blue Diamond perhaps. Bond stood up and held the chair for her and even as she sat down, the back of her shoulders sliding against his chest, he knew that there was only one way the evening could end.

Bond chose the food for both of them: Caesar salad to start, then grilled sole. He explained: 'I don't trust a menu that's in French unless I'm in France. Half these dishes are going to be pretentious and overcooked so let's go for something simple.'

'You go ahead,' Jeopardy said. 'Just make sure you choose a fancy wine. I don't usually get to go to smart places like this on my expenses. And as for the menu, I didn't even get past the swirly writing. It means they can double the prices.' She smiled and the strangely unmatched features of her face arranged themselves so that she was suddenly beautiful. 'It's great to see you, James. How are the ribs?'

'If you don't mean the ones on the menu, mine are doing fine.'

The waiter arrived with cocktails that Bond had already ordered: two Negronis made with sweet vermouth, Campari, gin and a slice of orange. He had decided to forego his usual martini because he didn't want to remind Jeopardy of the last time they had drunk it. They clinked glasses. In the corner of the room, half hidden behind pillars and pot plants, a pianist began to play.

They were easy in each other's company. They both knew that they were saying goodbye. Bond was returning to London the following morning while Jeopardy would be returning to Washington. She had already been given her next assignment, a tidying up operation that involved tracking all the cash payments made by Sin in the past year in case any more of the Bernhard dollars showed up. Twenty-four hours from now, there would be 3,500 miles between them. That meant there were no strings attached. Tonight was tonight and that was it.

It was Jeopardy who put it into words, after the coffee had been served and Bond was smoking his third cigarette of the evening. 'You have a room here,' she said.

'A suite. Your people have been looking after me.'

'Is that where we're going?'

'Is that what you want?'

'I suppose so.' She eyed him curiously. 'That's why you invited me, isn't it? It wasn't just for the fancy food.'

'I think you're wonderful, Jeopardy. You were always there for me. Without you, I'd have been gunned down at the Starlite or left behind in Coney Island. I'd say we're already more than friends.'

'And you're going to leave me with something to remember you by?'

'Well...' Bond couldn't quite work out the tone of her voice.

'You could have got me something from Tiffany's.'

'Is that what you'd have preferred?'

'No.' Again the urchin smile. 'I'm just teasing you. All right, then, Mr James Bond. Take me up to your suite. After everything we've been through together, don't we deserve to be happy?'

Jeopardy made love almost reluctantly to begin with. She let him take off her clothes and when she was naked, lay on the bed with her ankles crossed, one hand gently resting between her legs as if she were some delicate Venus posing for a classical painting. She watched as he undressed himself and only then did he see the appetite awaken in her eyes. Bond lowered himself onto her and kissed her softly on the lips. His hand explored between her breasts and continued down to the soft pit of her stomach. He felt the silky skin flutter. And then she clamped hold of his wrist. With a show of strength that he could never have expected, she pulled him sideways, at the same time rolling onto him so that her body lay full-length on his. She slipped her hands around him and gripped him fiercely, pressing the two of them together.

'Damn you,' she said. 'Do what the hell you want.'

Later, when it was all over, she was vulnerable again. Bond thought she was even sad. Holding her close to him, he turned to her. 'What is it?' he asked. 'What's the matter?'

'I'm just thinking that this is your way of saying goodbye.'

'It doesn't have to be.'

'Yes, it does.' She folded herself into him, moulding the

contours of her body into his own. 'It's been wonderful know-ing you, James. Not all of it. I almost died during that dinner with Sin – but somehow I knew we'd come through.'

'We were good together.'

'We were lucky – and you know it. But this is the end, isn't it? You're going to walk out on me. And I have to tell you, life's going to be a lot less interesting without you.'

'We can meet again.'

'I don't think so.' She lay in silence for a while. When she spoke again, her voice was level. 'I suppose I should have told you. There's a guy I know in the Treasury in Washington. He's sweet and he's reliable and we've been seeing a bit of each other. He wants me to meet his parents and I'll probably end up marrying him and we'll have two children and grow old together. I'm not sure it's what I want but I guess it's what's right for me. But you'll never be like that, will you? The best thing for you tomorrow morning would be to wake up and find me gone.'

'Jeopardy...'

'It's all right, James. That's the way it's got to be. I want you to make love to me again, right now. And then we're going to go to sleep and you're going to promise me you won't open your eyes until you've heard me leave.'

'You're running out on me again?'

'Yes. That's exactly what I'm going to do.' She turned and hooked her hands behind his neck. She was smiling at him, her eyes bright. 'You can remember me as the girl who ran away.'

He did as she wanted. He slept deeply that night. And the next morning, he lay there listening to her getting dressed and didn't open his eyes until she had gone.

*

Back in the traffic, in London, in the rain, Bond remembered the sound of the door closing. After Jeopardy had left, he had lain there for a while with her scent still on him. Then he had got up and taken a shower, dressed and gone down to breakfast on his own. By the time the taxi arrived, he had put her out of his mind. She had been right, of course. How could they mean anything to each other when they were 3,500 miles apart?

The Secret Service building was ahead. The rain still hadn't stopped and Bond realised he would be soaked by the time he reached the front door. He seldom carried an umbrella with him; it was such a stupid, clumsy invention and anyway it would be practically useless against a downpour like this. He eased himself into his usual parking space and sat there for a moment, listening to the water drumming against the roof. He had a long day ahead of him. First of all he would have to prepare a report on everything that had happened since he had left London. Loelia Ponsonby would type it up. And M would insist that he saw the MO for a thorough check-up. He would probably get an appointment this afternoon.

Bond noticed a man shuffling along the pavement, coming in his direction. The man was wearing a raincoat which seemed to have no buttons. His hands were stuffed into the pockets, holding it together. His head was bowed down and it was hard to tell with the rain distorting his image through the glass but he seemed to be in pain. A tramp? It was far too early for a drunk. Bond opened the door and at once the wind and the spray swept into the interior. At the same time, the man stepped into the road as if intending to go round the car. Bond's thoughts had been far away. The bad weather had distracted him. By the time he realised he was in danger, it was too late. He straightened up. The open door was between the man and him. The man had taken one hand out of his pocket. It was holding a gun. He looked up and Bond saw the bandages, damp and dirty, criss-crossing his face. He was staring out with eyes made more furious by the livid burns that surrounded them. A few strands of colourless hair were plastered across his forehead. He was wearing gloves but Bond saw more bandages around his wrists. The man had clearly walked out of the intensive care unit of some hospital. Bond knew instantly who he was.

Dimitrov. The Russian racing driver. Number Three.

'Bond,' he said. It would have been impossible to put more venom into a single word.

Bond said nothing. He had been unforgivably careless, parking where he always parked, even though the first rule of fieldcraft is never to repeat yourself, never to fall into a pattern of behaviour that can be interpreted by the enemy. Worse still, he had watched this man walk up to him. Could he have guessed that he was anything other than an innocent passer-by? It didn't matter. He should have acted – always – as if anything was possible. And now he had been left defenceless. Unless …

His mind was already racing ahead, weighing up all the possibilities. His gun, the Walther PPK, was in the secret compartment in the glove box of the Bentley. From where he was standing, it was an arm's length away and the whole piece of apparatus was designed to release it instantly into his hand. As if to steady himself, he reached inside the car and pressed his hand on the top of the walnut dashboard.

'Stop! Let me see both your hands.' Dimitrov raised the gun, standing implacably in the rain.

Why did nobody come along? No. That was the last thing Bond wanted. If anyone approached, the Russian would fire and that would be the end of it. Better that the two of them have a little time together. It was obvious that Dimitrov had things he wanted to get off his chest. What he didn't know was that Bond had activated a tiny button set into the surface of the dashboard. The secret compartment had opened electronically. He could see his own gun out of the corner of his eye. He was standing on the right of the car. He would have to seize it with his left hand. But the instructor had insisted that Bond should be ambidextrous on the firing range. After hours of practice, he could fire almost as fast with his left hand as with his right. It was a skill he was going to need – assuming he could actually reach the gun.

'You did this to me,' Dimitrov said. He spoke schoolboy English. The sort of English every SMERSH agent learned in some shabby room in the back of Moscow, and it was coming out distorted, through blistered lips. His accent was as heavy as the rain.

'I saved your life,' Bond replied. 'I could have left you to burn.'

'I did burn!' The Russian was furious. 'I burn all over!'

'You lost control. It was an accident.' It didn't matter what Bond said. The man was going to kill him anyway. But any dialogue was good. It bought time. It allowed him to make his plan.

'I know who you are, Mr James Bond.' He pronounced it 'Shems'. The moment of truth was coming fast. Bond could tell. The Russian levelled his pistol, water dripping off the muzzle.

'Do SMERSH know you're here?' Bond asked. It was unlikely. Even the Russians didn't usually send their agents into the streets of London and every instinct told him that it was a private desire for vengeance that had brought Dimitrov here. 'They're not going to thank you.'

'This is not for SMERSH. This is for me.'

Bond knew it was over. This was it. But he also knew what he was going to do. Even as he had been speaking, he had been lowering himself imperceptibly, inch by inch, simply by bending his knees. The rain had helped him. It was driving into the Russian's eyes. He hadn't seen what Bond was doing.

The Russian fired at point-blank range. He had been aiming directly at Bond's chest.

But Bond had been standing behind the Bentley's door. At the moment the bullet had been fired, the most obvious target was on the other side of a square of glass. And although the Russian couldn't possibly have known it, the window of the Bentley was bulletproof, one of the modifications that Q Branch had insisted on at the time and which had so annoyed Bond. The glass shattered but the bullet hadn't passed through and at the same time Bond was diving to one side, his left hand scrabbling for the gun. He grabbed it and now, protected by the lower half of the door, he twisted round and dived down. By the time Dimitrov realised what had happened, it was too late. He had taken aim but Bond had already fired. Three bullets spat their ugly farewells, driving into the Russian's chest and throat. Bond lay on the ground, sodden, his broken rib pounding. The rain beat down on him. A car drove past, spraying more water over him, but the driver noticed nothing and didn't stop.

Eventually, Bond stood up. He slipped the Walther PPK into his pocket and walked over to the dead Russian who was lying on the tarmac in a pool of rainwater and blood. He was still holding his own gun, a 9x18mm Makarov pistol, a sophisticated but ugly weapon used by the Russian army and police. He had come close to firing a second bullet. His finger was still curled around the trigger, already stiffening as his muscles began to contract.

Trigger mortis.

Bond remembered the phrase he had heard at the launch site on Wallops Island. It seemed appropriate that it should have all ended this way. As he stood over Dimitrov, he calculated that, even with the bulletproof glass, there could only have been a matter of microseconds between the shot that had killed this man and the shot that had been intended to kill Bond. Perhaps he had been a little faster. But he had been luckier too.

It would not always be that way. Bond knew that there would come a time, a moment in a mission, when his luck would run out. It was a mathematical certainty. No agent had ever survived long in the Double O section and one day someone, somewhere would have the edge and it would be he lying there dead, flat-out in the rain.

But not today.

Acknowledgements

Let me explain how this book came about.

I was delighted when The Ian Fleming Estate approached me in the summer of 2014 and invited me to follow some very distinguished authors in writing a new James Bond novel. But from the very start, I had something that they didn't.

Searching through Ian Fleming's papers at the time of the fiftieth anniversary of his death (12 August 1964), his family had rediscovered a number of outlines for a television series which he had been discussing in America. The worldwide success of the first Bond film, *Dr No*, in 1962 had made the television series redundant and Fleming subsequently used some of the stories in two collections – *For Your Eyes Only* and *Octopussy*. But five remained. I was allowed to see them and one of them immediately leapt out at me.

The episode was called 'Murder on Wheels' – I have used the same title for Chapter Seven of this book – and it placed Bond in the extremely dangerous world of Grand Prix. Reading it, I was actually quite surprised that although Bond had memorably played bridge in *Moonraker*, golf in *Goldfinger* and baccarat in *Casino Royale*, he had never, in any of the novels, taken part in the much more lethal world of Grand Prix. Better still – and this was really exciting for me – Fleming's treatment contained a scene with Bond meeting Bill Tanner and M at the Secret Service HQ. This means that some of the description and the dialogue in Chapter Two is actually Fleming's own work. It only adds up to four or five hundred words, but for me it was both an inspiration and a springboard. The truth is that trying to capture Fleming's style was not easy and I was grateful for any help I could get.

As has been reported, Fleming's original story makes Stirling Moss the target of SMERSH at Nürburgring. 'Switch to an English racetrack. Bond is getting instruction from Moss and we get various racing instruction sequences with Moss, or whoever might be chosen for the role, giving some real inside gen on top-class motor racing.' As much as I admire Sir Stirling, I decided not to use him in the story – real celebrities do not tend to make appearances in the Bond novels and anyway, he might not have been amused.

A great many people have helped me with *Trigger Mortis* – without their time and expertise, writing it would have been impossible. (That said, of course, any technical mistakes are entirely my own). First of all, my friend Nick Mason introduced me to the world of Grand Prix, gave me access to his superb library and allowed me to visit his amazing collection of vintage cars at Ten Tenths near Cirencester. While I was there, I was looked after by Mike Hallowes and Ben de Chair who showed me Nick's own Maserati 250F in action and helped me to understand what makes this car such a classic.

I travelled to Nürburgring with Marino Franchitti, one of the world's fastest sports-car racers and a winner of the Sebring 12-Hours, said to be the second toughest race after Le Mans. He gave me a fantastic insight into professional racing and drove me twice round the 20.8 km circuit – an experience I will not forget!

Doug Miller at the National Science Museum and Dave Wright, an expert on the technical aspects of missile defence and a co-director of the Union of Concerned Scientists, both introduced me to rocket science. Dr Tony Yang at the University of British Columbia gave me his thoughts on structural and earthquake engineering. I visited the impressive display at the New York City Transport Museum and the staff kindly allowed me access to their archive.

And then there were the books. I often wonder if non-fiction writers and academics are annoyed when people like me use their expertise for the sake of a thriller. Well, the least I can do is acknowledge some of the titles that helped me.

War and Peace in the Space Age – James Gavin
Countdown: A History of Space Flight – T.A. Heppenheimer
Vanguard: A History – NASA Historical Series
Space Race: The Battle to Rule the Heavens – Deborah
  Cadbury
The Limit – Michael Cannell
Maserati 250F, Owner's Manual – Ian Wagstaff
The Technique of Motor Racing – Piero Taruffi
Remembering Korea 1950: A Boy Soldier's Story – H.K. Shin
The Bridge at No Gun Ri – Charles J. Hanley
The Korean War – Max Hastings
Working Class New York – Joshua B. Freeman
Ian Fleming – Andrew Lycett
James Bond: The Man and his World – Henry Chancellor
The James Bond Dossier – Kingsley Amis

Finally, a few personal acknowledgements.

At a charity auction to raise funds for London's Air Ambulance, two bidders – Nigel Wray and Bernardo Hertogs – each paid a very large sum of money to appear as a character, the proceeds going towards the purchase of a much-needed second helicopter. It's actually shocking that this superb, life-saving service needs to be a charity at all. Nigel Wray subsequently donated his appearance to Henry Fraser who turns up in Chapter Two.

I am, of course, very grateful to Ian Fleming Publications Ltd and The Ian Fleming Estate for entrusting me with this iconic character – and in particular to Corinne Turner who first approached me. This has been a very happy collaboration, helped by Jonny Geller at Curtis Brown who represents Ian Fleming and by the ever-watchful Jonathan Lloyd who represents me. I am very fortunate to have had my own Miss Moneypenny in Lauren Macpherson, my assistant, and once again I have to thank my publishers, Orion Books; Kate Mills (my editor), Jon Wood and Malcolm Edwards.

Anyone who has read my work will know how much James Bond has meant to me throughout my life and so finally I have to acknowledge the genius of Ian Fleming, who got a teenaged boy reading and imagining and who has been influencing me ever since. In writing *Trigger Mortis*, I have tried to stay true to his original vision and to present the character as he was conceived back in the fifties, whilst hopefully not upsetting too many modern sensibilities. It's been – and I must be honest – a pleasure to write.

IAN FLEMING

Ian Lancaster Fleming was born in London on 28 May 1908 and was educated at Eton College before spending a formative period studying languages in Europe. His first job was with Reuters news agency, followed by a brief spell as a stockbroker. On the outbreak of the Second World War he was appointed assistant to the Director of Naval Intelligence, Admiral Godfrey, where he played a key part in British and Allied espionage operations.

After the war he joined Kemsley Newspapers as Foreign Manager of the *Sunday Times*, running a network of correspondents who were intimately involved in the Cold War. His first novel, *Casino Royale*, was published in 1953 and introduced James Bond, Special Agent 007, to the world. The first print run sold out within a month. Following this initial success, he published a Bond title every year until his death. His own travels, interests and wartime experience gave authority to everything he wrote. Raymond Chandler hailed him as 'the most forceful and driving writer of thrillers in England'. The fifth title, *From Russia With Love*, was particularly well received and sales soared when President Kennedy named it as one of his favourite books. The Bond novels have sold more than sixty million copies and inspired a hugely successful film franchise, which began in 1962 with the release of *Dr No*, starring Sean Connery as 007.

The Bond books were written in Jamaica, a country Fleming fell in love with during the war and where he built a house, 'Goldeneye'. He married Ann Charteris in 1952. His story about a magical car, written in 1961 for their only child, Caspar, went on to become the well-loved novel and film, *Chitty Chitty Bang Bang*.

Fleming died of heart failure on 12 August 1964.

www.ianfleming.com

BOOKS BY IAN FLEMING

The James Bond Books

Casino Royale

Live and Let Die

Moonraker

Diamonds are Forever

From Russia with Love

Dr No

Goldfinger

For Your Eyes Only

Thunderball

The Spy Who Loved Me

On Her Majesty's Secret Service

You Only Live Twice

The Man with the Golden Gun

Octopussy and the Living Daylights

Non-fiction

The Diamond Smugglers

Thrilling Cities

Children's

Chitty Chitty Bang Bang